WHEN THE
DEVIL
WHISTLES

**Center Point
Large Print**

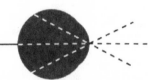

**This Large Print Book carries the
Seal of Approval of N.A.V.H.**

WHEN THE DEVIL WHISTLES

Rick Acker

CENTER POINT PUBLISHING
THORNDIKE, MAINE

This Center Point Large Print edition
is published in the year 2011 by arrangement with
Riggins International Rights Services, Inc.

The persons and events portrayed in this work of fiction
are the creations of the author, and any resemblance to
persons living or dead is purely coincidental.

The text of this Large Print edition is unabridged.
In other aspects, this book may vary
from the original edition.
Printed in the United States of America
on permanent paper.
Set in 16-point Times New Roman type.

ISBN: 978-1-61173-029-6

Library of Congress Cataloging-in-Publication Data

Acker, Rick, 1966–
When the devil whistles / Rick Acker.
p. cm.
ISBN 978-1-61173-029-6 (library binding : alk. paper)
1. Whistle blowing—Fiction. 2. Corporations—Corrupt practices—Fiction.
  3. Large type books. I. Title.
PS3601.C545W47 2011
813'.6—dc22
                                              2010051683

For the men and women of the False Claims Unit
at the California Department of Justice.
I am honored to call you my colleagues
and my friends.

ACKNOWLEDGMENTS

Books are rarely solo projects, and mine never are. Without the help of experts, test readers, paid and volunteer editors, and countless others, this book would never have been written. I've been assisted by more people than I can name, but the contributions of a few stand above the crowd. I would like to express my deepest gratitude and appreciation to:

Anette (wife)—for unceasing encouragement, exacting edits, and boundless love.

Lee Hough (agent)—for believing in this book, championing it, and landing it with the perfect publisher.

Barbara Scott (wearer of many hats, including acquisition editor and developmental editor)—for taking a chance on this novel and making it the best book it could be.

Maegan Roper and the Abingdon sales team— for your enthusiasm, creativity, and tireless efforts to get this book into the hands of readers.

John Olson (author)—for the seed of an idea and for the brainstorming sessions that made it grow into the book you're reading now.

Camy Tang (author)—for staying up all night (though you deny it) to help a suspense author write his first real romantic story line.

Randy Ingermanson (author and computer

expert)—for being an early and constant supporter and providing invaluable feedback.

Mark Talkovic (Chief ROV Pilot)—for reviewing and fixing the ROV scenes.

Monterey Bay Aquarium Research Institute—for generously letting the public have access to your ROVs, staff, and research.

Megan Sato and Marc Riera (IT gurus)—for debugging the computer-related scenes.

Jim Thomas (P-51 pilot)—for letting me climb around on your P-51 and answering all my questions about it.

Nick Akers (Captain, California Military Reserve)—for giving me all the unclassified help you could on nuclear weapons, Port of Oakland security procedures, and air raids.

Amy Akers (neurologist)—for giving Allie a neurology consult and correcting my medical mistakes.

David Dodson (Lt. Col, ret., USAF)—for lending a fighter pilot's eye to the scenes in the air.

Mo Park and Esther La (Korean-American colleagues)—for helping track down a crucial—but very hard to research—detail about South Korean culture circa 1990.

Sylvia Keller, Susan Palazzo, Charlotte Spink, Lucy Wang, and Maretta Ward (test readers)—for your candid comments and for catching an embarrassing number of typos.

Rel Mollet, Nora St. Laurent, Susan Sleeman, Christy Lockstein, Janna Ryan, Laurel Wreath, Carolyn Scheidies, and many others (bloggers and reviewers)—for all you have done to support and encourage me and other Christian authors.

Readers everywhere—for investing your hard-earned money in books and making it possible for authors to tell you our stories.

Prologue

Something Wicked This Way Came

SAMUEL STIMSON MADE HIS LAST TWO mistakes on March 23. Boredom caused the first. He had run the last network diagnostic on his task list, the servers were all up and running, and none of the marketing staff had crashed their computers or forgotten their passwords all day. So Samuel played solitaire and Minesweeper for a while. He IMed his gaming buddies, but none of them had time to talk. And then he did what he had always done when sitting in front of a computer with nothing to do: go looking for trouble.

He didn't have to look far. Two floors above him in a secure room sat his employer's secure server, the S-4. Samuel didn't have access to it. In fact, the only person in the IT department authorized to work on S-4 was Franklin Roh, an ex-Microsoft drone who had half of Samuel's skill, but double his salary. Not even Franklin's little toady, Rajiv, knew what was on it.

Guessing what the mystery server held was a favorite pastime for the IT staff, particularly when Franklin and Rajiv were in the room. Speculation ran the gamut from classified government contracts to evidence of executive tax fraud, but Franklin never reacted to any of their theories, no matter how serious or outrageous. He just sat there watching them with cool arrogance. Maybe he learned that look growing up in Korea. Maybe they taught it at Microsoft. Whatever—it bugged Samuel.

The image of Franklin Roh's impassive Asian face gave Samuel the final little push he needed to act. He had been an accomplished hacker in college and grad school—so accomplished that he had never been caught. He didn't vandalize systems or steal data files like some other hackers but always left the phrase "Something wicked this way came" buried in some unobtrusive spot to unnerve whatever systems engineer later found it. Four years had passed since his last foray into forbidden cyberspace, but he had kept up on recent developments in computer security, and he was pretty sure he could beat anything that Franklin could create.

He went to work. As he expected, the server was well protected by top-of-the-line commercial security software, which had been configured with perfect competence but no creativity. Just what he expected from a Microsoft guy.

He didn't even bother with a direct assault on the server. Conventional firewalls were good at spotting and stopping those kinds of attacks. Careless users were easy targets, and careless senior executives were easiest of all. He did a couple of discreet searches and found a list of the six senior executives with access to the S-4 server. Then he ran a user log and found that four of them were on the system. One, Richard Addison, had been logged in for seventeen days and fourteen hours, but his computer had been inactive for almost two days.

Samuel grinned. Time for a little stroll.

He got up and walked out of the warren of IT cubicles, grabbing a handful of random tech gear on his way out the door. He took the elevator up to the executive floor and held up his ID as he approached a security station manned by two alert, rock-jawed guards wearing body armor and toting M-16s. He licked his lips and felt tiny drops of sweat prickle his forehead. Those guys always made him nervous—the way their eyes locked onto him every time he got off the elevators and followed him across the lobby, the no-nonsense way they held their guns, the over-the-top SWAT team gear. He always had the feeling that they were just looking for an excuse to blow away a bike messenger or something. But they buzzed him through with only a perfunctory glance at his ID and the computer parts clutched in his hand. For once, he was grateful for the fact that IT staffers are invisible in the corporate world.

He walked down the oak-paneled hallways, his footsteps silenced by the rich burgundy carpet.

He scanned the brass plates on the office doors for Addison's name. There it was. He slowed down as he passed Addison's office and glanced in. It was empty and dark, but a green spark gleamed from the power button on his desktop computer.

Samuel's grin returned as he continued down the hall. As he had hoped, Richard Addison had decided to ignore the memo about turning off his computer when he left for the day. *Easier to just leave it on and not have to waste two minutes waiting for it to boot up in the morning, right Dick?*

Addison's unattended computer was a wide-open door in the pricy firewall Franklin Roh had built. This would be easier than Samuel had thought—almost disappointing.

Samuel meandered back to his cubicle and pulled up the keystroke logging program Franklin had installed. Getting into that was easy enough since he was on the IT staff. The keystroke logger had, of course, recorded all of Addison's passwords as he typed them in. Two minutes later, Samuel had the one for the S-4 server: "Richrocks1."

Samuel snorted and opened the utility on his computer that allowed him to take over any other machine on the system. A few seconds later, he had control of Addison's computer. If Addison had been at his desk, he would have noticed that his monitor had woken up from power-save mode and was acting possessed. Samuel realized that someone walking past Addison's office might look in and see the same thing. He should have turned off the monitor. His hands froze on the keyboard and for an instant he considered aborting. Then he smiled and started typing again. He felt the familiar adrenaline rush and tightening stomach muscles. He'd forgotten how much fun a little risk could be.

Addison had left open a link to the S-4 server on his computer, so Samuel just pulled it up, typed in Addison's password, and he was in. The server held a single folder with the innocuous title "Project Docs." Inside that were two subfolders titled "Financial" and "Operational." The "Operational" subfolder sounded the most interesting, so he opened that one first. It held dozens of PDFs of various sizes. He glanced around to make sure nobody was watching. Then he took a deep breath and opened the first PDF. *Now we're getting somewhere.*

Or maybe not. The PDF was some sort of form in an Asian language Samuel didn't recognize. So was the second PDF, and the third.

He clicked through half a dozen more files before coming across something in English. It was a checklist titled "6/16-8/16 Winch and ROV Spare Parts," and it cataloged various machine parts that meant nothing to Samuel. He tried a few more, but nothing juicy—no Navy memos labeled "Top Secret," no charts marking debris fields from lost Spanish galleons, and no fake executive tax returns. He couldn't even find a memo that would at least give him some inkling of what this project was about.

The "Financial" subfolder held nothing but a bunch of PDF invoices and a couple of Excel spreadsheets. They were all in English, but it didn't matter. The invoices were all one-line bills that said "For services rendered" followed by a number. And the spreadsheets were just lists of invoices with totals at the bottoms.

He stopped and rubbed the soul patch beard on his lower lip. The totals were each in the tens of millions of dollars, and some topped $100 million. He'd been in the company long enough to know that all marine engineering and salvage projects were expensive, but that was *a lot* of money.

He did a quick scan of the rest of the files, but found nothing useful. Whatever the company was getting all that money for, it wasn't at all clear from what was on the S-4 server.

Now thoroughly frustrated, Samuel got ready to minimize the server connection again and get out of Addison's computer. Before he did, though, he embedded "Something wicked this way came" as an anonymous tag on one of the PDFs. He also added an image to the PDF: a picture of Franklin

Roh's face Photoshopped onto the body of an obese woman in a bikini.

He finished and looked at the clock in the corner of his monitor. His little adventure had only killed an hour—still two and a half hours to go until he could head out. He stretched, checked his e-mail again, and started reading a twenty-three-page policy memo Franklin had just circulated on appropriate Internet usage while at work. After two pages, Samuel realized that reading the whole thing would just be too painful, so he skimmed it for rules prohibiting use of the 'Net to find pictures of fat chicks who would look good with a supervisor's head.

Five o'clock came at last. He slung his backpack over his shoulder and headed out. By the time he reached the elevator, he had already mentally left work and his mood brightened. He needed to find a new job—maybe one of his friends was putting together another start-up or something. He made a mental note to polish up his resumé over the next couple of weeks.

He was crossing the ground floor lobby and had almost reached the street when a familiar nasal voice called his name in a sharp, schoolteacher-on-the-playground tone. He turned to see Franklin Roh pushing toward him through the stream of departing workers. "Samuel!" he repeated as he got closer, his normally inscrutable face flushed and contorted. "Samuel, we need to talk!"

Looks like I'll need to get that resumé ready faster than I thought. "Sure thing. I'll stop by your office tomorrow morning."

Samuel turned to go, but Franklin stepped in front of him and grabbed his arm. "No, now!"

Samuel stared at his boss. He had expected Franklin to be mad if he found his artwork, but the guy was way beyond mad. His face looked strange and wild, the bland Microsoft mask completely gone. He panted and his hand shook on Samuel's bicep.

A cold ripple rolled over Samuel. He was tempted to yank his arm free and force his way past Franklin and out of the building. He was bigger and younger and there weren't any security guards around, so he knew he could do it. But he didn't. He was probably going to get fired anyway, and he really didn't need "assaulting a supervisor" tacked onto his list of offenses. So he allowed Franklin to lead him away.

That was his second mistake.

1

CONNOR NORMAN LOVED A GOOD FIRE-works show. He especially liked the ones that took place once or twice a year in the conference rooms at the California Department of Justice. Some executive or general counsel whose company was under investigation would come in for a witness interview, would lie, and would get caught. Then Deputy Attorney General Max Volusca would go off and the show would start. DAG Volusca did not suffer liars gladly. Fools he would tolerate, often longer than Connor. But if Max felt he was being misled, he soon lived up to his nickname, "Max Volume."

Connor didn't mind it when Max got loud. In fact, he liked the DAG's outbursts because they usually rattled whoever was sitting across the table from him. And that usually meant more money for Connor and his *qui tam* clients. A *qui tam* plaintiff is a whistleblower who sues on behalf of the government and gets a cut (generally 15 to 20 percent) of whatever the government recovers. Better yet, if the Department of Justice likes a case, it takes on the lion's share of the work. Envious defense counsel sometimes complained to Connor that he wasn't really litigating these cases, just riding a gravy train driven by DOJ. Though Connor never told opposing lawyers, the real fun wasn't the train ride so much as tying corporate criminals to the tracks in front of the engine.

Today, Connor's client was Devil to Pay, Inc., a shell company he had created to bring *qui tam* lawsuits while protecting the identity of its owner. Most contractors assumed that Connor was the force behind Devil to Pay and that he recruited new whistleblowers for every lawsuit. In fact, all those suits were the work of a single woman: a professional whistleblower named Allie Whitman.

The corners of Connor's mouth twitched. Allie was probably the most widely hated and feared woman in California's government contracting industry, even though no one knew she existed.

The person who probably hated Allie most at this particular moment was Hiram Hamilton, the CEO of Hamilton Construction. He was sitting at a cheap wood table in conference room 11436 at the San Francisco office of the California Department of Justice, where he was being grilled by Max Volusca.

Connor sat next to Volusca and let him do all the talking. While the DAG asked questions, Connor watched Hamilton and the brace of lawyers who flanked him. One of the lawyers was Joe Johnston, Hamilton Construction's general counsel. The other was Carlos Alvarez, a high-priced defense lawyer with a reputation for playing hardball with the government.

Hiram Hamilton was a gregarious, open-faced man of about fifty-five who smiled a lot when he spoke. But Connor suspected those traits were the result of practice rather than character, and that raised warning flags. In his experience, men who tried to appear candid rarely were.

"So, how many cost-plus state contracts has your company bid on over the past ten years, Mr. Hamilton?" Max asked.

"I don't remember—at least two dozen."

"And you do know what cost-plus means, right?"

"Sure," Hamilton said with a nod and a genial smile. "It means the contract price is my cost plus an agreed percentage of profit."

"Has your company ever inflated its costs in order to get a higher profit percentage than your contract allows?"

"No, of course not," the witness replied without letting his smile waver.

Max stared at him in silence for several seconds. "Do you or do you not realize that you're under oath, Mr. Hamilton?"

Alvarez grimaced and stirred. "Look, Max, we're trying to be cooperative and give you the information you want. There's no reason to badger my client."

Max kept his eyes on Hamilton. "Are you trying to be cooperative, Mr. Hamilton?"

"I . . . uh, sure."

"And provide the information requested in the state's subpoena?"

"Absolutely. We gave you everything you asked for."

Here we go. Connor glanced at Max. The DAG's face had darkened and his bull neck swelled against the collar of his white dress shirt.

"Then WHY didn't you give me these?" Max demanded, his voice rising several decibels as he thrust a stack of photocopied documents at the witness.

Hamilton's grin vanished and his eyes widened. "I, I . . . I'm not sure what these are."

"Really? Take a good look at them." Max leaned forward and pointed at the stack with an accusatory finger.

Hamilton flipped through the documents in silence for half a minute as Alvarez engaged in a staring contest with Max. Hamilton looked up again. "These look like the invoices backing up our costs for the work on the DMV building in Oakland," he said with strained nonchalance. "We gave you all of these already."

"No, you gave me FAKE invoices for that project! Invoices that had been doctored to make the numbers in them match the numbers you reported to the state," Max shot back. "These are the REAL invoices."

Alvarez put a hand on his client's arm to signal him not to respond. "I object to this harassment, and I'm not going to let it go on any longer. We came here in good faith to answer questions, not listen to you shout at Mr. Hamilton. If you can't behave civilly, we're leaving."

"Before you do, make sure to write down Mr. Hamilton's shirt and pants size."

"What? Why?"

"So we can have an orange jumpsuit waiting for him the next time we meet."

"This is outrageous!" Alvarez stood up and his client and the company's general counsel followed suit. Max also hefted his sizable bulk upright, his face now beet red. Connor stayed seated, letting his body language say that he was staying out of the fight. At some point, he might need to play "good cop," and it didn't hurt to start telegraphing his reasonableness now.

"It's outrageous alright!" Max rejoined, his voice now at near-bullhorn level. "This is a civil investigation right now, but if you and your client aren't real careful, there's going to be a criminal referral. Giving false evidence during an investigation by the Attorney General is a felony under Penal Code section 132."

Connor fought back the urge to smile as his ears rang. Max Volusca only hauled out section 132 when he was *really* mad. It was the legal equivalent of the old belt Connor's father had kept in the back of the hall closet to threaten particularly incorrigible sons. He almost never used it, but its mere appearance worked wonders of attitude adjustment.

Alvarez jammed papers into his briefcase. "I'm not going to dignify that with a response!"

Max put his fists on the table and leaned forward. "Yeah, well I'm going to dignify it with an indictment!"

Hamilton and his lawyers packed in frosty

silence for half a minute. Then Alvarez grabbed the stack of photocopied invoices.

"What do you think you're doing?" demanded the DAG.

"These are company property," said Alvarez as he shoved the invoices into his briefcase. "And I am reclaiming them."

"No they aren't, and no you're not!"

Alvarez ignored Max and walked toward the door, trailed by Hamilton and Johnston. Max pushed a button on the speakerphone on the conference room table. "Ruby, there are three men leaving conference room 11436. Ask security to arrest them and search them for stolen state property."

"Yes, Mr. Volusca," said the receptionist in a bored voice.

Hamilton and his lawyers stopped in the conference room doorway. "You can't be serious," said Alvarez.

"Go downstairs and find out," said the DAG. "I hope you brought your toothbrushes."

Alvarez's face turned the same shade of crimson as Max's, but he reached into his briefcase, pulled out the documents, and slammed them down on the conference room table. "You are nothing but a schoolyard bully," he said through clenched teeth.

"No, I am the state of California," Max thundered, "and I hit a lot harder than any bully you ever met! And I promise you that I will absolutely DESTROY you and your client unless I start getting REAL cooperation REAL fast!"

Alvarez opened his mouth, but Johnston spoke first. "Look, let's all take a deep breath and try this again. You've got questions about Hamilton Construction's billing practices and we want to answer them. If there's a problem with the documents, just send us a letter and we'll look into it. You mentioned the Oakland DMV project—were there any other contracts you'd like us to, um, take a second look at?"

"ALL of them!" The DAG turned his glower to the company's general counsel.

"Okay. All right. We'll do that," replied Johnston in the placating let's-fix-this tone Connor had come to expect from GCs caught in a fraud investigation. "Did you have any more questions for Mr. Hamilton? He is the company CEO and doesn't spend much time with the accounting paperwork, so I don't think he'll be able to help you much on this point. Was there anything else you'd like to ask him about?"

"Yes," said the DAG in a calmer tone, "but let's wait until this document problem has been solved. I also strongly suggest that you talk to your client about the importance of being completely candid in his dealings with DOJ. I wasn't kidding about the criminal referral."

"I understand." Johnston nodded as he spoke.

"Hopefully once we've got this document issue nailed down, there won't be any need to discuss referrals."

Hiram Hamilton and his lawyers packed up and left a few minutes later. Hamilton had begun to recover his composure and had forced his habitual smile back onto his face. But large rings of sweat adorned each armpit of his suit coat and he wiped his palms on his pants at least once a minute.

Once they were alone, Max stretched, sat down, and turned to Connor. "So, what did you think?"

"I was watching Hamilton, and he didn't look angry or surprised when you brought up orange jumpsuits. He just turned pale. And when you put that stack of invoices in front of him, I got the impression that he was shocked to see them but not shocked by your description of what was in them."

Max nodded. "He was in on it. I went into this thinking we might be looking at some low-level guy trying to boost his revenue numbers by ripping off the government on one or two contracts. But if the CEO is in the loop, it goes way beyond that."

Connor nodded. "And they're desperate to know what we know. First, Alvarez tried to walk out of here with your documents. Then Johnston tried to get you to give him a list of the projects you're looking at."

Max leaned back in his chair and stroked his jowls. "Good point. That's another reason to think this isn't limited to the Oakland DMV building. Plus, this guy Hamilton really ticks me off—sitting there grinning and making noises about how cooperative he's being, and the whole time he's lying through his teeth. I love hammering guys like that."

Connor smiled. "And we're happy to help in any way we can, Max. Any way at all."

2

ALLIE WHITMAN COASTED HER SNOWBOARD to the end of the Gunbarrel run at the Heavenly resort in Tahoe. She rode the board until it came to a dead stop. She sighed and popped it off. The last run of the day was always a little bittersweet.

But by the time she was on the bus she had stopped missing the snow and started looking forward to the casino. She wasn't much of a gambler, but the casino had a great nightclub and cheap drinks. Plus, Erik would be there waiting for her. She smiled and leaned back into her seat as the bus pulled out of the parking lot.

Twenty minutes later, she walked into her room and was greeted by the sight of Erik dressed for a night out—though that was more or less how he always dressed in the evening. After all, he was the lead singer in a band that was "on the edge of a big breakthrough" (and had been for five years) and needed to keep up appearances.

His handsome, angular face broke into his trademark brilliant smile. "Hey, babe, how were the slopes?" he asked as she stowed her gear in the closet.

"Sweet—best boarding of the season." She eyed the outfits hanging in the closet. Erik had on black pinstripe pants with sharp creases, a white shirt, and a black silk vest, so she needed to be a little more dressed-up than she had anticipated. The best she had was a gold minidress. She held it up. "What do you think?"

"Perfect. I managed to get us a VIP booth at Vex, so you'll want to wear something with a little flash and hot sauce."

She paused for a heartbeat. A VIP booth at Vex was not going to be cheap. "Wow, are we celebrating something?"

His smile broadened. "Just that Alex called to say that he's added more gigs to the tour. We're going to be playing two more dates in Kansas. One is at Kansas State and another one's at a town near there—Salinas or something like that."

"Hey, that's great! Let me get ready and then let's grab something to eat and hit Vex."

She showered, redid her hair and makeup, put on the dress, and evaluated the results. Not bad. She'd picked up a little color on the slopes, and it worked well with her shoulder-length blond hair and the shimmery gold fabric. She also liked the way her black cat tattoo peaked out over the neckline of the dress. Just the right look—what had Erik said? A little flash and hot sauce.

Something on the top of the toilet tank caught her eye. She walked over for a closer look. It was a glass pipe half-hidden by a towel. She picked it up and sniffed. The scent of fresh meth smoke assaulted her nose. She frowned and tapped the bowl of the pipe against her palm. Erik knew how she felt about meth, and he had promised not to get high while they were on vacation. She wanted to smash the pipe on the counter or walk out and throw it at him.

But she didn't. What would it accomplish? Nothing, except to ruin what was looking like a great night out. Why focus on the negative? That only caused problems.

She put the pipe in the glass that held his toothbrush. Maybe he'd get—and take—the hint.

He was lying on one of the beds and watching TV when she came out of the bathroom. "Okay, let's go," she said, hearing a cold tone in her voice.

"Cool." He got up and was walking toward the door when her cell phone started playing "Sympathy for the Devil."

"Hey, it's my lawyer," she exclaimed as she grabbed the phone out of her purse. Sure enough, Connor's slender face smiled back at her from the cell phone screen. She liked this picture of him: he had the same intelligent, confident expression that had made her trust him almost immediately at their first meeting. It was something about his brown eyes and the way he always seemed to know exactly what he was supposed to do or say.

"I was wondering when he'd call."

Erik frowned. "Just let it go into voicemail. I'm starved."

She ignored him and answered the phone. "Hi, Connor. So, how did it go? Did we have a good day?"

"A very good day. I tried calling you earlier, but you must have still been up at Heavenly. What did you think of Killebrew Canyon?"

"Loved it—perfect snow and it scared me half to death, just like you promised." She imagined being on those slopes with him, but then pushed the thought away. It could never happen, so why think about it?

"I'm glad to hear it. And glad you made it back off the mountain. When I couldn't reach you earlier, I was a little worried that you might have done some involuntary tree hugging at sixty miles an hour."

She laughed. "Yeah, I did come close to splattering myself a couple of times, but that's all part of the fun." Erik caught her eye. He pointed at his watch and glared. She realized she was getting too friendly and pulled back to safer ground. "But give me the skinny on what happened. Is DOJ going to intervene?"

Connor paused before going on in a slightly cooler tone. "They haven't made a decision yet. All that happened today was that Max Volusca and I interviewed the CEO of Hamilton Construction. He had some credibility issues that both Max and I noticed, and that seemed to irritate Max. The CEO also didn't have an immediate explanation for the discrepancy between the invoices you found and the ones they sent to the state. Also, by the end of the interview Max and I both thought that there might be more to this case than the Oakland DMV building contract. It's still early in the investigation, but overall today was certainly positive."

"Connor, is that all hypercautious lawyer-speak for 'yeah, they're probably going to intervene and it looks like there's serious money here, but I don't want to get your hopes up?' "

He gave a low chuckle. "Something like that."

"Excellent! Hey, I've got to go, but thanks for the call."

"Hot date with your pet rock star?"

She laughed, but felt a twinge deep inside. "Something like that. Talk to you."

She hung up, turned to Erik and kissed him hard, trying to convince herself that she really did want to be with him tonight. "Okay, now I'm ready to celebrate!"

3

CONNOR SAT BACK IN A CREAKY OLD WOOD and leather chair and looked out over the view from the back porch of what his family called "the California beach cabin." In fact, it was a 3,100-square-foot structure that had a part-time maid and was bigger than most nearby homes. It was only a cabin in comparison to "the California house" east of San Francisco, which was about twice as large.

Waves crashed on the stony shore, and a cool Pacific breeze riffled the sea grass and whispered over his head in the majestic redwoods dotting the lawn surrounding the "cabin." Two pelicans rode the breeze and watched the water just off shore for anchovies.

Connor's Blackberry buzzed intermittently on the table beside him, sounding like a dyspeptic bumblebee. He reached over and switched it to silent. He'd check his voicemail and e-mail when he felt like it, and he didn't feel like it right now.

The firm wouldn't mind his absence—the clique of senior partners who ran Doyle & Brown cared a lot more about seeing his contribution to the bottom line than about seeing his face in the office. Last year he'd brought in more money than any other partner under 40 and he was on track to do it again, so he could safely play hooky for a couple of days if he wanted. It was the prerogative of profitability.

Plus, he had an excuse for ignoring the outside world. There was a mediation scheduled for next week in the Hamilton Construction case, and he was here to get ready for it. That meant no distractions.

He leaned over and rummaged through his trial bag—a boxy, wheeled briefcase designed for carting large volumes of paper between office and courtroom. He pulled out Hamilton Construction's opening mediation brief and started to read.

Two months of intense scrutiny from Max Volusca and his team of auditors would be painful for any executive. And if the executive in question happened to run a company as corrupt as Hamilton Construction, his suffering would be severe. So Connor was not surprised when Hiram Hamilton and his lawyers requested mediation.

Even so, Connor was a little surprised by how weak the company's brief was. It did not include even a token protestation of innocence. It conceded up front that "a certain amount of accidental overbilling may have occurred" and then launched into a string of complaints about the methodology that the government's forensic accountants used to calculate the amount of the overbilling.

Connor finished the brief, smiled, and dropped it back into his bag. Any day his opponent's main argument was "well, we didn't steal that much" was a good day. Even though he was fifty yards from the ocean, he could smell the blood in the water.

Now that he thought about it a little more, the company's lawyers had probably done the best they could. During the two months since Hiram Hamilton's witness interview, the company had grudgingly coughed up a steady stream of damaging documents. They had to turn over the real invoices for the Oakland DMV contract, of course. But they didn't know what other projects DOJ might have dirt on, so they couldn't stop there without risking a few years wearing the orange jumpsuits Max Volusca had promised.

By the time they were done, it was clear that the company had ripped off the state of California to the tune of at least $1.5 million—maybe as much as $5 million depending on what kind of accounting assumptions were used.

And they had bragged about it. Some of their executives apparently hadn't learned the Enron Rule: e-mail is forever. So when Max managed to pry the e-mail archive tapes out of the company, he and Connor found choice quotes like, "Those morons in Sacramento don't audit, so you're fine as long as you don't do anything obvious. No $400 hammers." Connor imagined how that would play to a Sacramento jury and sat back with a contented sigh.

He relaxed and watched the breakers crash. Hamilton Construction clearly was willing to be reasonable at the mediation. The real problem would be managing Max, but Connor had plenty of experience at that.

4

ALLIE DIALED THE NUMBER OF HER TEMP agency manager and former bar-hopping partner, Trudi Wexler. They still kept in touch by phone and e-mail, but hadn't seen much of each other since Trudi got married and started shooting out babies like a Pez dispenser. She picked up on the first ring. "Hey, Al! What's up? Are you home yet?"

"I just got back yesterday. I would've called you earlier, but I was beat. I took out my contacts and just flopped down on my bed. I didn't wake up until, like, half an hour ago. Want to grab a cup of coffee?"

"Allie, it's nine o'clock at night."

"Okay, so get decaf. What do you say?"

Trudi laughed. "Let me ask Dave. He brought work home, but Maddie just went down and I've fed the twins, so I might be able to sneak out for an hour or so. Hold on a sec." Muffled voices for half a minute. "Okay, where do you want to meet?"

"How about the Starbucks on Powell just off of Market."

"Sounds good. The one right there on the corner?"

"No, no. The one a block to the north."

"Oh, okay. The one in the Nikko or the one on the street?"

"On the street."

"Got it. I'll see you there in fifteen minutes."

Allie got there first and ordered an Americano and a scone. While she was waiting for her order to come up, Trudi walked in. She looked different somehow. Older. Her hair was still jet-black and her face still belonged in an Oil of Olay ad, but she definitely looked older. Less makeup, shorter hair, flats instead of heels, naked lobes instead of gold hoops, a tired look around the mouth and eyes. It hit Allie: Trudi looked like a mom. How depressing.

Trudi gave Allie an affectionate hug and ordered a decaf latte with skim milk. She turned to Allie with a bright smile. "So, tell me about the tour! How was it?"

"It was great, but I'm wiped. We hit ten cities in two weeks and the band's manager threw out his back moving equipment after the first show, so I had to help out a lot more than I usually do—driving, dealing with little problems at the venues, and stuff like that. I slept four or five hours a night. It was fun, but I'm getting too old for this kind of thing."

"Mm-hmm," said Trudi as she picked up her coffee. She opened her mouth as if to say something more, but just took a sip of her coffee. They found an isolated little table in the corner and perched on a couple of bar stools.

"So, how's Erik?" asked Trudi. "How was it being with him 24/7 for two weeks straight?"

"Erik's fine," replied Allie. "He loves being on tour. The energy from the crowd just lights him up. The real trick is switching him back off afterward. He's so fired up after a concert that he wants to stay up all night."

Trudi nodded and looked Allie in the eyes. "Meth does that too, doesn't it? Is he still using?"

Yes. The image of postconcert Erik, chattering nonstop and stinking of sweat and meth mouth, pushed itself into Allie's mind. She looked down at her coffee. She'd also seen him and the other band members selling a few times. Fans—usually nervous young men with bad teeth and furtive eyes—would come up to the band's van when no one was around, and money and plastic baggies would exchange hands.

Allie forced a smile. "He'd better not be. He knows how I feel about that crap. So, how's business? Got any jobs for me?"

Allie could see the concern in Trudi's eyes, but she let the Erik issue lie. "For my best temp? Of course I've got jobs." She paused and bit her lip. "My boss would kill me if she heard me say this, but do you want something permanent? One of our clients is looking for someone who knows accounting software and government contracting rules, and you know both of those better than anyone I've ever met. The money and benefits would be better than you're getting now, and there'd be advancement opportunities. What do you think?"

Allie shook her head. "Thanks, but no thanks. I've tried that before and I get bored after a few months and quit. Or I want to take a month off and fry myself on a beach or go boarding or something. That's fine if I'm temping, but it doesn't work so well if I've got a permanent job."

Trudi laughed and shook her head. "You're amazing! Dave and I both work full-time, and we can just barely afford a week in Tahoe every year. You work part-time as a temp and you're always taking these exotic vacations and you've got a great apartment in Noe Valley. How do you do it?"

Allie smiled and took a long sip from her coffee as she searched for something to say other than *By secretly suing your clients, of course.* "Well, I own some stock in a little company that pays big dividends. That, and I clip coupons."

"Wow, I've got to buy some of that stock with my next bonus. What's the company?"

Allie cleared her throat and shook her head.

"Sorry, but it's . . . it's privately held. So the stock isn't for sale. Besides, the owner doesn't like to talk about the company. It, um, it does hush-hush government work. If word got out, there'd be the devil to pay."

5

THE *GRASP II* WAS THE BEST CIVILIAN DEEP-sea exploration and salvage ship on the West Coast—and her crew would argue that she was the best in the world. A twenty-ton crane towered over her deck midship. A smaller crane near the stern supported a complicated device called an ROV (short for "remotely operated vehicle") that explored the deep and guided the crane.

Today, however, the *Grasp II* was not exploring but waiting at her home dock in the Port of Oakland. "The wife and kids weren't too happy to hear there'd be no Hawaii trip again this year," commented Mitch Daniels, the *Grasp II*'s ROV pilot, as he helped stow extra cable for the ROV winch.

"Take 'em to Yosemite. It's closer and cheaper." Ed Granger eyed Mitch's work critically. "Hey, don't put that cable there. Too close to the spare cameras. Don't want to bust one of those."

Mitch thought the cable was fine where it was, but he didn't protest. Ed's official job title was simply "ROV Chief Pilot," but he was in fact master of all things related to the ROV, and he knew it better than he knew his children. He had even given it a name: "Eileen," after his ex-wife's divorce lawyer. Both of them were expensive, ugly, and very good at poking around in the muck.

"Tried Yosemite," Mitch grunted as he moved the massive spool of metal cable where Ed wanted it. "Wife didn't go for it. She said she'd promised the kids dolphins and volcanoes and what was I going to do about it? So I said, 'What am I supposed to do, miss the ship and get left behind? I'll lose my job.' And she gets all mad and says, 'You can't just make me break promises to the kids!' So I tell her to go—" he broke off in a curse as the cable got stuck on a crate. After he got it loose, he continued, "So anyway we had a pretty good fight about it."

"You guys fight a lot," Ed observed.

Mitch shrugged and grinned.

Ed grinned back. "You like the way she fights, huh?"

Mitch laughed. "I guess you could say that."

"Sign of a good marriage. Well, this trip should be worth the fight."

Mitch stopped working and looked up. "Why's that? You know something?"

Ed looked around and lowered his voice conspiratorially. "They had me put some new sensors on Eileen. Metal detecting stuff."

He patted Eileen gently. To the untutored eye, the ROV was a chaotic seven-foot mass of cables, pipes, propellers, and cameras. To a marine engineer, however, the *Grasp II*'s ROV was a masterpiece—a cutting-edge array of depth-resistant sensors and cameras, a Swiss-army-knife array of tools and manipulators that could probe deep into ocean floor mud or perform delicate surgery on oil rig parts, and half a dozen powerful thrusters that could hold it virtually motionless above the bottom of the sea even when buffeted by deep water currents.

Mitch noticed the new bank of sensors on Eileen's tool sled. "So you think we're looking for a shipwreck?"

Ed nodded. "But not just any shipwreck. There's already a magnetometer on Eileen and we've got sidescan sonar. The new metal detector looks for nonferrous heavy metals."

Mitch stared at him blankly.

Ed rolled his eyes. "Metals like gold, Mitch."

6

LAST SUNDAY, CONNOR'S PASTOR HAD preached on Matthew 5:9: "Blessed are the peacemakers, for they shall be called sons of God." The pastor's central message had been that if God blesses peacemakers, we also should honor and respect them. The pastor did a nice job with the sermon, but Connor thought it was a little obvious. After all, who doesn't like peacemakers?

Now he knew.

Connor was in no mood to bless the retired judge who was mediating *State of California ex rel. Devil to Pay, Inc. v. Hamilton Construction Corp.* The mediation had been going on for nearly five hours, and Connor was seething.

The problem wasn't that the mediator was incompetent. Quite the contrary. The mediator was a wily old trial judge named Abraham Washburn who had retired to the greener pastures of private mediation, where he could do half the work of a judge for twice the money. Unfortunately, he was proving entirely too good at his new career for Connor's liking.

"A good mediator only looks for one thing: weakness." So another judge-turned-mediator had told Connor several years ago as he was preparing for his first mediation. Connor had seen the weaknesses in Hamilton Construction's case perfectly clearly, but he had missed a serious weakness on his side of the table: Max Volusca.

Connor had figured that he could count on Max to take a hard line throughout the negotiations but ultimately allow himself to be talked into whatever deal Connor could get. That sort of tag-team effort had worked well in the past and had shaken loose handsome sums in half a dozen prior settlement negotiations.

Max was taking a hard line this time too, but Judge Washburn had persuaded him that it was more important to fight over principles than dollars. "You represent the Department of Justice, not the Department of Finance, counsel," he had told Max. "And isn't justice better served by a comprehensive deal that includes a criminal plea and a public apology, even if that means a little less money?" That resonated with Max, even once it became clear that "a little less money" really meant "nothing more than repayment of the most egregious overbilling"—a number that Hamilton Construction insisted was less than $1 million.

Connor protested, of course. A criminal plea and apology would look great in a press release from the Attorney General's office but would have little real effect. Companies like Hamilton Construction didn't give a rat's rear end about bad publicity as long as it didn't interfere with business.

Unfortunately, Connor and his client had very little leverage in these negotiations. That was the downside of suing on behalf of the state. It was great to have Max Volusca thunder about orange jumpsuits and terrify defendants into doing the right thing. But if Max decided that the right thing was little more than a public shaming, there wasn't much Connor or Devil to Pay could do to stop him.

The mediator fully understood the dynamics of the situation and did everything in his power to keep Connor from talking Max out of the deal that was beginning to gel. First, he took Connor with him as he shuttled back and forth between Max and the Hamilton Construction team, who were in separate conference rooms at either end of a short hallway. Then he parked Connor by himself in a third conference room on the pretext that there were certain matters related to confidential investigative documents (which Connor could not legally see) that needed to be hammered out.

Connor spent half an hour cooling his heels and admiring the spectacular view of the Golden Gate Bridge afforded by the conference room window. Late afternoon fog softened the outlines of the graceful spans of the bridge and cast halos around the headlights of the cars coming south out of the rugged Marin Headlands, which were graced by picturesque (and very expensive) towns. It was a soothing view. But Connor was in no mood to be soothed.

Judge Washburn opened the door and poked his head in. "Connor, great news!" he said, his bright white smile contrasting with a deep golf tan. "We've got a deal!"

Connor raised his eyebrows in surprise. "Really? How can you have a deal without my client's agreement?"

The mediator's brow furrowed in a disingenuous show of surprise and concern. "Oh, I thought that the whistleblower just gets a share of whatever the state gets. Did I misunderstand that?"

"That's technically how the law works," Connor conceded, "but as a practical matter we're always part of the negotiations. Plus there's the issue of attorney fees."

"Ah, well your fees are taken care of," interjected Judge Washburn, his smile returning. "Every penny. You've billed just over $200K, correct?"

"That's right, but fees aren't the only issue that concerns us."

The mediator opened a black leather notebook. "Did you want to go over the terms of the deal now before I read them to the whole group?"

Connor thought for a moment. "Actually, that's okay. I don't want to keep everyone waiting. If Max is comfortable with the settlement, I'm sure it's in the best interests of the state."

Judge Washburn's grin widened. "Great, I'm glad you see it that way. Let's head to the big conference room. I think everybody else is already there."

Connor followed him down the hall and into the conference room. It held a broad walnut table surrounded by about twenty leather chairs. Most of these were empty and the lawyers had spread out some. Max looked tired, but satisfied. The Hamilton Construction team across the table was exultant. Its inside and outside counsel, Joe Johnston and Carlos Alvarez respectively, were both smiling and talking quietly, and Hiram Hamilton was beaming and making small talk with Max about the 49ers.

Connor sat down right next to Max, who moved some of his notes to make room. Judge Washburn walked to the head of the table and the room fell silent as the negotiating teams looked toward him expectantly. "Okay, now that we're all here, I'm going to read the settlement term sheet and then, if what I have written is acceptable to everyone, I'll have my secretary type it up so you can all sign it before you go home." He glanced around the table, opened his notebook and began to read.

As Connor expected, the settlement was long on press release fodder (a wordy apology and a meaningless guilty plea to a record-keeping infraction) and short on money. Even with Connor's attorney fees, the defendants were only paying $1.5 million—or about a quarter of Connor's private estimate of what the case was worth. To call it a slap on the wrist would be an overstatement.

Judge Washburn stopped reading and looked up. "So, does that accurately reflect your agreement?"

"It does," said Alvarez.

Max started to nod, but Connor leaned forward and said, "That's not the whole settlement, is it?"

The mediator frowned at Connor, and Max turned to him in surprise. "What's missing?"

"Well, the fact that they'll be barred from public contracting in the future, of course. I mean, they're publicly admitting that they stole taxpayer money, right? They're even pleading guilty to it. The government can't very well turn around and do business with them after that, can it?"

"Of course not," replied Max nonchalantly.

"And someone will need to notify all the cities, school districts, and so on to make sure they know who they're dealing with before they hire these guys," Connor continued. "So there should be some sort of notice provision in the settlement agreement and—"

There was a choking sound from across the table. Hiram Hamilton's mouth was opening and shutting soundlessly and his lawyers both wore expressions of mixed shock and outrage.

"That was *not* part of our deal!" said Alvarez. "We're not agreeing to debarment!"

"You don't have to!" Max shot back, his face reddening. "The State of California does not do business with criminals."

Alvarez glared at Max. "You are acting in remarkably bad faith, Mr. Volusca! I—"

"As long as we're talking about bad faith—" began Max, his voice rising.

Judge Washburn held up his hand. "Counsel!" he said in a stern tone cultivated through twenty years on the bench. He gave Connor a quick look that made him glad that retired judges can't jail anyone for contempt.

Max and Alvarez subsided, though both continued to glare at each other like feuding fourth graders.

Connor relaxed and suppressed a smile. That had been a gamble. Despite Max's comments, the government often did business with companies that had previously been caught overbilling. Max didn't like that and had grumbled to Connor about it from time to time. Connor had therefore bet that his friend would rather walk away from the settlement than admit that a dirty company could be allowed to land state contracts in the future.

"All right," said the mediator. "It looks like I was a little premature in thinking we had a deal. I'd like both sides to go back to their conference rooms while we sort out this little hiccup."

Connor hung back as the room cleared. Once he and Judge Washburn were alone, he said, "Sorry about that."

The mediator looked at him darkly. "No, you're not."

"Actually, I am. I want a negotiated settlement

too, but I don't think either of us wants one that's based on a misunderstanding."

Judge Washburn scowled at Connor for several seconds, then shook his gray head and broke into a rueful grin. "I think both of us understand the situation perfectly."

7

ALLIE NIBBLED HER WAY THROUGH ANOTHER handful of white cheddar popcorn and washed it down with a sip of Diet Coke. The bowl held only crumbs and a few duds, so she opened another bag (her second) and poured it in. A nearly empty package of Keebler Deluxe Grahams sat on the table between the popcorn and a nearly empty 2-liter Diet Coke bottle.

She ate when she was nervous, and she was always nervous when Connor was trying to negotiate a settlement of one of Devil to Pay's lawsuits. She understood why she couldn't be at the negotiating table with him, but that didn't make it any easier to sit in her apartment and wait for a phone call.

The waiting was particularly hard this time. She needed the money more than she usually did—the last settlement had been a little smaller than she expected and she had been living a little larger than maybe she should have.

Plus, Connor had called late in the afternoon to

tell her that he was stuck in a conference room by himself. The mediator had been trying to freeze him out of the negotiations and wanted to settle the case for peanuts. He said he'd call her back if they ever got to the point of negotiating a whistleblower share.

That had been three hours ago, and she had been putting away about 1,000 calories an hour since then. She wondered how long it would take to eat herself to death like a goldfish. Not a bad way to go, actually.

The opening notes of "Sympathy for the Devil" played from her phone and she grabbed it from the table. She bit her lip and looked at Connor's picture on the phone's screen. "I hope you've got good news for me, bud." She clicked the answer icon and held the phone to her ear. "So?"

He laughed. "It's good to talk to you too, Allie. How's life treating you?"

"You tell me."

"Life isn't bad." He sighed and she could hear him stretch. "In fact, life is pretty good right now."

"*How* good?"

"Oh, all right. Ten million dollars good, plus attorney fees. Max is offering twenty percent to Devil to Pay as a *qui tam* share. We could try to negotiate with him for a bigger cut, but—"

"Woooooo-hooooo!"

"Hey, Max," she heard him call, "I think she's okay with twenty."

She did some quick calculations in her head. Connor got a twenty-percent contingent fee in addition to his hourly rate and then there were taxes to pay. Still, she should net about a million, which was almost double what she had hoped for—enough to pay all her bills, keep living the good life for a couple of months, send a couple hundred thousand back to her mom, and still have some left over to invest. "So, how did you do it?"

"Remember how I told you the mediator was trying to put together a mostly noncash deal? Well, that blew up when the Hamilton team realized that Max would try to debar them from public contracting. So everybody went back and started over and this time the mediator didn't try to keep Max and me apart. We talked it over and decided that Hamilton didn't need to be debarred so long as they paid a substantial price for their misconduct and had an independent auditor go through their bills on any future government contracts."

"Very nice! I knew my lawyer could beat up anyone else's lawyer."

Connor laughed. "There's an old saying at the bar: 'good facts make great lawyers,' and you always give me great facts to work with. So, are you up for a victory dinner tonight?"

She bit her lip. These dinners always made her stomach do somersaults even when she hadn't just filled it with junk food. The thought of an evening alone with Connor at a five-star restaurant filled her with all sorts of conflicting feelings that she wasn't ready to deal with. "Um, sure. Eight o'clock at the usual place?"

He laughed again. "Perfect. By the way, now that this case is wrapping up, we should start thinking about the next one. Do you have anything in the pipeline?"

"Nothing yet, but I just lined up a new job through my temp agency. I'm starting on Monday. Two-month assignment, so I should have plenty of time to look around."

"I'll have my paralegal do some background research on them. Who is it?"

"Hold on a sec." She dug in her purse and found the notes from her last conversation with Trudi. "Okay, here we go: Blue Sea Technology. They do a lot of maritime salvage and engineering work for both Defense and the State of California. Big-ticket stuff like that turbine project under the Golden Gate Bridge. They're checking my fingerprints and criminal record right now. By the way, my agency says their books are a mess, which is why they're bringing in me and a couple other CPA temps."

Connor whistled. "My, my, my. Classified government contracts, lots of money, and messy books. Sounds like an excellent prospect. Happy hunting."

"Thanks. I've got a good feeling about this one."

8

"ABOUT AS GOOD AS WE'RE GOING TO GET," Connor told his reflection. He'd managed to make his wavy brown hair look casual rather than unruly—a feat that usually only his stylist could accomplish. The collarless white Dior shirt looked as good with the black V-neck sweater as the sales clerk had promised, and they both went well with his favorite light gray slacks. He could use a little more chin and a little less nose, but there wasn't much he could do about that.

He checked his watch: only an hour until his reservation at Wente. Time to get going. He took a deep breath and headed for the door.

There were higher rated restaurants a lot closer to his San Francisco apartment, but Wente was where he went to celebrate. It was a special place—the rolling vineyard hills that surrounded it, the concerts on the lawn on summer nights, the memories of dozens of family dinners there over the years. And they had a superb reserve cabernet to go with their excellent filet mignon. He doubted that Wente was Allie's type of place, but so what? He wasn't going to let that spoil his dinner.

His powerful Bentley convertible purred through the clogged streets of San Francisco. They gave way to urban highway at the Bay Bridge, and that in turn gave way to grass-covered hills, populated only by cattle and the occasional deer. Then the hill country opened into a wide valley that held the aptly-named Pleasanton, where Connor had grown up. Ten minutes later he was in the Livermore wine country. And in the heart of the wine country lay the cluster of brightly lit buildings that made up the Wente winery and restaurant.

Connor put the Bentley in park, tossed the keys to the valet, and walked up to the hostess. "Evening, Christine."

"Good evening, Mr. Norman." She smiled brightly and glanced at her reservation book. "Table for one tonight?"

"Yes. There's a concert starting in about fifteen minutes, isn't there?"

She nodded. "A Grammy-winning jazz trio. Your table has an excellent view." She picked up a menu and wine list and led him back.

"Good, but don't put me so close that I can't carry on a quiet conversation."

Christine stopped and turned. "I'm sorry. I thought you wanted a table for one."

He smiled. "I do."

"Umm, okay."

She seated him and he ordered a glass of champagne. Once he was alone, he put on his Bluetooth headset and took out his cell phone. He started to dial but stopped. No, wait for the champagne.

A moment later, a waiter appeared with a tall flute of sparkling wine, took Connor's order, and left. Connor discovered that his palms were damp and he wiped them on his pants. Then he picked up his phone and dialed.

Allie picked up on the first ring. "Hi, Connor. Thanks for dinner. I love this place!" He loved the silvery energy in her voice. It was the perfect complement to the champagne in his hand and the evening deepening around him.

"Where are you? Tell me about it."

"I'm at Gary Danko. I'm sitting by the window and watching the fog coming in through the Golden Gate. I just ordered their tasting menu. I've always wanted to do that."

"You'll love it. I'm sitting on the patio at Wente. It's an old school restaurant out where I grew up. It's surrounded by hills covered by grapevines. The sun has already set and they're starting to light the gas heaters, but the hilltops are still bright gold and green." He wanted to add *like your eyes,* but stopped himself. They were friends and colleagues—and that was all. Anything more would cause him serious problems at work. Doyle & Brown had a draconian policy against personal involvement with clients. Even these dinners pushed the envelope.

"Sounds beautiful. What are you having?"

"Filet mignon with the house reserve cab. Oh, and I've got a glass of champagne in front of me now. Do you have yours?"

"Um, yeah."

"Excellent, I'd like to propose a toast." He lifted his glass. "To making the devil pay."

"To making the devil pay."

He took a sip and savored the crisp, not quite sweet taste. "Ahh. There's nothing quite like taking down a bad guy, is there?"

"It's not a bad way to make a living."

"Oh, it's a lot more than that, don't you think? For every dollar we get paid, three or four dollars of stolen taxpayer money go back into state coffers. Plus, the companies that stole it get to have Max wash their dirty laundry—while they're still wearing it."

She laughed. "I'd love to see that sometime. Too bad I can never sit in on any of those meetings."

"It is too bad. Just like it's too bad that we can never have these victory dinners together." He wondered whether he was trying to convince himself or her. He deepened his voice and imitated the narrator of the old Batman reruns he'd seen as a child. "But we must protect your secret identity at all costs."

"That's me: mild-mannered accounting temp in the eyes of the world. But I'm really Qui Tam Girl, fighter against fraud and injustice!"

He chuckled. "We joke about it, but it really is true. You are doing great things, and I'm proud to know you."

"Thanks, and likewise. I couldn't do it without you."

"Yes, you could. Any decent lawyer could set up a shell company for you and tell you what evidence you need to build a good case. You're the one who actually goes and gets it. You put it on the line every day by going into these companies undercover, finding the fraud, and never getting caught. Hey, I'm going to propose another toast." He lifted his glass again. "To Qui Tam Girl."

"And her crime-fighting partner, Lawyer Boy."

"I'll drink to that." And he did.

"Cheers!"

He set down his glass. "We really do get to fight crime. I love that. I wish everyone took the law as seriously as we do. If you commit a crime, you should pay the price. Every. Single. Time. No excuses, no compromises."

"Uh-huh. By the way, is that PI still tailing you?" she asked, referring to a detective who had been following Connor during a previous case.

"I don't think so. I'm pretty sure he was working for Three C, and we settled with them six months ago. I still can't believe they had someone going through my garbage. Good thing I shred *Us* magazine before I put it in the trash."

She laughed. "It's amazing what dirty contractors will do to figure out who I am. Who knows, maybe some lucky investigator is getting a free dinner at Wente right now, courtesy of Hiram Hamilton."

"Maybe." He saw his waiter approaching with a loaded tray. "Speaking of dinner, mine is arriving."

"Mine too, so I'm going to let you go. It was good talking to you."

"And it's always good talking to you, Allie. Have a great dinner. Danko's is the best place in the city."

Connor took off his headset and was truly alone for the first time that night. He looked around the restaurant and realized he was the only one eating by himself. He must look a little pathetic.

He shook off the feeling. Tonight was a time to celebrate. He took a bite of his filet mignon. As delectable as always. The jazz trio was just starting to play, and the sky overhead had darkened to deep sapphire, with a few early stars glimmering in it like diamond chips on blue velvet. Maybe Allie would like this place after all, at least tonight. He smiled at the thought and took another bite of his steak.

• • •

Allie closed her cell phone and put it down on a cluttered counter. She sighed and shook her head slightly. It really would be fun to be dressed up and sitting in Danko's right now.

Instead, she was wearing sweats and standing in her kitchen. Erik hadn't liked the idea of her "going out" with Connor, even though they would have been miles apart. He had promised to buy her lobster and champagne to make it up to her. But somehow that hadn't actually happened.

She looked over to the sofa and saw Erik watching her with a smirk. "Qui Tam Girl and Lawyer Boy? Excuse me while I go puke."

She wadded up a piece of junk mail and threw it at him. "Oh, shut up. I thought you were asleep."

"Why'd you tell him you were at Danko's? I thought we agreed that . . . uh . . ." She watched his smirk fade as he remembered the lobster and champagne.

She shrugged and turned away. "It's what he wanted to hear, and there's no harm in letting him hear it."

"So, how often do you lie to me?"

"Hmm, let me see . . . Never—as far as you know."

9

THE MAN LOOKED DOWN AT THE PASSPORT in his hand as the line snaked toward the customs checkpoint at San Francisco International Airport. It identified him as Cho Dae-jung of Seoul, Republic of Korea. Other papers in his wallet and luggage reversed family and personal names in the Western fashion, calling him Dae-jung Cho. Some even informally Westernized it to David Cho.

He reminded himself that he was Cho so long as he was in America. Cho couldn't be just an *act*— it had to be *him*. He needed to lose himself in this identity as long as he was in enemy territory. He needed to be utterly convincing to the outside world. So from now on, he would think of himself as Cho.

Cho was a sailor employed by Incheon Marine Industries, a South Korean marine exploration and mining firm—or so his documents said. He was here to make a voyage aboard the *Grasp II*, an American vessel with advanced technology unavailable in South Korea. The trip would begin and end across the San Francisco Bay at the Port of Oakland. He doubted that the customs clerks would be chatty enough to ask about the exact purpose of his trip, but if they did, he could give an honest answer: he didn't know. His superiors were keeping the exact destination and goal of their trip confidential—which was not unusual among the secretive fraternity of ocean bottom explorers.

The line moved forward and he was at the front. The clerk in one of the customs booths motioned him over. His heart quickened, as it always did at these moments. His papers and cover story were both solid, but what if his name had been added to a TSA watch list? What if the South Korean National Intelligence Service had discovered he was here and told the CIA? What if the clerk simply didn't like his looks and had him pulled aside for fingerprinting and a thorough background check?

He walked forward and held out his documents to a bored-looking overweight woman whose nametag said "Sandra." She looked at them quickly and glanced from his passport picture to his face and back. "Anything to declare, Mr. Cho?"

"No."

"How long will you be in the United States?"

"Two or three weeks. It depends on the weather and how many days my ship voyage takes."

She gave him a quizzical look. "You here for a cruise?"

"No. Perhaps I am unclear." He made himself smile and look a little embarrassed. "My English is not so good. I am here for a business voyage.

My company rents the ship, and I am crew."

She looked at his papers again, studying them closely. Lines of concentration formed around her mouth and between her eyebrows. He felt the muscles in the back of his neck stiffen and performed mental calming exercises to prevent himself from sweating.

After nearly a minute, the woman turned and waved over a beefy man wearing a blazer and tie. She handed him the documents and the two of them had a conversation that the visitor couldn't quite hear. They were both poring over his documents now, shooting quick glances at him as they spoke.

He looked past the customs checkpoint and spotted an exit about twenty feet away. He was confident that he could get past these two and through the door in no more than fifteen seconds, but what then? He would be on the run in a strange country with no safe houses, no weapons, and his only cover identity blown.

The conversation ended and the woman looked up again. The lines on her face relaxed. "Okay, I see. All right." She handed the documents back to him and smiled. "Welcome to America, Mr. Cho."

10

AMAZING. ALLIE SHOOK HER HEAD AND leaned back in the chair in her cubicle at Blue Sea. During her orientation, the HR director had bragged about how the company had grown from a little salvage and commercial diving outfit twenty years ago into a billion dollar company today. Maybe they were worth a billion dollars, but their accounting system wasn't worth the week-old leftovers in the back of Allie's fridge. She had literally seen gas stations with more financial sophistication.

Based on what her supervisor told her, five years ago the company had tried to modernize their records by computerizing everything. They bought an accounting software package that they didn't really understand and hired some temps to convert all of their financial information to the new program. They left the job of keeping it current to secretaries—none of whom had any accounting training, naturally.

The result, of course, was a colossal mess. Now the company was a finalist for a $360 million government contract and, in the words of Allie's supervisor, needed to "tidy up the books a little" before submitting their final bid. And that bid was due in just over two weeks.

This was all music to Allie's ears. All the

permanent employees around her would be distracted, so no one would have the time to pay close attention to what she was doing. Better yet, Blue Sea would need to have people working on this "tidying up" project around the clock, so no one would find anything suspicious about a temp poking around in the files after hours. And Allie didn't mind working after hours. Not at all. Work was an easy way to keep her mind focused on the here and now—which was exactly what she wanted this week.

Allie scanned her computer's directory and pulled up half a dozen project files at random. Each was supposed to contain an Excel spreadsheet showing every transaction and PDFs of all backup documents. Three of the spreadsheets featured at least one phantom entry with no accounting backup. Another spreadsheet was completely blank. Only one file held a spreadsheet that actually matched the supporting PDFs.

Then Allie pulled up the electronic general ledger to see whether the numbers in it matched what the spreadsheets showed. Surprisingly, they all did. Allie surmised that the IT staff had linked the spreadsheets directly to the general ledger to prevent errors. Not bad.

Having a good general ledger system wouldn't save them, though. If all the files were as bad as the ones she'd seen, the general ledger was garbage. Blue Sea had no idea whether its invoices were accurate, which almost certainly meant they were overbilling some of the time. They'd be on the hook for triple the amount of each overcharge *plus* $10,000 for each inaccurate invoice they sent the government.

Allie grinned. This would be easier than a slow run on the bunny slopes. Almost as boring too, but she could live with boring if she was well paid for it.

The only potential problem was that none of the files she'd pulled were for government projects. She pulled up the directory again and scanned it for telltale words like "U.S.," "State" or "base." Nothing.

She decided to risk running a few searches. There was a chance that an alert IT staffer might spot what she was doing, but it was a small chance. Even if they did catch her, there wasn't anything particularly suspicious about an accounting temp who had been hired to help the company get ready for a government contract running searches for government invoices in the company's accounting database.

"Your search has located 0 records," her computer informed her.

She frowned and did a little more digging in the directory. There was a secure server she couldn't access. That must be where all the government files lived.

She drummed her fingers on her fake wood desk as she weighed her options. Ask someone to give her access to the secure server? No, the connection would be too obvious when the documents she found there later appeared in Devil to Pay's court filings.

Try hacking into the secure server? Maybe. She'd helped configure security software for an accounting database during a previous assignment and had learned a couple of tricks in the process. At the very least, she could poke around and see whether the system administrator had left an unlocked "back door" in the security barriers. She'd be careful, and she doubted that they'd be on the lookout for internal hackers. After all, how many employees were likely to try to hack into a bunch of customer files? Still, it would be risky.

Was there time to take a quick trip into forbidden cyberspace, or was she done for the night? Allie glanced at the clock on her computer: 6:23 p.m. She hesitated, her fingers poised over the keyboard. She needed to call Mom and Sam tonight, and she really couldn't put it off any longer. It was already 8:23 back home in Illinois, and Mom usually went to bed by 9:30.

Thinking about calling Mom got her thinking about Dad. She'd been trying not to think about him all day and most of yesterday, but she couldn't hide from him anymore. His blood-spattered face filled her mind, repeating soothing lies over and over.

She closed her eyes and took a deep breath. Worries about secure servers and dreams of easy money vanished, burned away by memories bursting out of a locked box buried in the back of her mind. Tonight was their night, and she couldn't keep them away. Tomorrow she'd force them back in, close the lid, and lock the box again. But tonight was their night.

Yeah, she was done. She wiped her eyes and opened them. The computer screen glowed expectantly, showing a list of Blue Sea's servers and their file paths. Tomorrow. She sniffed and turned off her computer.

11

THE EARLY EVENING SUN ARCED OVER THE canopy, casting splintered gleams as its light caught imperfections in the thick old Plexiglas. Then shadow filled the cockpit as Connor nosed the *White Knight* over into a power dive, making sure to keep the sun directly behind him to blind antiaircraft gunners on the ground.

The deep roar of the single Packard V-1650 engine thrummed through the entire plane. The airspeed gauge climbed fast, racing past 200, 300, 400. The airframe shook with speed and the altimeter plummeted. A familiar adrenaline rush hit Connor and a wide grin spread across his face.

The Japanese airstrip rushed up at him. Zeroes and Oscars lined up in neat rows on either side of a dirt runway. Camouflage-painted buildings and fuel tanks hid among palm trees. Uniformed men scrambled for cover or ran for their planes. Machine guns blazed away from behind sandbag rings that looked like brown snow forts, sending streams of phantom bullets toward Connor and his plane.

Connor returned the sentiment, firing a sustained burst from the six .50-caliber guns in the *White Knight*'s wings. The force of the guns rattled his teeth and slowed the plane sharply, pushing Connor forward into his harness.

He dragged back on the stick, killing more airspeed and pulling the plane out of its dive. G-forces crushed him back into his seat and his heart struggled to pump blood to his brain against the unnatural gravity. He flew over the base at treetop level, so close that he could see the bright red star of the Imperial Japanese Army on the gunners' helmets. He kept his finger on the trigger the whole time, aiming roughly at a group of Zeroes, which duly exploded.

Suddenly the camp was behind him and he was flying over a sea of warehouses and parking lots. He wheeled around and headed back toward the jungle camp. He leaned toward his mic. "Okay, here I come again. I'll be flying in low from the north, and I'll be shooting at the oil tank."

"Roger that," said a voice in his ear.

The line of palms flashed below him and a large oil tank came into view. He pressed the trigger, but no bullets came. He swore and tried again. Still nothing. The oil tank blew up on cue anyway, but Connor was not happy. He pulled the stick back and to the right, veering smoothly around the fireball. "Sorry about that," he said into the mic. "A wire must've pulled loose or something. I've never had that happen before."

A few seconds passed in silence. Then the director's voice came on. "Don't worry about it, Connor. You did great. We just looked at the roughs, and we got some terrific footage. It'll be easy to have the FX guys add muzzle flashes. Besides, we don't have another oil tank ready to blow up."

"Okay, Steve. Well, if you change your mind later, let me know. I'll be happy to bring the *White Knight* down free of charge for a reshoot. I want to make sure you get your money's worth."

"Oh, we did. Cindy will be in touch with you in a couple of weeks about scheduling the dogfight scene."

An hour later, Connor was at the Bob Hope Airport in Burbank, crouching on the wing of the *White Knight* and peering down into the machine gun feed mechanism in her left wing. The guns hadn't jammed. He smiled even though that meant more work later. He was proud of those guns, and it pleased him that they were still working smoothly over two generations after they came off the assembly line.

The problem lay somewhere between the trigger on the control stick and the guns' firing mechanism. Since all six guns had failed, he suspected a wiring problem in the cockpit. He'd have to tear it apart once he had the plane back at its home airport in Livermore.

"Is that a P-51D?" asked a young voice behind him.

Connor turned and saw a boy of about twelve, staring at the *White Knight* with bright blue eyes.

Connor stood and smiled. "It is indeed. How did you know it was a D?"

The boy pointed to the bubble canopy. "It doesn't have that big thing behind the pilot that the A, B, and C models had." He gestured at the wings. "And it's got six guns, not four."

"Very good. I'm impressed."

"Do the guns still work?"

"They do. In fact, I was just firing them today. A movie studio is making a war movie called *Blood on the Sun*, and they paid me to fly down and shoot up a Japanese airstrip—or pretend to shoot it up anyway. I loaded the guns with blanks

70

today. The real bullets are locked up back at my hangar."

"Cool, I'll have to see that movie when it comes out."

Connor tapped the metal skin of the wing. "You know, my grandfather actually built the guns in this plane during World War II."

"Whoa, he built P-51s?"

"Well, not quite. He owned a company called Lamont Industries that made all sorts of machinery. One of the things they made was machine guns for the P-51. When the war was over, he bought one of the planes that had his guns in it."

"I wish my grandfather had a P-51."

"Stein!" called a pretty blonde woman who had just emerged from an office building. "Time to go!"

"Hold on just a sec." Connor felt around inside the wing and found a small loose cylinder. He pulled it out and handed it to the boy. "Want an empty cartridge from today's movie shoot?"

The boy's eyes widened. "Thanks!" Then he turned and ran to his mother, showing her his prize as soon as he reached her.

Connor chuckled as he watched them go. Twenty years ago, he had been exactly the same. He pestered Grandpa Lamont for a ride in the *White Knight* at least once a week, and when they were in the air, he always begged to shoot the guns. Grandpa had soon learned to keep them unloaded whenever he took his trigger-happy grandson for a ride.

Grandpa had been convinced that Connor would be a fighter pilot and had given him the P-51 when he got his pilot's license. Grandpa hadn't exactly said he was disappointed when Connor chose Stanford over the Air Force Academy, but he had made Connor promise that he wouldn't let the *White Knight* get rusty.

That hadn't been a hard promise to keep. Connor loved the old plane and kept it in mint condition. He flew it at least once a month when he was in California and had trained himself to be a competent P-51 mechanic.

As for Grandpa Lamont's desire that Connor spend his life shooting down America's enemies, Connor liked to think that he was doing just that—even if he generally didn't get to use machine guns on them.

12

OKAY, MIGHT AS WELL GET THIS OVER WITH.

Allie picked up the phone and hesitated. She eyed the bottle of margarita mix in the liquor cabinet, but decided against it. Better to do this sober.

She took a deep breath and dialed. The phone rang three times. Four. Five. She began to hope that Mom and Sam had gone to bed early.

But no. "Hello, Allie."

"Hi, Mom."

"Thanks for calling, sweetheart. It's so nice that you remember to call every July twenty-third." She paused. "It's ten years today."

"I know. Sometimes it feels like a hundred years ago—sometimes it almost feels like it's still happening. How are you and Sam doing?"

"We're fine." She sighed, and Allie could hear the tired smile in her voice. "Samantha and the girls made oatmeal-raisin cookies and we sat around the kitchen table and ate them and looked at pictures of Grandpa."

"Wow, he would be a grandfather now, wouldn't he? It's weird to think of him like that."

"I know. He's forever young, isn't he?" Mom's voice got rougher and softer. "He'll always be the man in those pictures."

"Which pictures were you looking at?"

"The ones from our last trip to the Dells. The girls loved the one of you and Sam on his shoulders. Do you remember that one?"

"Oh, sure." She and Sam, each wearing bikinis and each standing on one of Dad's shoulders in the hotel swimming pool. All of them wet and laughing in the sun. Dad was a big man, proud of his size and strength. One of his favorite pool or beach stunts was to balance his two teenage daughters on his shoulders like a circus strongman. Sometimes they even stayed up long enough for Mom to snap a picture. That had been the last time.

Less than forty-eight hours after that picture was taken, he'd been lying next to Allie in a pile of twisted steel and shattered glass, his face too pale and—

Waves of guilt crashed over Allie, driving her down and suffocating her. She squeezed her eyes shut and swallowed hard. Her eyes were suddenly wet and she fought back sobs. "So, how are you and Sam doing?" she forced out.

Mom paused a second before answering. "We're fine, dear. How are you?"

She sniffed and took a deep breath. "I'm good. Just started a new job. Lots to do. These guys can build an underwater power plant, but they can't balance a checkbook." She laughed, a brittle and harsh sound. "So anyway . . ."

"Are you sure everything's all right, Allie?"

No. "Yes. I'm just . . . work is just really busy and I'm kind of distracted and tired." She faked a yawn. "Sorry."

Mom paused again. "All right. Well, I'll let you get some rest then. Have a good night, honey. I love you."

"I love you too, Mom." She sniffed again and wiped her eyes on a sheet of paper towel, leaving little smears of mascara. "Give Sam and her girls hugs from me, okay? And if you need any money or anything, just let me know."

"Thank you, but you're already too generous. We still have over twenty thousand from the last wire transfer you sent."

"When that starts to run out, let me know."

"Good night, Allie."

"Good night, Mom."

She hung up and took out the margarita mix. She dumped some ice in a big plastic mug, filled it halfway up with mix, and then the rest of the way with pure tequila.

Last year had been a lot easier. She had held it together for nearly two hours, chatting and reminiscing about Dad with no problem. Come to think of it, the year before hadn't been too bad either. Maybe this year was rough because it was the ten-year anniversary of the crash. She took a swig from her mug, and the strong tequila aftertaste promised a powerful buzz by the time she reached the bottom. Good.

The annual Dad calls were like going to the dentist for a checkup. Sometimes all that poking around was basically painless. But other times, ka-BLAM—it hit a nerve with no warning. It felt like being slapped with an oven mitt covered in broken glass.

She popped her iPod into the stereo and set it to shuffle. She took another swallow of super-charged margarita and flopped down on the sofa as the first song came on: "Novocain for the Soul." She laughed and tipped back the mug again. How appropriate.

13

Predictably, the call came at 7:00 on a morning when Mitch Daniels was trying to sleep in. First Mate Randy Jenkins told him that the *Grasp II* was sailing in 24 hours, and anyone not on board would be left behind. Mitch said he'd be there, hung up the phone, and rolled over. His wife, Sherrie, was snoring vigorously. He thought about trying to roll her onto her side, but if she woke up she'd yell at him, insist she didn't snore, and they'd have a fight. Too early for that. He put on his headphones and buried his head under a fat down pillow. He had just started to drift back to sleep when the phone rang again.

Mitch groaned and dragged the handset to his ear. "Hello?"

"Mitch, pick up a can of WD-40 on your way to the dock, okay?" said Ed Granger's voice. "I'll see you there at eight."

Out of deference to the sleeping Sherrie, Mitch didn't yell. Instead he whispered, "It's seven in the morning, Ed. Go do your own shopping."

"Can't. Jenkins told me Tuesday he didn't think we'd be sailing until next week, so now I gotta get down to the G-2 and do four days' worth of work on Eileen in twenty-four hours."

"Yeah, well that sucks for you. I'm going back to sleep."

Ed gave an exaggerated sigh. "Okay, fine. If you don't want to know what else Jenkins told me when he called me this morning, that's fine."

"What'd he say?"

"I'll tell you when we're on the G-2."

Mitch flopped his head back on the pillow and stared at the popcorn ceiling. There was no way he'd be able to go back to sleep now. "This better be worth it."

Ed cackled. "Oh, yeah. And don't forget the WD-40."

"Up yours, Granger."

The familiar scent of bunker oil, seawater, and diesel exhaust met Mitch as he stepped out of the cab he had taken from the 12th Street subway station to the Port of Oakland. The sharp, incessant cry of sea gulls mixed with the sound of the sea breeze and the rumble of the trucks that were picking up or dropping off shipping containers.

The *Grasp II* lay in her berth, her freshly painted hull gleaming blue and white in the morning sun. She was squat and low, and her two cranes looked like mismatched mantis arms on her deck. The G-2 wasn't a beautiful or graceful ship, but she had a certain magnificent ugliness that Mitch liked.

He picked up his duffel and stainless-steel mug and walked across the stained concrete dock to his ship. First Mate Jenkins leaned against the gangplank railing, a clipboard in one hand and an Egg McMuffin in the other. He wore a clean uniform shirt, but didn't look like he'd showered. So even he had been surprised by their sailing date and time. Interesting.

Jenkins checked him in and confiscated Mitch's cell phone and laptop. When Mitch asked why, the second officer just shrugged. "Captain's orders."

"Any idea why? We've gone on some pretty hush-hush trips before, but the captain never ordered us to turn in computers."

Another shrug. "He's ordering it this time."

Jenkins didn't seem to be in a talkative mood, so Mitch gave up and went below to stow his gear and find Ed Granger. As he expected, Ed was in the machine shop tinkering with Eileen. Man and machine looked remarkably alike: ugly, powerfully built, and bulging in odd places.

"Hey, Ed." Mitch pulled a can of WD-40 out of his jacket pocket and tossed it to his friend.

Ed caught it nimbly. "Thanks, Mitch."

"Just make sure you pay me back." Mitch drained the last inch of lukewarm coffee from his mug and yawned. "So, what did Jenkins tell you?"

"Hey, you want a reload?" Ed pointed a greasy finger toward a battered orange Thermos. "I got some Italian roast in there. Not the garbage you get from Starbucks—roasted and ground those beans myself. Pretty good if I do say so—that's as full-bodied and sensuous a cup of joe as you're gonna find."

" 'Full-bodied and sensuous'?" repeated Mitch as he poured himself a steaming mug. "What, am I supposed to drink it or take it to a hotel room?"

"Do both for all I care." Ed snorted and turned back to Eileen. "Last time I give you good coffee."

Mitch took a sip. It really was good coffee. "Sorry, man. This is good stuff. It really is, uh, sensuous and full-bodied."

No response from Ed.

"So, *what did Jenkins tell you?*"

Still no response.

"Oh, come on, man! You wake me up, make me get your stupid WD-40, and come all the way down here—and now you're not going to tell me because I made a joke about your coffee?"

"Don't make fun of my coffee."

"Fine. I'm sorry, okay? I won't do it again."

Pause. "Okay."

"So, what did Jenkins tell you?"

Ed stood slowly, wiped his hands on a towel that was almost as dirty as they were, and motioned for Mitch to come closer. "Okay, so I went down to Jimmy's last night," he said in a thick whisper. "Jenkins is already there, so I sit down next to him and we start talking. He's had a few, and you know how he is when he's had a few. So I figure this is a good time to ask him what the big mystery is and why they wanted all that new equipment on Eileen. And he says, 'Ed, you know I can't talk about that.'

"So I say, 'Come on, it's me. Who am I gonna tell? Besides, I already know we'll be looking for gold.'

"And he says, 'Who told you that?'

"And I say, 'Oh, I figured it out, but if you tell me the rest of it, I promise to keep quiet.'

"So he tells me. At the end of World War II, the Nazis have all this gold and jewels they took from the Jews and the French and other people, right? They want to hide it where the Americans and Russians can't find it, so they put a bunch of it on their biggest submarine and send it to Japan. They stuff it so full they even put loot in the torpedo tubes."

Mitch grinned. "But the submarine never reached Japan, am I right?"

Ed grinned back. "You are correct, sir. No one knew what happened to it until a fishing boat found some wreckage in its nets a couple of months ago."

"Wow." Mitch pondered for a moment. "Wait a sec, who owns it? The French and the Jews because it's their gold? The Germans because it's their sub? Or is it really finders keepers?" He took a sip of coffee and shook his head. "There's gonna be a huge lawsuit over this."

Ed's smile narrowed and a crafty gleam came into his eyes. "Only if someone figures out that we've found their gold."

14

ALLIE TOOK A SIP OF HER FOUR-SHOT VENTI white chocolate latte and tried again to focus on the spreadsheet on her monitor. She needed to reconcile it against a stack of customer files but was making slow progress. She had done about ten minutes' worth of work in the hour she'd been in the office.

A bartender had once explained to Allie that pure tequila wouldn't cause a hangover the next day because of the chemical structure of the sugars in the liquor. Based on extensive experience since then, Allie had concluded that the bartender was a liar trying to sell her pure tequila, which was a lot more expensive than the mixto stuff bars ordinarily use. Either that or lime juice caused pounding hangovers.

Whatever caused her hangover, the result was impressive. It hurt to stand up, it hurt to sit down, it hurt to think, and it hurt to talk. It even hurt to blink.

"Allie, please come with me," said a woman's voice behind her.

Allie jumped and turned to see her supervisor, a large and open-faced Hispanic woman named Sabrina.

"Hi, Sabrina. You startled me." She pointed at the screen and smiled, trying hard not to wince. "These spreadsheets are a little too interesting, I guess." Lame, but it never hurt to make sure her temporary employers knew they'd caught her working when they surprised her. They'd be less likely to keep a close eye on her in the future.

Sabrina didn't smile back. "Uh-huh."

They know! Panic shot through Allie, cutting straight through the hangover fog. She froze. Had she copied any hard files? No. Had she downloaded any of the screwed up on-line files she found? No. Had she accessed any locked files? No, but she had started looking for them. She'd had that secure server up on her computer screen last night—had she left it on? She couldn't quite remember. *Think! Think! Think!*

"Allie?" prompted Sabrina.

"Yes?"

"Could you come with me, please?"

"Oh, uh, okay. Just let me close out of this and I'll be right there."

"Don't worry about it. You can finish what you're doing later."

"Um, all right."

Allie stood slowly and followed Sabrina down the hall, several sets of eyes following her as she went. At least there were witnesses in case she never came back. She caught herself and smiled. Maybe she was being just a *touch* melodramatic.

Then she remembered that she had indeed turned off her computer last night. Her smile widened and the lump of ice in her stomach began to melt. She hadn't done anything remotely suspicious. Maybe this was nothing. In fact, it almost had to be.

She had mostly relaxed by the time Sabrina stopped at a conference room, gave a tight smile, and motioned for her to go in.

Allie returned her smile and walked in. Two men sat at a medium-sized oak table. One was Sanford "Sandy" Allen, one of the founders of Blue Sea. He had thick white hair and a wide, lined face that had made Allie think "grandfather" the first time she met him. Her only interaction with him had been on her first morning at Blue Sea. Sandy had greeted her and the other new temps and told them a few funny but pointless stories before turning them over to Sabrina.

He looked more like a prison warden than a grandfather today, and he frowned as she entered. The other man in the room was a younger, but equally grim, Asian with a crew cut. Allie didn't think she'd met him before.

She heard the door shut behind her and Mr. Allen said, "Have a seat, Miss Whitman."

Allie picked a chair near the door and perched

on its edge, the ice refreezing in her gut. "Why are you here?" asked crew cut man without bothering to introduce himself.

"Um, what do you mean?"

He glared at her. "You know what I mean. Why are you at this company? You're clearly overqualified for the work you're doing."

"Oh, well, I like the flexibility of temping and if I took a permanent job, I couldn't—"

He snorted. "Couldn't make nearly as much because you'd only have one company to sue, isn't that right?"

Her heart stopped and she gaped at him soundlessly.

Mr. Allen's frown deepened, turning the lines on his cheeks and forehead into shadowed crevices. Crew cut man's mouth twisted into a confident, predatory smile as he continued his cross-examination. "Yesterday, you were running searches for words like 'state,' 'federal' and 'government' in our customer files. Why?"

"You're—Blue Sea is trying to get a federal contract, so I—I figured that I'd see what your government contract files looked like."

Crew cut man waved his hand dismissively. "You're doing this after hours, with no one asking you to? That's an awful lot of initiative for a temp, but it makes perfect sense for a whistle-blower hunting for her next lawsuit, don't you think?"

"I—"

"And before you deny it," he said, raising his voice to talk over her, "think about whether you'll also deny working for every company ever sued by Devil to Pay."

She opened her mouth, but before she could speak, he added, "Oh, and I'm also interested to hear you explain how you afford that apartment and all those Tahoe and Vail trips on your temp earnings."

Her ears roared and she felt dizzy. "I don't understand. Why did you bring me in here and make all these . . . these accusations?"

Crew cut man leaned back and Mr. Allen leaned forward. His grandfather face was back, but it was somehow worse than crew cut man's open malice. "Oh, we're not making accusations, just—" he paused and rubbed his jaw. "Just observations. That's all. Now, we could share those observations publicly. We'd be very popular with a lot of our business partners if we did. And you'd never blow another whistle."

She struggled to ignore the adrenaline shouting in her brain. "But you haven't."

Mr. Allen smiled and nodded. "That's right. We haven't. We're the only ones who know about you, and we're willing to keep it that way."

"What do you want me to do?"

"Just keep doing what you're doing, but not here."

Now she saw where this was going. "And where do you want me to do it?"

Mr. Allen chuckled warmly and shook his head. "You're a clever young woman. Our main competitor is a company called Deep Seven. We're convinced that they're cheating the government, and we'd like you to go put a stop to it."

"Um, okay. No problem. What evidence do you have?"

Mr. Allen's smile faded and he raised his eyebrows, sending a network of wrinkles up into his snowy hair. "Finding evidence is your job, isn't it?"

She paused. "Are you saying you don't have any evidence?"

Crew cut man scowled and opened his mouth, but Mr. Allen raised his hand. "I'm saying that we're quite certain that Deep Seven is defrauding the government and that you can catch them."

She twisted sweaty hands below the table. She wanted to ask what would happen if she couldn't find evidence of fraud at Deep Seven, but she was afraid of what the answer would be. Better to leave it alone and cross that bridge if she came to it. She looked down at the highly polished table, avoiding her own reflected gaze.

"Do we understand each other, Ms. Whitman?"

She took a deep breath and looked up. "We understand each other, Mr. Allen."

He smiled with every part of his face except his eyes. "Please, call me Sandy."

15

SOMEONE RAPPED THE OLD "SHAVE AND A haircut" knock on Connor's office door.

Connor recognized that knock. "Two bits. Come on in, Tom."

Tom Concannon walked in. He was a tall, fit man of fifty-five with close-cropped gray hair, brown eyes, and an animated face. He had the easy manners and confidence of old money and good society—the sort of man who is equally comfortable in a neighborhood sports bar and at a formal embassy dinner. He also happened to be the managing partner of Doyle & Brown, though he never let that fact come between him and Connor.

Tom sat in one of Connor's leather office chairs, a smile on his face. "Nice work on the Hamilton matter. You make it look easy."

Connor shrugged modestly. "That one *was* easy. You know the old saying: 'good facts make great lawyers.'"

"But it often takes a great lawyer to find good facts."

"Not this time, but I won't argue with you."

"Not an argument you'd really want to win, I suspect." He crossed his legs and smoothed his tailored slacks in one fluid motion. "You should know that ExComm is very happy with your success in these *qui tam* cases. You've carved out a profitable new niche for the firm. You've also made invaluable connections in both state and federal government."

Connor nodded. "Thanks, I've tried to pick good cases, and I'm glad they've turned out well."

Tom paused and his face grew a little more serious, telegraphing that he was about to make his real point. "How would you feel about doing something outside that niche? There are some big cases coming down the pipe that could give you a real opportunity to step into the limelight and show off the skills I know you've got."

"Sure, I'd love to. What did you have in mind?"

"We've been asked to represent a company that's been indicted for bribery related to their, ah, contributions to a congressman. We'd like you to first chair the defense team."

"First chair?" Connor leaned back and let that sink in. "Wow, that's quite an honor. It's pretty far outside my field, though. You know I don't have any criminal experience, right?"

"We'll give you someone from the white collar crime team, but I really don't think this case is going to trial."

"Plea bargain?"

Tom nodded. "The client is anxious to start negotiations as quickly as possible."

Connor's eyebrows shot up. "*Start* negotiations? Weren't there any negotiations before they got indicted?"

Tom made a sound that was part sigh and part dry chuckle. "That depends on how you define 'negotiations.' Their GC used to be a litigation partner at an aggressive New York firm, and it shows. I'm sure he thought he was negotiating, but the Department of Justice seems to think he was grandstanding, stonewalling, and lying."

"Once they get that impression, it's very hard to change their minds." Connor bit his lip and replayed what he'd just been told. "And I'm guessing that there might be some pretty serious bad blood between their general counsel and the government. True?"

"Yes, in the same way that the Pope might be Catholic."

Connor laughed and shook his head. "If it's that bad, why not just take the case to trial? I mean, negotiations aren't likely to lead any place the company will want to go."

"Because a trial would mean a lot of publicity; they'd lose big, and they'd never get another government contract again."

"So they're guilty?"

"As sin."

Connor frowned. "Hmmm."

"Within these four walls, they haven't got a prayer at trial," Tom continued. "That's why they need you. You've got a good relationship with DOJ. They know you. They like you. You've even taken the local U.S. Attorney herself up in your plane, haven't you?"

"Her husband too."

Tom smiled and spread his hands out toward Connor. "See? You're exactly what they need— someone who can come in and talk the government down. Get them to agree to something reasonable."

Connor didn't like it. He didn't like that he would be helping exactly the type of dirty company that he spent most of his time taking down. He didn't like that his opponents would be the prosecutors he usually worked shoulder to shoulder with. And he particularly didn't like the idea of schmoozing people he considered friends to get them to go easy on a company that was guilty "as sin."

But he also didn't like the idea of saying no to Tom. He had no problem turning down the firm's managing partner, but he hated turning down a friend. Still, it was the right thing to do. The firm might choose to rain down its benevolence equally on the wicked and the righteous, but Connor was going to leave the wicked high and dry when he had the option.

Besides, what would Qui Tam Girl say if she found out that her crime-fighting partner had gone over to the dark side?

Connor smiled and Tom, mistaking the reason, smiled back. "So, you'll take the case?"

Connor shook his head. "Sorry to disappoint you, but I don't think I can."

Tom blinked and his smile vanished. "Why not? If you're too busy with your other cases, I'm sure we can get you help."

"That's not it. I just . . ." He paused, hunting for the right words and not finding them. "Look, there's no easy way to say it. I fight companies like this. I'm not going to represent one of them."

Tom said nothing, so Connor went on. "Rules matter. When someone intentionally breaks the rules, I think they should pay the price. I know everyone's entitled to a lawyer, even if they're guilty as sin. But they're not entitled to me. I'm sorry."

Tom's face hardened and he nodded. "I understand."

"I really am sorry, Tom. I hate saying no to you or the firm, even about this."

Tom's smile returned, but its warmth was gone. "Don't worry about it, Connor."

"I just want to make sure that we really do understand each other on this, Tom. If someone else in the firm wants to represent this company,

I'm fine with that. I wish them well. I'm just not comfortable doing it myself."

Tom uncrossed his legs and his smile became a little more natural. "We understand each other, Connor. You've got strong principles, and I admire that."

16

THE *GRASP II* WAS EVERYTHING CHO HAD expected. It had state-of-the-art technology throughout and a powerful winch and claw that should be more than sufficient to lift whatever they found on the ocean floor. His commander, who was going by Mr. Lee on this trip, had told the Americans it was a treasure-filled German submarine. Maybe that was true and maybe not. "Mr. Lee" had been extremely tight-lipped about the details of this trip for months.

Cho and Mr. Lee sat on one side of a small table in the *Grasp II*'s galley. The captain and first mate of the ship sat on the other side. The captain was Harry Wither, and he fit his name. He was a stooped white-haired man of at least seventy. He had a neatly trimmed beard, watery blue eyes, and a prominent nose laced with red veins. Perhaps he had been a strong captain once, but those days appeared to be long behind him. As far as Cho could tell, First Mate Randy Jenkins more or less ran the ship now. He certainly was trying to run the conversation they were having right now.

"Are all these men necessary?" Mr. Lee asked, pointing to a list of the ship's crew.

Jenkins folded thick tattooed arms across his broad belly. "Yeah. They are."

Mr. Lee's eyebrows went up two millimeters. "Please explain."

Jenkins frowned at the demand, but took the list of names and ticked them off with a stubby pencil. "Adams is Chief Engineer. Sanford is the Engineer's Mate. Curtis—"

"I can read their names and titles," Mr. Lee cut in, speaking in the precise and commanding tones Cho had heard many times before. "We have men who can perform all those duties. They will be here soon. Your men can give our men whatever information is necessary."

Jenkins snorted and scratched his thick red beard. "Let me explain how things work on this ship." He pointed to the captain. "This is the captain." He poked a meaty finger into his own chest. "I'm the first mate. We decide who comes on board and what jobs they do. And when this ship sails, we're 100 percent in command. We are both God and the devil to everyone on board. You are our guests, but we run this ship. Got it?"

Neither Mr. Lee's expression nor his authoritative tone changed. "You are mistaken." He pinned the captain with a hard look. "Captain

Wither, I believe your employer sent you a copy of the contract by e-mail last week."

The captain made a vague throat-clearing noise, and his eyes moved from Mr. Lee to his first mate. "Well, I don't know about that. I don't, ah, always read my e-mail."

Mr. Lee looked into the captain's eyes until the American dropped his gaze to the table.

Mr. Lee turned back to the first mate. "Perhaps you had a different role on other trips. This time, you are owner's representative only. We are renting this ship and will control. The contract will explain this to you." He plucked the crew list from Jenkins's hand with a quick motion. "We do not have someone to operate the ROV," he said as he read it. "How many men are required for this job?"

Jenkins turned red and his eyes flashed. "Three, but we can make do with two."

"Acceptable." He looked at the list. "Chief Pilot Granger and Assistant Pilot Daniels will come. The rest of the men are unnecessary and will not come."

The muscles of Jenkins's jaw clenched and unclenched. "I'll look at the contract."

"Very good. Your men are to be off the ship in two hours to make room for our men."

Mr. Lee stood without waiting for a reply and walked out. Cho trailed him.

When they were out of earshot of the

Americans, Mr. Lee turned to Cho and spoke in Korean. "Make sure that stupid red-haired *geseki* does what I told him to."

"Yes, sir. I doubt that he will properly understand his role even after he reads the contract."

Mr. Lee considered for a moment. "Once we are at sea, find an opportunity to educate him."

"Yes, sir."

17

THE LOBBY AT DEEP SEVEN MARITIME Engineering was an airy, high-ceilinged room decorated with pictures of ships and chunks of vaguely threatening machinery, each accompanied by a small plaque. A scattering of bulky leather furniture and glass-and-steel coffee tables faced a reception desk ruled by a sixtyish woman with distrustful eyes who reminded Allie of the librarian at her grade school.

Allie sat at one end of a leather sofa, clutching her purse and a small sheaf of forms from TempForce, her temp agency. She wore what Erik called her "costume"—a conservative navy suit, simple black flats, and cream blouse that hid her tattoos. She had also dyed her hair back to its original mousy brown and pulled it back into a responsible-looking bun. Her look screamed "accountant" to her when she saw it in the mirror this morning. Depressing, but reassuring.

The first day of a new temp job was usually an exciting time. She was a spy setting foot in an enemy country for the first time—an undercover Jane Bond who had tricked her way into the heart of a malevolent conspiracy to steal taxpayer dollars. The contrast between her blah cover and her secret mission—spiced with just a touch of danger—was absolutely delicious.

Or it had been delicious until today. Sour fear and bitter desperation filled her now. She had been *caught*. That changed everything. Worse, it could easily happen again.

Blue Sea had caught her before she did anything suspicious. Something must have tipped them off before she ever walked in the door. Most likely, they had put two and two together and realized that an accounting temp who specialized in government contracting would be ideally placed to feed information and documents to Devil to Pay. Since all of the defendants were Bay Area companies, they also could guess where she lived and worked. And once they figured that out, it would be simple to have a private detective investigate anyone with those characteristics who came to work for them.

Unanswerable questions crowded her mind. How many other companies had had the same epiphany as Blue Sea? Had Deep Seven? Would Blue Sea keep their promise about not blowing her cover—or would they expose her as soon as she took out Deep Seven? Was there anything she could do to wriggle out of the trap she was in?

She wanted to talk to Connor. Badly. She had almost called him a dozen times over the past two weeks. But every time she pulled her cell phone out and rested her thumb on the speed dial for his number, the same fear stopped her: he would tell her not to take a job at Deep Seven. He would insist. He'd say that even if they were dirty, she shouldn't play Blue Sea's game. He'd tell her to fight them. Then he'd start plotting legal strategy and he'd have the case half planned before she could get a word in.

Allie didn't doubt that Connor would beat Blue Sea, but so what? Her whistleblower career would be over and she doubted Connor could get enough money out of Blue Sea to make up for her loss. He could live with that, of course. There were plenty of other corporate dragons for him to slay, and she knew he didn't need the money.

The problem was that she *did* need the money. And she didn't need a dragon slayer right now. She needed someone who would make a deal with the dragon and keep it from burning up the princess's dollar-printing machine. Unfortunately, that wasn't Connor.

Besides, if Blue Sea *did* blow her cover, she could always tell Connor then. He probably wouldn't like the fact that she hadn't told him earlier, but he'd be furious with Blue Sea.

"Welcome to Deep Seven, Allie. My name is Janet Sheldon."

She looked up and saw a tall woman of about forty smiling down on her. She stood and smoothed her skirt. "Hi, thanks. I'm happy to be here."

"And we're happy to have you. We've heard a lot about you."

An icy finger stroked Allie's spine. She looked carefully at the other woman, but her face revealed nothing more than a plastic HR smile. "I, um, thanks."

"Let's head back to my office. We'll go over your paperwork, and I'll tell you more about the job."

Allie followed her back to her office. She took Allie's forms and looked through them while Allie sat silently and tried not to fidget. Janet Sheldon's office was a small, cheerful room decorated with children's artwork and framed motivational posters bearing uncomfortable captions like "AMBITION—Create the life of your dreams with every choice you make!" A catalogue titled "Successories" lay on her clean, organized desk.

Three minutes later, Janet looked up. Her lips were pressed together into a bright pink line and there were little furrows between her perfect eyebrows. "Hmmm. Your work history shows that your most recent assignment was at Blue Sea Technology. Is that true?"

Allie had expected that question, but she felt her heart rate spike anyway. "Yes, is that a problem?"

"It might be. They're bidding on a big project that we're bidding on too—the Golden Gate turbine. If you worked on their bid, you might have been exposed to confidential information. I'd feel uncomfortable hiring you."

Allie gave the answer crew cut man (aka Andy Duong, she had learned) had coached her to give. "I knew about their bid, but I didn't do any work on it. In fact, once Trudi told me you had an opening, I actually called Blue Sea and asked if it would be okay for me to work here. They said yes. You can call Andy Duong to confirm that."

Janet brightened. "Wow, great initiative, Allie! The agency said you're one of their best employees, and I can see why."

Allie made herself smile, but said nothing.

"All right, now that we've got that out of the way, let's talk a little bit about the work you'll be doing. Once you're done with your orientation, we're going to plug you into the team that's setting up Quickbooks Premier files and stuff for our Golden Gate bid. You've done that sort of work before, haven't you?"

Allie guessed that reviewing their files on

earlier government contracts wouldn't be part of her job description, but she could work with it. "Sure. I've worked with that software dozens of times."

"Great. I'm sure you'll fit right in. Do you have any questions for me?"

"Um, nothing I can think of right now."

"Okay, then I'll take you to meet with the head of our IT department. His name is Franklin Roh."

18

CONNOR POLISHED OFF THE LAST OF HIS chicken/pepper/mushroom stir-fry and put his wok in the sink to soak. He stretched and let out a contented sigh. Time for the evening e-mail check and a phone call before turning on the movie Netflix had just sent him. He was a little suspicious of the film because it was French and billed as "a powerful drama," but Netflix insisted that he would "♥ it!" Well, maybe. He checked to see whether the Giants were playing tonight—just in case.

He walked into the spare bedroom that served as a combination home gym and home office. He plopped his laptop onto the small oak desk beneath the window and plugged it into its power cord and the Bose speakers on the corners of the desk. Classical music from KDFC streamed out of the speakers as he went through the two dozen e-mails that had come since he left the office an hour and a half ago.

Then it was time for the call. He turned down the music, sat up a little straighter, and dialed.

Allie's voice appeared a few seconds later. "Hi, Connor. What's up?"

"Just checking in. I'm having lunch with Max tomorrow, and I was wondering if you had any news about that new prospect—Blue Sea, right?"

"Oh, I'm not actually there anymore. I'm at a new place now: Deep Seven Maritime Engineering. Just started."

"We'll do some backgrounding on them. What happened at Blue Sea? I thought your assignment was going to last two months."

"Um, nothing in particular. They just didn't . . . my part of the assignment wrapped up early."

Connor frowned and drummed his fingers on his desk. "Think they suspected you?"

"No, no, no. Not at all. They even talked about having me come back sometime."

"Let's talk if they ever offer you another job. I don't like the fact that they just let you go like that with no explanation."

"Uh, yeah. Absolutely. I was thinking the same thing. So, what's up with you—other than lunch with Max tomorrow?"

"Oh, not much. Just keeping busy at work."

"*And* going to some very fancy parties. You were dancing with the governor's wife at something not too long ago, right? How did he feel about that? Did he have some guys beat you up in the parking lot afterward?"

Connor laughed. "He was the one who asked me to dance with her, so the guys in the parking lot let me off with a warning. How did you know about that?"

"I was just clicking through pictures on some news website and came across one of you two together. You looked great in your tux, by the way. Very dashing."

Connor's face warmed at the compliment. "Thanks."

"Hey, I could use an excuse to buy myself a new dress. How do I get myself invited to one of these things?"

It was on the tip of his tongue: *Do me a favor and go to one with me.* But he swallowed it back. "Easy. Buy a ticket to the ball put on by the governor's favorite charity. They start around five hundred and go as high as ten thousand if you want to sit at his table. You could probably even get your picture taken dancing with him. Just make sure to wear steel-toed shoes."

"Which would go great with the new dress. No thanks, I can think of better things to do with ten big ones than spend the evening dancing with clumsy politicians. Still, it would be fun. I've never been to a real ball."

"I'll take you to one sometime. And you won't

have to dance with anyone but me." He felt his face flush and shook his head.

Can't believe I just said that.

She laughed. "As if I'd want to dance with anyone else."

19

A BRAIN SMOG FOLLOWED ALLIE HOME FROM Deep Seven. She'd been there for three weeks now, and it was getting to her. Something about it left her feeling tired and tainted at the end of the day, and each day was a little worse than the one before—as if there was a subtle poison in the office air that was slowly building up in her.

Only one week left on the project. Reminding herself of that helped, but it also raised a different discomfort. The end of her time at Deep Seven wasn't only a goal. It was a deadline.

She opened her apartment door and a wonderful smell greeted her. She smiled and inhaled deeply. Spices. Fried veggies and beef. Sweet-and-sour sauce. Heaven in a box.

Erik appeared in the hall, a such-a-good-boy-am-I smile on his beautiful face. "Welcome home, Allie."

"Tang Dynasty?"

He nodded. "Just got home two minutes ago."

"I love you."

"Love you too, babe." He stepped up to her,

slipped a hand behind her head, and kissed her. For a few seconds, she almost forgot about the boxes of Chinese food calling to her from the kitchen.

Their lips parted and he smiled down on her. "Let's eat on the balcony—first clear evening in I don't know how long."

She followed him out onto the wide, tiled balcony. The evening sun warmed her face and hands. Ranks of $2 and $3 million row houses marched across the gentle slope below her, interrupted by upscale cafes, shops, and restaurants. She sank into a cushioned redwood deck chair as Erik disappeared back into the apartment. Incessant coastal fog had cast a pall over San Francisco nearly every evening for the past month. A sunset dinner for two on the balcony would be wonderful.

Erik reappeared a few minutes later clutching chopsticks and a cluster of white paper buckets stamped with the red Tang Dynasty label in one hand and two Tsingtao beers in the other. He set his burdens down on a small table next to Allie's chair and plopped into another chair on the other side of the table.

Allie found a container of beef stir-fry and another of rice. "Mmmm. You are the best."

"You seemed pretty beat when you called, so I figured . . ." His words trailed off in a shrug. He patted her arm and smiled. The slanting light caught in his pale blue eyes so that they glowed in striking contrast to his tousled black hair. Allie wished she could freeze time so she could just look at him like that forever.

"You figured right. This is exactly what I needed."

"Job's that bad, huh?"

She frowned and took a sip of her beer. "Not exactly bad. More weird."

"Weird?"

"Yeah. Little things mostly."

"Like what?"

"Like there are more security cameras than I've ever seen in an office. Like they have these 'red' projects that people can't talk about, even inside the company. Like the security guards all look like extras in a GI Joe movie."

Erik stiffened and his eyes widened. "Hey! I'll bet the whole thing is a CIA front or something—like in *24*."

Allie shook her head. "I thought of that, but it doesn't work. Why would a front company hire temps with no security clearance? Why would they put a front company in America? Wouldn't they put it someplace like Iraq? I don't even think the CIA is allowed to operate here."

Erik nodded as if she had said exactly what he expected. His hair fell into his eyes and he flipped it back. "It's all part of the front. So they can fool people like you and me." He tapped his temple and smiled. "But we're too smart. We know everyone's got their guilty little secrets."

"Uh-huh." She made a mental note to talk to Connor about this later. "So, how was practice today? Hear anything more about that record contract?"

"Great session today. Toob had a new guitar riff that really rocked, and they loved those lyrics I showed you last night. Alex thinks we should cut a new CD for that executive down in LA, but . . ." He glanced at her and continued quickly. "We don't have enough money to rent a studio, so we were wondering if, you know, you could spot us a couple grand."

"And you'll pay me back as soon as you land your record deal, right?"

He fidgeted with his beer and leaned forward. "Uh, yeah."

"Hmmm. I'll think about it. You guys already owe me from your last studio session."

He smiled nervously.

Allie smiled back. She'd already decided to loan them the money, but she didn't want Erik to start expecting it. She paid for enough of his lifestyle already. Besides, he was more attentive when she made him sweat a little, and she liked being attended to.

Allie woke with a jolt. She must have fallen asleep on the couch after Erik left. A big meal and a couple of beers tended to do that to her, even when she wasn't already tired. She opened her eyes and winced at a familiar sting. Her optometrist had warned her that she'd have to give up contacts if she kept falling asleep with them in her eyes.

Her cell phone blared Beck's "Loser" from the coffee table by her head. She groaned. That was the ring tone she had given Andy Duong. She'd been ignoring his calls for nearly a week, and his messages had grown increasingly agitated.

She picked up the phone. "Hello?"

"You're lucky you answered. If you didn't, I was going to send out an e-mail blast with that press release we discussed."

Not likely while I'm still poking around Deep Seven for you. "Nice to talk to you too, Andy. What do you want?"

"Tell me that you've sued Deep Seven."

"No can do."

"What? Why not?"

She smiled in the darkness. After the meeting where he and Sandy Allen ambushed her, she had realized that they wouldn't follow through on their threats while they still had something to gain from letting her keep her secrets. Blowing her cover while she was still investigating Deep Seven would be stupid. And if Devil to Pay did wind up suing, it would be stupid to give Deep Seven her identity while the lawsuit was pending.

After that, they'd probably send out their press release no matter what she did. And then she'd tell the whole story to Connor, and he'd find a way to shred them in court.

Once she had gamed out all of that, she had lost all fear of Andy and Sandy. Which meant she could yank Andy's chain if she felt like it. "False claims complaints are sealed. I can't even tell you whether or not one has been filed."

"Don't mess with me, Allie! You either tell me whether you've sued them or that press release goes out now."

"Relax, Andy. If they're as dirty as you say, we'll sue them when we're ready. But if they're *not* dirty—or even if I just can't prove they're dirty—I'm not going to sue them. DOJ investigates every lawsuit we file, and I'd have to lie to them about Deep Seven. Not going to do it. There are worse things than your press release."

"Like going to jail."

"Exactly."

His thin, unpleasant chuckle dribbled through the phone. "Does the name Jason Tompkins mean anything to you?"

She sat up. "Should it?"

"Jason was a sixteen-year-old boy who lived in Salina, Kansas. Eagle Scout, according to his obituary. Liked going camping with friends. Sounds like a nice kid." He paused for emphasis. "Six weeks ago, he died in the emergency room at

Salina Regional Health Center. Meth overdose. You wouldn't happen to have been in Salina then, would you?"

Allie's heart pounded and she tried to breathe. A cold and familiar weight crushed down on her chest. "I don't know what you're talking about."

"Let me try jogging your memory. It seems Jason bought the meth at a concert. No one knows who sold it to him." He paused. "No one except us."

The memory forced itself into her mind: Erik in the parking lot after a show. He was behind the band's van, out of sight except from the stage door, where she stood. His handsome face was pale in the streetlight and his forehead gleamed with sweat. His hair was lank and tucked behind his ears. He didn't see her because he was talking to a group of teen boys. She had thought they were fans basking in the glow of her "pet rock star," as Connor called him. She had smiled to herself. And then she saw Erik handing them little baggies.

After a moment, Andy went on. His voice was smooth and satisfied now. "You know, if anyone knowingly helped the dealer who sold that meth—say by driving the dealer around or paying the dealer's hotel bills—that person could be guilty of Jason's death just the same as the dealer. Exactly the same."

The room spun and Allie put her head in her

hand. Bile burned in the back of her throat. "I've got nothing more to say to you."

"But you do have something more to do for me. I don't care how you do it, but you will find evidence that Deep Seven has been ripping off the government—unless you'd rather spend a long time in a Kansas jail."

She hung up and started to cry.

20

A SHARP WIND WHISTLED THROUGH THE *Grasp II*'s superstructure and drove bullet-like raindrops against the windows of her lounge. Inside, First Mate Jenkins, Mitch Daniels, and Ed Granger talked over a table bolted to the floor, sitting on the U-shaped bench that was also bolted down. It had been a long, cold, wet day, and they were all drinking Irish coffee.

They had the lounge to themselves, which was a relief. Mitch had nothing against Koreans, but being surrounded by foreigners all day every day was beginning to wear on him—the buzz of incomprehensible language, the stink of strange foods, the unspoken rules that everyone understood except him. Pile all that on top of the hush-hush nature of their trip (they *still* didn't know where they were going), and . . . Well, it was good to have a couple drinks with guys he knew and who only spoke English.

Ed apparently felt the same way. "I don't like it," he announced. "All these Koreans."

Jenkins chuffed. "What's to like? Buncha jerks."

"Yeah, but that's not what I mean." Ed sipped noisily from his drink. "Why are they here? Why not let us handle this? They aren't the first ones to hire the G-2 crew for a treasure-hunting trip. No one ever brought their own crew before. Why'd they do that?"

Mitch shrugged and stretched. "Maybe they don't like Americans."

Jenkins's mouth twisted. "They don't—and it's mutual." He swirled his coffee and stared down into his mug. "But is that a good enough reason to bring a whole crew from Korea?"

Mitch's irritation with the Koreans bubbled higher. "They don't trust us. They think Americans will screw up whatever it is they're doing."

Ed gave a lopsided smile. "So your reputation precedes you, Mitch."

"If I wanted crap from you, Granger, I'd squeeze your head."

Jenkins and Ed both started to laugh, but a clipped Asian voice interrupted them.

"Mr. Granger and Mr. Daniels, you should sleep. We will arrive at the search area tomorrow and the remotely operated vehicle and other devices must be ready to go down as soon as possible."

Mitch looked up and saw David Cho standing behind Jenkins, who stood to face the newcomer. Cho was a tall man of around thirty-five. He was about the same height as Jenkins, but the first mate outweighed him by over fifty pounds—at least half of it muscle.

"We're almost there?" Jenkins swayed slightly, either from the wave action or the whiskey in his coffee. "Why didn't you tell me?"

"You did not need to know." Cho turned back to Mitch and Ed. "You will need—"

"What do you mean, I didn't need to know?" Jenkins leaned toward Cho. "I'm the first mate of this ship!"

Cho placed a hand in the middle of Jenkins's chest and pushed him back. "Leave! I am done speaking with you."

Jenkins stumbled back several steps, then grabbed a chair and steadied himself. His face was as red as his beard and shaggy hair. He bared his teeth and took a step toward Cho. The Korean moved sideways into the open part of the lounge and stood waiting, feet apart and hands up and open. He didn't look mad or scared, just . . . expectant.

Jenkins stopped and the two men stared at each other for several seconds. Mitch held his breath and waited for the burly first mate to pound the obnoxious Korean. But Jenkins narrowed his eyes and folded his arms across his chest.

Without taking his gaze off of Cho, he said, "Better get to bed, guys. Since our *guests* screwed up and didn't give us advance warning, you're gonna have a busy day tomorrow."

21

CONNOR WAS WORKING ON HIS SECOND cup of Peet's when his cell phone rang. He didn't recognize the number, though he could tell from the 415 area code that it was in San Francisco. "Hello, Connor Norman."

"Hi, it's Allie."

He smiled and swiveled his chair to face the spectacular view of the San Francisco Bay outside his office window. Sailboats meandered lazily across the sparkling blue surface like giant white gulls, keeping well clear of the occasional lumbering freighter. Real gulls flew in sinuous flocks across the water or rested on the numerous docks and wharves that jutted out into the water like fingers of the land grasping the Bay and holding her tight. The view always made Connor want to go for a walk along the waterfront, but he could rarely take the time off work.

"Hey, Allie. It's good to hear from you. Where are you calling from?"

"I'm at a pay phone in the Ferry Building. Want to get together for a cup of coffee or something?"

Get together? In public? He was about to object

when he realized what she was telling him by calling from a pay phone and calling his cell rather than his office number. Concern knotted his stomach—what kind of danger was she in? "Uh, sure. I'll meet you in front of the Ferry Building in ten minutes. Bye."

Ten minutes later, he walked across the Embarcadero and scanned the crowd in front of the Ferry Building. She emerged from the building and walked toward him. She wore jeans that complemented her slender legs and a hooded UC Davis sweatshirt. Her shoulder-length hair was black. He wondered whether that was supposed to make her harder to recognize or whether she had gotten tired of brown and blond. Either way, it looked good.

"Hi, Connor." She gave him a just-friends hug. He was disappointed and relieved at the same time. "Want to walk down the Embarcadero? There are enough people, but not too many."

"Sounds like a plan. Let's head north. More good coffee places that way."

They turned up the wide sidewalk, bordered on the right by the busy Embarcadero, which carried automobiles, cable cars, and streetcars between its curbs. On their right were shops, restaurants, wharves, and occasional glimpses of the blue waters of the San Francisco Bay and the distant shoreline of Treasure Island.

After they had gone a couple hundred yards, the

tourist crowd began to thin. Connor glanced around to make sure no one was too close. "So, is my phone bugged, your phone, or both?"

She rewarded him with a bright smile. "I love having a smart lawyer. Maybe both, maybe neither. Maybe I'm just being paranoid."

"About what?"

She pursed her lips and shook her head slightly. "I'm not totally sure. The last place I worked— Deep Seven—was . . ." She shrugged. "There's something off about them."

"How so?"

She recounted the incidents she had described to Erik and concluded, "So basically they're very security conscious, very suspicious."

Half-formed fears woke in his stomach. "Suspicious of you?"

"Suspicious of everyone. But yeah, me in particular." She paused and shoved her hands deep into her sweatshirt pockets. "You should also know that I, uh, I heard one of the secretaries from their legal department talking about having a quote unquote shred first and ask questions later policy. She was talking about how they'd done that to kill a lawsuit a couple of years ago. Raised the hairs on the back of my neck."

"Not good. You'd better keep a low profile until I've had a chance to look into this. And don't take any more jobs in the meantime. Oh, and send me a list of former employees for interviews—make sure to include some executives and security guys if you can."

"Okay." She smiled and winked at him. "Thanks for watching out for me."

"Couldn't let anything happen to my best client, could I?" He returned the smile. *Get that protectiveness under control, buddy. Remember, she's just a client.* Back to business. "So, how did their books look? Are they hiding anything?"

She nodded and pulled an envelope out of her purse. "It looks like they're padding each bill by about ten percent. I could only pull a couple because of all the Big Brother stuff, but I hope it's enough to interest DOJ."

She handed the envelope to Connor and he opened it. It held only ten sheets of paper: two invoices to the California Department of Water Resources for underwater repair work at a reservoir, two pages of itemized billings supporting each invoice, and an Excel spreadsheet showing lower amounts for most line items. Nice, simple documents—the kind that would be easy to explain to a jury.

"These are great docs, Allie. But there's only about $20K of fraud here. With trebling, that's sixty thousand. Add a penalty of ten thousand per invoice and we're still only at eighty. That's too small for Max, and it's too small for my firm."

She wrinkled her forehead and pressed her lips

together. "Hmmm. Would it be big enough if I told you that they had over two hundred million dollars in government contracts? How about if I also told you that over half the invoices I saw had padding?"

Connor did some quick mental calculations and gave a low whistle. "Then I'd tell you that I'm very interested, and I'll bet DOJ will be too."

She grinned. "Thought you might. Hey, didn't you say something about coffee?" She stopped and tilted her head toward an espresso cart bearing the name "Wilson's Expresso Espresso." A tall man with an earring and a goatee watched them hopefully.

"I did indeed." Connor bought an Americano for himself and a complicated chai-based drink for Allie that took Wilson five minutes to make.

After they had their drinks, they turned around and headed back toward the Ferry Building. "So, what else is up?"

"My bank account for starters. Your accounting department just sent me the last installment from Hamilton."

"That should pay for a few nice trips to Vail or Tahoe for you and Erik. Come to think of it, that should pay for one of those ski-in condos. And some bunny slope lessons for Erik." Connor allowed himself a small grin as he pictured Allie's oh-so-cool boyfriend wobbling on his first pair of skis.

Allie didn't smile. "Uh, yeah. Anyway, what's up with you?"

Connor winced inside. *Should've kept the Erik thing to myself.* "Um, you know that World War II fighter I've got? I took it down to LA for a movie shoot." Allie's face wore a distant, slightly glazed look and Connor instantly regretted bragging. "Other than that, just the same old boring grind at the office."

"Uh-huh. Say, could you give me a referral for a detective?"

"Sure, but if this is for a case, we'll hire one ourselves."

A chill ocean breeze gusted between two buildings. Allie's hair whipped around her face and she hugged herself. "No, it's not for a case."

Connor waited for her to go on, but she just tucked her hair behind her ears and watched the sidewalk as they walked.

He wanted to ask what was wrong, to tell her that he was her friend and he wanted to help. But he didn't. *I've done enough damage for one day.* He stuck hands in pockets and looked away. "Okay, I'll send you a couple of names."

22

THE RAIN HAD STOPPED BY THE TIME MR. LEE summoned the team to the *Grasp II*'s lounge, but the ship still rolled in heavy seas. It was late and the Americans had all gone to bed. Nonetheless, Mr. Lee put a guard outside the door.

The men were tired, but fully awake as Mr. Lee rose to speak. This was the first full meeting he had called since they had boarded the ship in Oakland, over five thousand kilometers to the east. There could be only one reason: they were only hours from their goal, and he was finally going to tell them what it was.

He surveyed the dozen men crowded around the two tables and smiled, exuding real affection. He was the perfect picture of a leader—wise and warm eyes, lines of experience and endurance etched into his strong face, an iron jaw, thick shoulders that would have been the envy of a man half his age. Cho could not help admiring the man right now.

Mr. Lee extended his right hand to the team. "What a glorious group of men! What a noble, chosen few! You are finest sons of the finest people on this planet. You have done everything I have asked and more. At great peril, you have followed me faithfully over air and land and sea, even though you did not know where I was leading you. You have trusted me with your lives and your honor."

He walked as he spoke, riding the shifting deck with the unconscious grace of a man who has spent his life at sea. "Now your trust will be repaid. I will tell you a great secret—a secret so great that I have spoken it to no one." He pointed to the rolling floor. "Down there lies the treasure that will destroy our great enemy. A gift from heaven buried in the depths of the sea. It is the key that will unlock the cage of fear that has held our nation for generations and kept the two halves of our country apart."

He paused and looked every man in the eye. His gaze was like a jolt when he met Cho's eyes.

Then he told them.

When he finished, the room was silent except for the whistle of the wind outside and the rhythmic creaking as the ship rode up and down the swells. The men continued to stare at him, as if frozen by the enormity of the news they had just received. Cho had difficulty comprehending what he had just heard. Could this be true? Could Mr. Lee really mean to do what he had just said? Horror and disbelief swirled inside his head, shrouding his mind in a thought-choking miasma.

The silence stretched for nearly a minute. Mr. Lee gave a low chuckle. "Have you nothing to say? Not even any questions?"

The engineer's mate—a burly, profane man

who was called Park on this mission—stood and bowed. "Sir, I am honored to be here with you, doing this thing that men will talk about a thousand years from now. Thank you." He bowed again and sat, surrounded by murmurs of approval and agreement.

Mr. Lee caught Cho's eye. "How about you? What do you think?"

Cho stood and bowed. As he did, the cloud in his mind lifted and he knew what he must do. A wave of regret swept over him, but the path before his feet was clear. "Sir, your plan astounds me. It is brilliant. It is subtle. And if it succeeds, it will change everything we have ever known forever."

"With all of us standing together, it cannot fail."

"No, sir." Which was why one of them would have to fall.

23

CONNOR HIT THE "SAVE" BUTTON AND glanced at the clock on his computer's task bar. 1:46 a.m. He yawned, leaned back in his desk chair, and stretched until he heard cracks from his neck and both elbows. He picked up one of the open Red Bull cans on his desk and shook it to make sure it wasn't an empty.

He drained the can in one long swig and steeled himself for one more read through the two documents on the screen. The first was a *qui tam* complaint consisting of numbered paragraphs that recited a bare bones description of Allie's story about Deep Seven's fraud. It ended with three boilerplate causes of action for breach of the California False Claims Act and a ritual demand for "damages in an amount to be proven at trial."

The second document was a disclosure statement. This was where the action was. In the disclosure statement, Connor laid out everything he and Allie knew about the case: names, dates, dollar amounts, invoice numbers, estimates of recoverable damages—anything that might make DOJ like the case.

And they would like it. Connor had no doubt about that. This was as close to a perfect false claims case as he had ever seen. It had obvious fraud, lots of government money, and an in-state defendant with deep pockets. It would have been nice if Allie had been able to copy some more documents, but Connor could live without them and he suspected DOJ could too. The disclosure statement told a good story, and DOJ had learned to trust Devil to Pay's stories.

By 3:00, he had the documents in final. Filing them with the superior court could wait, but he needed to get these to the Attorney General's office by first thing tomorrow morning.

This morning. He sighed and closed his eyes.

He PDFed the complaint and disclosure statement and sent them to Max Volusca with a red-flagged covering e-mail that said, "Max, call me on my cell as soon as you get this. We may have a spoliation problem."

Then he went home, where he fell asleep on the sofa with the cell phone next to his head.

Connor was more or less awake when his phone rang a few minutes before 8:30. "Morning, Connor," Max's voice boomed. "So, what was so urgent that you were sending me high-priority e-mails in the middle of the night? What's the spoliation issue?"

"Hey, Max." Connor rubbed gummy eyes and held the phone away from his ear. "Big new case. About twenty million in fraud, and that's before trebling or penalties. Allie thinks the defendant may destroy documents as soon as they catch wind of your investigation. She heard someone from their legal department talk about having a shred first, ask questions later policy."

Max snorted. "Yeah? Well, it's tough to run a shredder when you're wearing handcuffs. I'll tell that to their president when we serve him with a subpoena."

Connor chuckled and walked into the kitchen to start the coffeemaker as he talked. "I'm sure that'll get his attention, but what about the account executives who are going to have their careers destroyed when this comes out? One of them may try to shred himself out of trouble or start wiping hard drives. Also, that person from legal who Allie overheard was saying they'd done it before to kill a case."

"Hmmm. Yeah, that's a problem." Max was silent for a moment. The coffeemaker gurgled and the blessed aroma of fresh espresso curled around Connor. "I've got an idea. Can you get Allie to swear out a declaration repeating what you just told me?"

Connor smiled and poured himself a cup of thick black coffee. "I'll have it to you by noon. Mind telling me what your idea is?"

"Can't—this is a sealed investigation. Just watch the evening news tomorrow and find out with everyone else."

Allie's home phone (which Connor had had swept for bugs) rang and the computerized caller ID voice announced that "Norman, Connor" was calling. She popped up from the kitchen table, where she was busy on her laptop, and grabbed a handset. "Hi, Connor. What's up?"

"Lots. I put together a complaint and disclosure statement yesterday and sent them to Max Volusca early this morning."

Her heart skipped a beat. "Wow, that's fast. What's the rush?"

"You kidding? This is a big case and the target

has a history of document destruction. We had to get this into Max's hands as fast as possible."

She wiped sweaty palms on her jeans. "Okay, I was just a little surprised is all. I like to see the papers and sleep on them before we file."

"Sorry about that. I'll get you a copy ASAP and we can file an amended set if we need to." His voice was distracted and she could tell he wanted to get to something else. "But anyway, I just got off the phone with Max. He sounds ready to jump in with both feet, but he's going to need a little help from us. He wants a sworn declaration repeating the story you told me about shredding at Deep Seven."

She stiffened. "Why?"

"Max wouldn't say and I'd rather not speculate, but he hinted that whatever he's up to will probably make the local evening news tomorrow."

She winced. This just kept getting better and better. "I don't know. Isn't the idea to keep my name out of these cases?"

"It is, but this will stay under seal. Forever. Besides, Max will get suspicious if you say no."

She said nothing. This was all moving too far too fast. She felt like she was in a driverless car that was picking up speed. She desperately wanted to get out, but didn't see how she could.

"Allie?"

She closed her eyes. "Okay, send it over with a messenger and I'll sign it."

Allie switched on the TV at five the next day and perched on the edge of the wide leather sofa facing her television, sipping from a can of Diet Coke. She'd been as high-strung as a caffeinated cat ever since she talked to Connor yesterday morning.

The lead story on the local Fox station was about two baboons that had escaped from the Oakland Zoo. She clicked over to CBS. They were also covering the baboon story. ABC—more baboons. Apparently their names were Gavin and Arnold. When she found their hairy faces on NBC too, she jumped up and started pacing. "Come on! If I want to see baboons, I'll go to a nightclub!"

Click. ". . . Forty-Niners quarterback controversy flared up again, which . . ."

Click. ". . . plan was endorsed by heavyweight political groups like the Harvey Milk Gay, Lesbian, and Transgender Club . . ."

Click. ". . . elderly woman reported having feces thrown at her by Gavin and Arnold . . ."

Click. ". . . raid carried out by the California Bureau of Investigation, acting on a warrant obtained by the Attorney General." The screen showed the main entrance to Deep Seven's headquarters. Half a dozen men in blue jackets emblazoned on the back with "CBI" were carting boxes out through the glass and steel doors. "A company representative denied any wrongdoing," intoned a female newscaster over the video clip "and insisted that the company would be completely vindicated."

The scene switched to a photo of two familiar simian faces. "Now for an update on the search for the Oakland Zoo's escaped baboons."

Allie turned off the TV and dropped the remote onto the teak coffee table. It clattered loudly, making her jump. She took a deep breath and ran her fingers through her hair. "Okay," she said to the empty room.

The air in her apartment suddenly felt thick, stale, and unwholesome, like the atmosphere inside a long neglected attic in summer. She walked outside, but once on the balcony she felt eyes watching her.

She went back in, but left the sliding glass door to the balcony open. A fresh breeze flowed in, and that helped. A little. "Okay," she repeated. She took another deep breath. "Okay, this is working." Now came the hard part.

24

CONNOR DECIDED THAT HE COULD DO A little investigating of his own without too much risk. Now that the complaint was on file and Max had, in his subtle way, alerted Deep Seven to the fact that they were under investigation, there wasn't much to lose by interviewing former employees. The worst they could do was say they didn't want to talk to him.

He pulled out the list of Deep Seven ex-employees that Allie had given him. A low-level marketing vice president, an accountant, an IT guy, and a security guard. He tried the accountant first.

After two rings, a cheerful woman's voice answered. "Hello?"

"Hi, is this Janet Lee?"

"Yes, who is this?"

"My name is Connor Norman. I'm an attorney with the law firm of Doyle & Brown, and I'm investigating a matter related to a former employer of yours. It doesn't involve you at all, but you may be a witness. Do you have a few minutes to talk?"

Unlike most witnesses he cold-called, she didn't suddenly become more reserved after learning she was talking to a lawyer. "Oh, sure. A friend of mine works at Doyle & Brown. Susan Mendoza."

Connor knew her friend—a perky, social forty-something who never missed a firm party. "In our billing department. Right. I'll tell her you said hi."

"Thanks. So, what can I do for you?"

"I'd like to ask you a few questions about Deep Seven."

Silence. Then, "I can't really talk about that."

Connor pulled out a legal pad, plucked a pen out of a pewter mug on his desk and got ready to take notes. "Okay. Can you tell me why not?"

"I signed a nondisclosure agreement."

An NDA? Interesting. "Did they say why they wanted you to sign it?"

"I'm sorry, but this conversation is making me uncomfortable. I have to go. Goodbye."

Click.

Connor put the receiver down slowly. Then he dropped the pen on his pad and stared at it. Well, that had been different. He'd had lots of witnesses refuse to talk to him, but he'd never had one go from hot to cold that fast. One second they're chatting about a mutual acquaintance, the next she clams up like a door slamming. And the second after that, she hangs up on him.

He tried the marketing veep next, but that conversation was even shorter. As soon as Connor identified himself as a lawyer, the man politely ended the conversation. He also had signed an NDA and didn't want to talk about it. A little on the paranoid side, but Connor wouldn't have thought anything of it if not for the oddness of the first call.

His third call went to the IT guy, but the line was disconnected. Connor jotted down a note on his to-do list: "Do search on Samuel Stimson & find good number."

The ex-security guard was next. Unlike the first two, he didn't immediately end the conversation as soon as Connor revealed who he was and why he was calling. But Connor's conversation with him was hardly a normal witness interview: "So you're investigating Deep Seven, huh?"

"That's right. Do you have time for a few questions?"

"Let me ask you one first. Does this have anything to do with that raid at Deep Seven yesterday?"

"Yes."

"But you're not with the government, right?"

"No, I'm with a private law firm."

"You might want to let the government do the investigating."

"Really? Why is that?"

"It might be healthier."

"What do you mean?"

"You know what I mean."

Connor swallowed hard. "Well, thanks for the tip, but I'd still like to talk to you. My first question for you is—"

"Weren't you listening to me? Look, buddy, I just answered every question you need to ask."

Click.

25

THE PACIFIC OCEAN SPREAD CLEAR AND FLAT, a plane of polished glass under an empty sky. Mitch stood on the bow of the *Grasp II*, enjoying the view and the gentle breeze as the ship cut through the still air at five knots. The horizon was so sharp and distant that he thought he could see the slight curve of the Earth.

Or was it an optical illusion? Another sailor had once said any curve in the horizon was so slight that it couldn't be seen. Mitch had nothing better to do, so he decided to test that claim. He fished a piece of paper out of his pocket, smoothed it out, and held it a foot from his face with the corners touching the rim of the ocean. Then he stared over the center, trying to decide whether he could see a sliver of dark blue above the paper. There it was. No, one corner had slipped down a hair below the horizon. Now there was nothing but bright sky above the blurry white of the paper. Was he holding it too high?

After ten minutes, he gave up and looked for something else to do. He had a lot more free time on this trip than he had expected.

He had thought he would be down below working with Ed Granger on the search for Nazi treasure. But after one busy day getting the ROV, sidescan sonar, and dive equipment ready, he was suddenly a fifth wheel.

Jenkins had pulled Mitch aside and told him the "good news" that David Cho would be working with Ed, which would give Mitch plenty of time to "relax" and "kick back." Nothing against Mitch, of course. The passengers just wanted Cho, that was all. They insisted that he was good at this sort of thing, whatever Ed might say. Ed had said plenty, of course, but it hadn't changed anything.

So Mitch watched the ship's scratchy collection of James Bond DVDs for the dozenth time. He fished out the old Nintendo console in the lounge and played Super Mario Bros. until he had rescued Princess Peach twice. He stared at the horizon. And through it all he chafed at not being down below with Ed, surrounded by monitors, keyboards, and joysticks—all feeding him dozens of types of information. He knew more about the ocean bottom sitting in his battered old swivel chair than a diver on the sea floor. That's where the action was. And Mitch was shut out.

Well, he'd know soon enough. They had reached the search area three days ago. They had deployed the sidescan sonar and the sensor arrays, and now they were slowly sailing back and forth in long sweeps criss-crossing a jagged undersea mountain range with roots miles below on the ocean floor and peaks just a few hundred feet below the surface.

Mitch walked over to the railing and looked down into the small bow waves. The Nazi treasure sub must be down there somewhere among those rocks. They would have been running silent and deep to avoid American destroyers and anti-sub planes. Their sonar would have been off, and they would have been relying on charts to navigate. The German sailors wouldn't have had any warning. They would have been working, eating, sleeping, and playing cards over coffee. Then a sudden shock and water roared in. Maybe they were crushed to death or maybe they had time to drown.

Mitch crossed himself unconsciously, a habit he had picked up from his Mexican mother. Salvaging a shipwreck, especially one filled with bones, always made him uncomfortable. It hit too close to home.

"Hey, I've been looking all over for you."

He turned and saw Ed Granger coming toward him. Ed was breathing heavily and his low forehead was damp. He hauled his fireplug frame up a short flight of steps and tugged at Mitch's arm. "Come on!"

Mitch saw the excitement in his friend's eyes. "You found it?"

"Maybe. I found something that's about the right size and shape. Don't wanna jinx it, but . . ."

"That's great! So, when are we sending Eileen down?" Envy stabbed him as he suddenly remembered. "Or, I mean, when are you sending her down?"

Ed laughed and punched him in the arm a little harder than was necessary. Mitch was about to complain, but the words came tumbling out of Ed. "It's we, buddy! That's why I was looking for you. As soon as I saw it on the sidescan, Lee says, 'You must send down the ROV at once.' So I say, 'Yeah, right. No way I'm sending it into a wreck without Mitch backing me up.' And Lee says, 'You have Mr. Cho.' Then I tell him, 'That's not good enough. Not with a wreck. Do you know how many things can go wrong? We lose the ROV down there and we're done. D-O-N-E. We can turn around and head back home. I do this with Mitch or I don't do it at all.'"

"Thanks, man! So they agreed with you?"

"No, they called Jenkins and wanted him to order me to do it with Cho. Jenkins turns to me and says, 'If I order you, you'll just disobey, right?' And I say, 'You think?' So he tells Lee, 'If he does that, I'll have to confine him to quarters and the ROV still won't go down. You'd better let him use Daniels.' Then they jabber away in Korean for a while. And then they said yes."

Mitch felt a warm glow in his chest. He grinned. "I'll try not to screw anything up."

Ed snorted. "Oh, you'll screw up, down, and sideways. You always do. But you'll be better than Cho."

26

CONNOR SAT BACK IN HIS OFFICE CHAIR AND reread the search results for Samuel Stimson, the final Deep Seven ex-employee on Allie's list. No wonder his phone was disconnected: he had vanished.

According to the one-paragraph news item Connor found in the *Oakland Tribune*, Deep Seven's security records showed that Stimson left the building at 5:11 p.m. on March 23. He didn't show up for work the next day or the day after that. His parents had filed a missing person report for him on April 3. The police called his disappearance "suspicious."

That was all. No follow-up item announcing that his body had been found or that the police had opened a murder investigation. No new phone number or address indicating that Stimson had reappeared. Nothing. It was as if the ground had opened beneath his feet as he walked out of Deep Seven, swallowed him up, and closed over his head.

The search results also contained a list of Stimson's known addresses and phone numbers. Most were clearly obsolete (university dorms, his parents' home, etc.), but his last place in Oakland still had a phone number listed as "current."

Connor's eyebrows went up. That wasn't the number Allie had given him. Maybe she had found Stimson's cell number and this was a landline that he shared with someone. Whoever it was, a call was in order. Probably a waste of time, but worth a shot nonetheless.

He dialed the number and it rang. And rang. Connor kept waiting for voicemail to pick up, but it never did. After ten rings, he was about to hang up. But as he reached for the "Call End" button on his phone, a loud clattering came through the receiver. Then came a loud thunk and a scratchy male voice swearing in the background. Then more clattering. Finally, the male voice—clearly an old man's—said, "Hello? Who's this? What do you want?"

Connor slouched back in his chair and wondered how long it would take this guy to hang up on him. His record for this case was about two minutes. "My name is Connor Norman, and I'm an attorney at Doyle & Brown. I'd like to ask you a few questions about Samuel Stimson. Do you know him?"

"Sam's my grandson. Why do you want to know about him?"

"Well, I'm working on an investigation of Deep Seven Maritime Engineering. I understand that Sam worked there, and—"

"You work for Deep Seven, do you?"

"No. I'm not at liberty to say whom I represent,

but it's not Deep Seven. I'm looking into whether Deep Seven committed certain wrongdoing, so—"

"Well, good. I'm glad somebody finally is."

Connor sat up a little straighter and started taking notes. Maybe this wasn't a wasted call after all. "Why do you say that?"

"Because they murdered my grandson."

Connor's pen stopped in mid-word. "How do you know?"

"Things he told me before he disappeared. They had this secret computer, see." The old man's voice grew excited and quick as he talked. "The S-4 or something like that. No one could look at it, not even Sam—even though they hired him 'cause he was a computer genius."

"Any idea what's on the computer? Could it be evidence of fraud on the government?"

"Could be, could be. They've got all sorts of secrets over there."

"And you think they killed Sam to protect those secrets?"

"I *know* they did!"

"Okay. Do you mind telling me how you know that?"

"Sam would never just run off like that. I don't care how much money he owed."

"Sam owed money to someone?"

"Yes, but that's not the point."

"Was it a lot of money?"

"It doesn't matter! The credit card companies didn't kill him."

So Sam Stimson had unpaid debts. That detail hadn't made it into the database Connor had searched. "So the reason you think Deep Seven killed him is that he disappeared? Do you have any other evidence?"

"What more do I need? You're starting to sound just like the police. Bunch of masons." His voice turned suspicious. "Are you a mason?"

"A what?"

"Don't play dumb! You're a free mason, aren't you?"

A free mason? Where did that come from? "Uh, no."

"You tell all your mason buddies down at the lodge that I'm on to them! I've been down to the docks. I've seen what Deep Seven is up to."

"And what's that?" Connor half expected the answer to involve aliens or Nazis.

"Tell them I've got pictures! I can prove what they were putting on that ship, the *Grasp II*. And I know about the Nazi submarine too. I heard those two talking about it in a bar. Granger and Jenkins. Got that on tape. And it's all in a very safe place in case anything happens to me."

Connor smiled. Nazis it was. "Uh-huh. Can I see the pictures and listen to the tapes?"

The man scoffed. "You just tell them."

Click.

27

ALLIE SAT ON THE EDGE OF THE DIRTY GREEN couch in the lobby of Clayton Investigations, one of the firms Connor had recommended. Julian Clayton was a former police detective who had specialized in undercover homicide investigations for two decades before leaving the police force "because he wasn't very rules-oriented," as Connor had put it. Exactly what she was looking for.

Clayton opened the door and motioned for Allie to come in. He was a handsome black man with a bald head, long beard, and piercing eyes—the sort of man who would have intrigued Allie if she had met him at a jazz concert but frightened her if she had met him on a deserted street.

Once they were seated in his office, he pulled out a yellow notepad covered with crabbed handwriting. "There's still one loose end, but otherwise I'm pretty much done with my investigation."

"And?"

"The story you heard pretty much checks out. A kid named Jason Tompkins did die in Salina, Kansas, last month. The cause of death was a methamphetamine overdose." He handed her a picture of a boy with long brown hair, braces, and wide blue eyes. "That's him."

She looked at the picture quickly, avoiding the

eyes, and handed it back to him. "When did he die? What was the date?"

He paused and regarded her with those burning eyes. "He was admitted to the hospital on May third. He died the next day."

So he was in the hospital the day after Erik's band played in Salina. She wanted to throw up and then crawl into a hole. Why was she paying this guy to tell her things she didn't want to know?

All thought of telling Connor vanished. His words rang in her mind: *If you commit a crime, you should pay the price. Every. Single. Time. No excuses, no compromises.* He wouldn't help her; he'd do everything he could to get her locked up.

She forced her face to stay blank and nodded. "Okay. Sorry, go on."

"The local police are investigating. I don't know whether they've got any leads, but I doubt it."

She examined her fingernails and kept her voice nonchalant. "Why's that?"

"Because of an article I found in the *Salina Journal*. It said no one saw Jason buy the meth that killed him. If there are no witnesses to a drug deal, it's almost impossible to prosecute the dealer."

Allie looked up, doing her best to hide her relief. "Got it. Okay, anything else?"

He looked through his notes for half a minute, then put the pad down. "That's my entire report."

She stood. "Thanks, Julian. Just send me your final bill. I won't need a written report or anything."

He didn't get up. "Please sit down, Allie. We're not quite done."

She sat, butterflies beginning to take flight in her stomach. "Oh, I thought you'd finished your report."

"I said there was a loose end." There was iron in his voice and stone in his eyes.

"The thing about nobody seeing the deal wasn't it?"

He shook his head slowly. "You were in Salina on May second."

Her brain froze and there was a roaring in her ears. "I don't . . . I didn't . . ."

"I've known plenty of drug dealers, and you don't fit the profile. You don't use. You're not in a gang. You've got no money problems."

She sat motionless, unable to think or speak.

His face softened. "Allie, I don't think you sold meth to Jason Tompkins. But I think you know who did. In fact, I don't think you know. I know you know."

"What are you going to do?"

He leaned forward, rested his elbows on the desk, and steepled his fingers. "What am *I* going to do? Isn't the real question what *you're* going to do? A boy is dead and you know who sold the drugs that killed him. Are you going to cover for that person? Are you going to let him keep dealing? Maybe kill another kid?" He was talking fast, almost pleading with her. "Or are you going to do the right thing and call the Salina police?"

"I—" Her voice shook and she took a deep breath to calm herself. "It's not that simple."

A weary frown crossed his face. She thought she saw disgust in his look too. "Do you mean 'simple' or 'easy'? It's true that, depending on your role, there might be . . . consequences for you. But don't you owe it to Jason Tompkins and his family to step up and do the right thing? Don't you owe it to yourself?" He scribbled on the bottom of his notebook, tore off a scrap of paper and handed it to her. "Here's the number of the Salina Police Department. Call them."

She took the slip of paper from him with numb fingers. But as she folded it and put it in her purse, she felt a fire flare to life deep inside. The ice in her brain melted and her face was suddenly hot. "Listen, I'm paying you to answer my questions, not play Oprah. If I wanted your advice, I would have asked, okay? I didn't, so keep it to yourself. You gave me the info I wanted. We're done now. Thanks. Bye. Send me the bill."

She got up and walked out, leaving him sitting at his desk with his notepad and his sanctimonious judgments about what she should and shouldn't do.

28

EQUIPMENT AND MEN JAMMED THE ROV control room on the *Grasp II*. A space designed for two or three men held five: Ed, Mitch, Cho, Mr. Lee, and Jenkins. Ed sat in a heavily duct-taped swivel chair with a steel Thermos, and a no-spill coffee mug at his elbow. Mitch perched on a stool beside him. Each man had an array of controls in front of him. Ed "flew" the ROV, controlling its multiple thrusters and keeping his eyes glued on the video input from Eileen's cameras. Mitch would be responsible for the manipulator arm when the little robot reached the bottom. For now, he was mostly a second set of eyes watching the various data feeds from the ROV and the other equipment they had deployed.

The other three men crowded around behind them, wedging themselves into the narrow space between Ed and Mitch's backs and the overflowing steel cabinets bolted to the wall behind them. They all stared at the monitors showing live feeds from Eileen's cameras.

Right now, the video screens showed only dark water and occasional fish that swam through the cones of light cast by Eileen's powerful lamps. The ROV hung motionless in the water almost five hundred feet below them, connected to the ship by a long tether that unspooled through a crane on the ship's stern. She was about two hundred yards from the nearest crags of the underwater mountain range, waiting as Ed and Mitch readied their approach to the wreck.

Ed jabbed a dirty, thick finger at a sonar printout that provided a workable map of the invisible terrain below. "I'm going to take her through here." He traced a path between two massive boulders between the ROV's current position and a long lozenge shape that lay at an angle on the mountainside.

Mitch craned his head for a better view. "Currents?"

Ed exhaled pungently. "Bad, but should be better in the lee of those boulders."

Mitch nodded. "What do you want me to do?"

"I'm gonna need all my attention on the cameras to keep from crashing. You watch everything else."

"Got it."

"All right, here we go."

Ed pushed the joystick on the ROV controller forward. The featureless black on the monitor didn't change at first. Then flecks of something began to flow across the screen, and soon the ROV's lights cast swirling, glowing cones like a car's headlights driving through wind-blown fog.

"Hitting some turbulence," Ed announced. "Mitch, we okay so far?"

Mitch glanced over the sonar readouts. "We're good, but you're coming up on something pretty soon. Looks like a—"

Ed suddenly swore and Mitch jerked his gaze back to the monitor showing the camera view. A blurry close-up of a wall of rock.

Ed invited the boulder to commit a number of obscene acts as he worked to move the ROV away from the rock and out of danger. He hunched over the joystick and stared at the monitor from less than a foot away. Dark rings grew in the armpits of his shirt.

At last, the image of the boulder shrank and faded on the monitor. Ed leaned back, took a deep breath and blew it out slowly. "Well, that was fun. I think we fouled a propeller. Must've sucked a rock into one of the thrusters or something. Motor might be damaged too." He pointed to the image on the screen, which had started quivering. "Looks like we picked up a shimmy."

Cho cleared his throat. "So we must stop and repair the ROV?"

Ed shook his head. "Don't have a spare forward motor on board. We'd have to order one and make port somewhere to pick it up. That would take weeks. Probably quicker to just go back to Oakland and get one from the warehouse."

"But without the motor—"

"Who flies this thing, you or me?" Ed demanded, cutting off Cho.

Mr. Lee leaned toward Cho and said something in Korean.

Cho nodded. "Please proceed."

Ed grunted and turned back to the bank of monitors. "Okay, Eileen's a little banged up in front. Everything else good to go, Mitch?"

"Good to go, Ed. Gonna drop her over the top this time?"

"Yeah. The current around those boulders was stronger than I expected. Better to just come straight down and take our chances."

They all watched silently as Ed maneuvered the ROV up to a point roughly a hundred feet above the target. "She's still shaking some, but not bad . . . Okay, we're going down. Eighty feet. Sixty. Fifty—hitting that current again, but it's steady. Forty. Current's picking up. Mitch, watch our sonar. Twenty-five. Current's not so steady anymore—getting some turbulence. Twenty. Fifteen. Lots of sediment, but we should be getting visual any second. Here's the moment of truth."

"Jackpot!" Jenkins crowed as a shape appeared out of the glowing clouds of silt on the screen. The stern of a submarine.

But there was something wrong with the picture on the screen. This was not the heavily corroded, narrow craft that Mitch had expected. It was too round, too big, and the propellers were intricately sculpted. This was nothing like any Nazi u-boat that Mitch had ever seen. Yet he *had* seen it before.

Mitch's mind raced. He recognized that wreck—but from where? Something he'd seen in a museum? During his stint in the Navy? On TV? He plumbed the dark waters of his memory, hunting for the answer.

Ed moved Eileen over the top of the wrecked sub. Her conning tower, still intact, came into view. Then Ed tilted Eileen's cameras down toward the wide deck in front of the tower. Pairs of large hatches punctuated the deck every few feet. The entire bow had been torn open like a Christmas cracker, its contents spilled out on the jagged rocky floor of the ravine.

Colored wiring and bits of metal and plastic lay scattered like streamers and confetti. And resting in the middle of that glittering carpet was a haphazard scattering of massive tubes. Most were crushed, twisted, bent, or torn in two. But not all. Two or three looked undamaged, and a blunt object peeked from one.

Typhoon. The word appeared in Mitch's mind a split-second before he realized what it meant. Then everything clicked into place and he knew exactly what he was looking at.

Mitch stared at the screen, hardly believing his eyes. Sweat prickled his palms and forehead. Electric tension hummed in his brain. He realized he was breathing fast and made an effort to slow down his respiration.

No one had said anything. Maybe they didn't recognize the wreck. He glanced around the room, gauging the reactions of the other men. Jenkins leaned at an awkward angle and craned his neck for a view of the screen. Ed's face was an expressionless mask of focus as his hands danced over the ROV's controls. Cho and Mr. Lee stood perfectly still, watching with bright, black eyes. Cho's face was unreadable, but Mr. Lee's eyes looked hungry and a slight smile curved the corners of his mouth.

29

CONNOR EASED HIMSELF INTO HIS USUAL chair in conference room 11436 at the California Department of Justice. Max Volusca sat on his right, a stack of documents and an interview outline in front of him. The witness sat across the table from Max with Carlos Alvarez at his side. Connor was a little surprised to see him handling another false claims case after his performance on the Hamilton Construction lawsuit. Apparently he'd managed to spin it into a success story. Well, Connor would be happy to help him add a similar line to his resumé for this case.

The witness was Franklin Roh, whom Allie had identified as the IT chief at Deep Seven. Roh looked the part. He wore a conservative gray Brooks Brothers suit with a burgundy tie. His shirt was so stiffly starched that it looked like he was dressed in white cardboard. Designer glasses that would have been stylish ten years ago hid his almond eyes. His hair was suspiciously pure black despite the fact that he was at least fifty.

Roh's face was bland and expressionless. In fact, it was almost motionless except for the mechanical movements of his jaw as he sucked cherry cough drops.

Max went through the preliminary background questions with his typical speed. Roh graduated from Seokyeong University in Seoul, South Korea, in 1976. He worked for the Korean Ministry of National Defense for ten years before emigrating to the United States and getting a master's degree at MIT. Then he worked at Microsoft for a decade. In 2005, he accepted the position of chief information officer at Deep Seven.

Once Max was through the preliminaries, he reached for the top document on his stack. Connor glanced at it, expecting to see one of the invoices Allie found. But instead he saw half a dozen lines identifying what appeared to be computer files.

Max handed it to Roh. "Is this an accurate list of all the drives in Deep Seven's computer system?"

Roh looked at it for nearly a minute, long enough to read it several times. "It appears to be, yes."

Max nodded and checked an item off his interview outline. "And where do you keep customer billing and payment records?"

Roh licked his lips quickly. His tongue was brilliant red from the cough drops. "Those are, ah, in multiple locations. I believe most are on the G drive."

Max jotted down a note. "Which server?"

Again his crimson tongue darted around his mouth. "Number three."

Another scribble on the outline. "Anywhere else?"

"I . . . I am not sure. Perhaps if you ask someone from accounting they can—"

"Are there billing or payment records on that encrypted server, number—" Max hunted through his notes, but Connor kept his eyes on Roh. The man sat motionless, breathing rapidly. Sweat rings began to form in his armpits and his cheeks fluttered as he dissolved another cough drop in his mouth. Max found what he wanted and looked up. "Sorry about that. Server number four. Any customer billing or payment records there?"

"Perhaps Korean. I mean, perhaps there are records from a Korean client. But no government money. None." The words came tumbling out of Roh's mouth, stumbling over each other in their haste to convince Max Volusca. "So there's nothing for you to care about because there's nothing government there."

The DAG stroked his second chin thoughtfully and looked at Roh for several seconds. Then he glanced down at his outline. "How often does Deep Seven back up its servers, and where do you keep the backup tapes?"

Max then launched into a long series of questions about Deep Seven's computer infrastructure. For some reason, he seemed to be trying to establish that CBI had seized every accounting database at Deep Seven. Roh recovered his composure after a few minutes, and soon Connor had to take notes to keep his mind from drifting. *Come on, Max. Why are you screwing around with this stuff?*

Finally, Max pulled an invoice out of the stack of documents in front of him. Connor glanced over and recognized it as one of the ones Allie had found. Connor perked up and made a conscious effort not to smile.

The DAG handed it to Roh. "Do you recognize this document, Mr. Roh?"

Roh studied it for several seconds. "This appears to be one of our invoices."

"An invoice to the state of California, correct?"

"Yes, the Department of Water Resources."

"Is the invoice accurate?"

"I assume so."

Max arched his eyebrows. "Do you really? Well, if you wanted to check on whether it was accurate, what would you do?"

Roh smiled and swept his ruby tongue over his upper lip. "I would ask someone from accounting."

"Okay, assume they're all out at lunch. Every one of them. And you need to know right now. What would you do?"

"I can't imagine that happening. But if it did, I suppose I would look at the other, ah, materials in the customer file."

"Materials like this?" Max tossed three pages of billing detail record across the table.

Roh glanced at them and held them up against the invoice. "Yes."

"And this?" Max handed him the smoking-gun Excel spreadsheet.

"Yes." He picked up the billing detail and began comparing it to the spreadsheet. "I—these numbers don't, ah, they don't appear to match."

Alvarez leaned over and whispered to his client. Max folded his arms and watched with a satisfied look on his face.

Connor couldn't hear what Alvarez and Roh were saying, but they didn't look happy. Roh kept studying the documents, as if he could somehow make the fraud go away if he looked at the numbers hard enough. Alvarez knew better and sat back, his face flushed and grim.

Losing sucks, doesn't it, Carlos? Connor felt a little sorry for his opponent, but not much. Carlos Alvarez was smart and very competitive, but he played by the rules and was a decent guy outside the courtroom. Connor appreciated that. There were other lawyers he'd rather see take sucker punches from Max Volusca.

But Alvarez had it coming. He was a good lawyer, but he didn't stick to representing good people. The wicked lay snares for their own feet, and if Alvarez wanted to walk with the wicked, he'd get caught with them too.

Roh finally looked up with a light of dawning comprehension in his face. "This is why you are investigating us?"

"I ask the questions here," Max replied. "And I'm asking why the numbers on that spreadsheet don't match the numbers on the bill your company sent."

"I cannot imagine how this could have happened."

Max snorted. "I can."

Alvarez's face reddened under his immaculate silver hair, but Roh hardly seemed to notice the DAG's sarcasm. "No, I mean I don't understand the technicalities. The computer procedures. The invoices are generated directly from the spreadsheet. Someone would have to go in and manually alter the invoices after they were generated."

"So you're saying this couldn't have happened by accident?"

Roh turned toward Alvarez again.

"Answer the question first!" Max boomed.

"Can I talk with my attorney?"

"Not while there's a question pending."

Alvarez looked as though he had just swallowed something sour. "I'm afraid that's how the rules work, Franklin."

Roh dropped his eyes to the documents and slowly shook his head. "I cannot think of . . . of an accidental scenario."

Bingo! After that little admission, Connor had trouble imagining what Deep Seven's defense would be. This case was going to settle faster than he had anticipated.

Max smiled. "Okay, *now* you can talk to your lawyer."

Alvarez and Roh left the conference room, and Connor turned to Max. "Nice work. So, when are you guys going to intervene?"

Max glanced out the conference room window. "Yeah, we need to talk about that."

"What do you—" The door opened and Connor broke off in mid-sentence.

Alvarez and Roh resumed their seats. Alvarez nodded. "Go ahead, Max."

"Okay. I've only got one question left." The DAG shoved a small stack of paper across the table. "Can you think of an accidental scenario for these invoices and spreadsheets?"

Roh looked at the documents for several minutes. Then he sighed and shrugged. "As I am

154

sitting here today, I cannot think of such a scenario."

Max checked the last item off of his outline. "All right. That's all I've got. Thanks for coming in today."

They all stood and the lawyers began to pack up their notebooks, pens, and other paraphernalia. Unlike last time, Alvarez made no effort to take any of the documents Max had shown to his client.

Roh cleared his throat. "Excuse me, Mr. Volusca. Now that the interview is over, may I ask a question?"

Max shrugged. "Sure. Go ahead."

"When can we have our computer equipment back? It is inconvenient to use our backup servers."

The restrained eagerness in Roh's voice made Connor look up. The man's face wore an unmoving and carefully casual smile. But his knuckles were white as he dug his fingers deep into the chair in front of him.

"Tough to say," Max replied. "We should be done with the investigation soon. Maybe a couple of weeks."

Roh nodded sharply and his smile looked more genuine. "Ah, very good. Thank you."

Once Roh and Alvarez were gone, Connor turned to Max. "That went about as well as could be expected. Weird, but well."

"Uh, yeah." He paused and took a deep breath. "Listen, I appreciate all the cases you and Allie bring in. You've brought us a lot of winners over the years, but this isn't one of them. I'm going to recommend against intervention."

Connor sat in stunned silence. He'd figured out that something was bothering Max, but he would never have guessed this. "Max, I don't get it. Why? You saw how he reacted to those invoices."

"Yeah, but those are the only ones we found. That's what—twenty thousand? Not worth fighting over."

"That's it? You've looked at all the invoices and those three are the only bad ones?"

Max nodded. "We sent a team of auditors through every one of those databases." He pointed at the invoices on the table. "Those are the only fraudulent ones."

Connor shook his head. "That doesn't make sense. This isn't a twenty-thousand-dollar case. No one hires Carlos Alvarez to solve a twenty-thousand-dollar problem. And did you see Roh? Your investigation scares the snot out of him. He's hiding something big."

Max pressed his lips together and tapped his pen against his notebook for several seconds before responding. "Yeah, I did notice that."

"And what about those witnesses I talked to? It was like I was talking to ex-mafia types and asking them about the mob."

Max arched his bushy eyebrows. "Maybe they were masons or Nazis."

"That was one guy, and his grandson *did* disappear. And he was right about that server four."

"All true."

"So you've *got* to keep digging."

Max reddened slightly. "No, I don't. Not unless this company is stealing from the great state of California."

"So you're going to drop it? Seriously?"

"Yes, I am. In case you forgot, I work in the False Claims Unit." Max's face darkened further as he spoke and his voice rose. "We prosecute false claims cases. Big cases. Cases that are worth spending the taxpayers' money on. This isn't one of those cases, Connor. If you want to go after these guys on your own, be my guest. And if you think there's something criminal going on, call the cops."

"But don't call you."

"Not unless you find a lot more stolen state money."

Connor bit back an angry retort. "Come on, Max. This is the Department of Justice, not the Department of Finance, right?"

"Yeah, but it's also not the Department of Running Down Connor Norman's Hunches That Something Funky Is Going On."

Connor held his tongue between his teeth and counted to ten. "Thanks for your time, Max."

30

THE PHONE RANG AGAIN. "HANSEN, ERIK" announced a robotic voice from Allie's phone.

She rolled her eyes and walked into her bedroom. When was that loser going to get the hint? The phone stopped ringing and the voice-mail kicked in. "Allie, just pick up the phone, all right? I know you're there."

She went into her closet and started sorting shoes into "keep" and "give to charity" bags. She tried hard to ignore the voice coming from her answering machine.

"Aarrgh! Just tell me what I did wrong, all right? Seriously, just pick up the phone and tell me."

Keep last summer's flip-flops? No, they were scuffed. Into the charity bag.

"I love you." His voice was soft and warm, full of the promise of candlelight and champagne.

She dropped the shoes and put her head in her hands. She soooo much wanted to pick up the phone.

"I need you."

She turned and glared at the phone. "Yeah, you need me to give you a ride and pay your hotel bill so you can sell meth to kids!" She said it loudly to drown out the voice inside her that said *I need you too*.

"Fine. Have a good life." Click.

She turned back to the pile of shoes and tried to ignore the ache in her throat. Her eyes blurred and she rubbed them harshly.

Man, the apartment felt empty. Come to think of it, her whole life felt empty. She suddenly felt a strong urge to call her mom just to not be alone for a while.

Focus. She had to focus. She had to get through all her clothing today. Otherwise she would fall behind schedule and wouldn't be done in time. The gold stilettos were keepers and went in the box labeled "Shoes #3." So did the underused cross-trainers. The black flats could go—she had two pairs just alike.

Three hours later, the closet was more or less empty. A few forlorn outfits hung among discarded hangers and empty dry-cleaning bags, but everything else was either in boxes destined for the mover or garbage bags destined for the Goodwill store. And Allie had gotten a workout despite not having put on her cross-trainers.

She admired her work and stretched. Time for a break.

The phone base on the black granite kitchen counter was empty and the mobile handset was nowhere to be seen. Okay, where did the phone fairy hide it this time?

She pressed the "Find" button and a muffled beeping came from the balcony. She walked out and dug the handset out of a stadium blanket on one of the Adirondack chairs. Two bars on the battery icon. That should be enough.

She pressed her mom's speed dial, and a few seconds later Mom answered. "Hi, Allie. I was just about to call you. Sam was paying bills and told me there was five hundred thousand more in our account than there should have been. Did you put it there?"

"I did." She settled into the chair and pulled the blanket over her as she spoke. "We settled a big case not too long ago and I thought you could use the money more than me."

"Thank you, dear. That's very sweet and very generous. But I can't accept it. It's just too much. Besides, we're fine. I'm going to send it back to you."

She was going to have to tell Mom sometime. Might as well do it now. "You can't. I closed my bank account and I'm about to move."

"Oh." She could hear the surprise and worry in her mother's voice. "Where are you going?"

Connor had assured her that her phone was safe, but that had been weeks ago. "I can't say, but I'll let you know when I'm there."

Long seconds ticked by. "Are you in trouble?"

Allie bit her lip and squirmed in her seat. "Not really. It's just that . . . I can't really talk about it now, but don't worry. Seriously, don't. Everything's fine. Oh, and don't worry about the money either. I won't be able to send any more for a while, so I wanted to send a big chunk now. Besides, I'd just blow it on a snowboarding trip in the Himalayas or something." She laughed, but it came out all jittery.

"Now I really am worried. What's happened? Why can't you tell me where you're going?"

"Really, Mom. I'm fine. Completely fine." A lie, but one Mom needed to hear. "Seriously. I'll give you a call in less than a week, okay? If you don't hear from me by then, you can worry, all right?"

Mom sighed. "I just wish you could tell me what's going on."

"So do I." Time to find something else to talk about. "Hey, did I mention that I broke up with Erik?"

"Oh, my. How are you feeling?"

Allie pulled the blanket tighter around herself. "I'm good. It's been a long time coming. Glad I finally did it."

"I'm glad too, sweetheart." To Allie's relief, her mother's voice had lost the I'm-worried-about-my-little-girl tone. "He wasn't the kind that makes a good husband."

Allie sat up, hot indignation burning through her chilly loneliness. "Mom, please! I never even considered marrying him! The guy's a rock star wannabe with a drug problem. I liked him and we had fun together, but that's it."

"Well, you two were together for a long time. And you're at the age where you can't afford to waste time with someone you wouldn't marry."

Maybe changing the subject of conversation to Erik hadn't been such a good idea after all. "Not everyone gets married by thirty these days, for your information. And why are you so sure I want to get married at all? It didn't work out so hot for Sam. She had the big wedding, started popping out kids, and now she's manless again and back at home living with you."

Allie immediately regretted bringing up Sam's divorce. Sam wasn't the one calling her an old bag who dated losers and would never get married. But it was out there now and Allie wasn't going to back down. She steeled herself for her mother's counterattack.

It still hit her like a gut punch. "I just don't want you to be alone and lonely. That's all. I love you and I want you to be happy."

The ache was back in Allie's throat, almost strangling her. "I know, Mom," she forced out, her voice thick. "I love you too. And I'm sorry I said that about Sam. Don't tell her, okay?"

"I won't." She paused and Allie could hear a child's voice in the background. "I'll be right there. Sorry, Allie. Sam and the girls just made dinner and Andrea just told me that they're ready to eat."

"Okay. I should get going anyway. Give them all hugs from me."

"I will. And call me as soon as you reach wherever it is you're going. One week, remember?"

"I remember. Bye, Mom."

"Bye."

Allie clicked off the phone and turned to go back inside. All alone and lonely.

She suddenly couldn't bear the thought of spending another minute by herself. But who could she call? She'd met most of her friends through Erik, so they were all out. Trudi? And have to talk about her happy marriage and precious little twins? Not exactly what she had in mind. Okay, who else?

She scrolled through the contact list on her cell phone and stopped on Connor Norman. Now there was an interesting idea.

Kind of sad that her lawyer was the one person she could think of to call when she was feeling like this.

But still. She always had a good time when they were together. And she'd always wondered, just a little, what would have happened if she'd met Connor before Erik. Besides, she'd be gone in less than three days, so there wasn't much to lose if this turned out to be a bad idea.

As the idea became more real, she started to get nervous. She laughed at herself, and the sound of her own voice startled her.

That settled it. If just thinking about Connor made her feel better, seeing him certainly would. She dialed his number before she could change her mind, then bit her lip as the phone rang.

31

Connor's cell phone vibrated in his shorts pocket as he wiped down the nose of the *White Knight*. Even in the hangar, the dust from the Livermore hills managed to reach the plane and dull its gleaming stainless steel finish.

He pulled the phone out and his eyebrows went up when he saw who was calling. "Hi, Allie. What's up?"

"Hey, Connor. I was wondering what you're doing tonight."

"Right now I'm out at the Livermore Airport working on my plane." He wiped his hands on a rag, switching the phone from hand to hand as he spoke. "Did you want to talk about Max's decision? I can't right now, but give me half an hour and I'll be ready."

"Uh, that's okay. We're scheduled to talk about that tomorrow morning, aren't we?"

"Yeah. 11:30."

Silence.

Something was weird. "Is anything wrong?"

"No, no. I was just thinking that it might be fun to get together for a glass of wine or something. Not publicly, of course. Go to an out-of-the-way little bistro or bar, walk in separately, and sit in the back. No one will see us. What do you say?"

He had no idea what to say, so he stalled.

"Sounds like fun, but I've already got plans tomorrow. I don't have my calendar with me, but I might be free Friday."

"Uh, Friday is bad for me. How about tonight? You're always bragging on the restaurant at that one winery out in Livermore—what's the name?"

Tonight? His heart started beating faster. The firm wouldn't like it, but then the firm didn't really have to know. "Wente."

"That's it. And I'd love to see your plane. Antique, isn't it?"

"Yeah, P-51. World War II fighter."

"How cool! So, is tonight good?"

Connor blinked and stared at the hangar wall without really seeing it. He knew this was a bad idea, but he couldn't bring himself to care. Besides, one of the perks of having a family like his was that he could afford a bad idea every now and then. "Um, sure. Tonight is great." He glanced at the cockpit, which his grandfather had modified to seat two. It was a tight fit, but would that be so terrible? "Hey, would you like me to take you flying?"

She didn't hesitate. "I'd love it!"

"Great!" He glanced at his watch. 5:00. "If you can be out here by seven, I can take you up for a ride before we head out to Wente."

"I'll be there."

"Excellent. I'll see you at seven. I'll meet you in the parking lot outside the main building."

He clicked off the phone and sucked in a deep breath. He blew it out slowly and ran his fingers through his hair. Wow.

Two hours later, Connor stood in the airport parking lot playing Brickbreaker on his Blackberry and trying not to think about the evening ahead. But the unanswerable questions kept sneaking back into his mind. What exactly were Allie's intentions? For that matter, what were his? What would tonight mean tomorrow when he was back behind his polished walnut desk and Allie was his client?

Better to just relax and let the evening unfold.

A red Cooper Mini pulled into the lot and he recognized Allie behind the wheel. She spotted him, smiled, and waved. He waved back. "And here we go," he said to himself as he walked over to meet her.

32

ALLIE PUT THE CAR IN PARK AND TURNED TO see Connor approaching her. He looked like an Eddie Bauer ad—crisp khakis, white polo glowing in the early evening sun, light tan, easy smile crinkling the corners of his chestnut eyes.

She got out of the car and gave him a hug. She held it a little too long, but didn't care. "Good to see you."

"You too." He put a hand in the small of her back and guided her around the corner of the building. "We've got an 8:30 reservation, so let's get right up in the air. I've got the plane out and ready to go."

They reached the open area behind the building and Allie saw the plane. She didn't know much about World War II aircraft, so she had vaguely expected Connor's plane to look old. Maybe a biplane or something with an open cockpit and a boxy, cloth-covered fuselage. But what she saw looked more like a steel shark with wings. She smiled in anticipation.

Connor turned to her and grinned. "Ever get sick on a roller coaster?"

"Nope. Iron stomach."

"Good."

They got closer to the plane, and she could see *White Knight* painted on the nose in Gothic script. She stifled a laugh.

Connor gave her a startled look. "What's funny?"

She nodded at the plane. "White Knight. It's just very, very you." If only he could save her. No, she wasn't going to think about that. Just enjoy today.

His smile returned. "Thanks. It was also very much my grandfather. He named it in honor of the fighter pilots he knew. Called them knights of the air."

He gestured to a spot on the wing with the words "Step Here" stenciled on it. "In you go.

The rear seat is yours. Sorry it's a little cramped. P-51s are single-seaters, so it wasn't designed for that jump seat."

Allie carefully squeezed into the narrow space, regretting that she hadn't spent more time in the gym. But once she was in, it was surprisingly comfortable. The custom leather seat cocooned her nicely between the rear of the cockpit and the back side of the pilot's seat.

Connor climbed into his seat, put on a headset, and buckled himself in. He started the engine and taxied to the runway. Then he opened the throttle and a deep roar filled the plane. Allie's entire body thrummed with the power of the P-51.

The plane jumped forward and accelerated down the tarmac. A giant invisible hand pressed Allie back into her seat. She felt the plane tip forward as the tail left the ground. A second later, the P-51 left the ground and soared into the bright azure sky.

Allie had flown dozens of times before, but those had all been commercial airliners. Those were about as similar to Connor's fighter as a commuter train is to a Corvette. She could really *feel* that she was flying in this plane—not just sitting in a cramped bus seat that happened to have a 30,000 foot view out the window.

"We've got clearance for aerobatics," Connor shouted over his shoulder. "Want to have some fun?"

"Sure!" she yelled back.

The word was hardly out of her mouth when the plane nosed up and the world wheeled under her. She suddenly found herself hanging from her seatbelts and she looked up—down?—through the canopy to see vine-covered hills rushing by. Then the plane rolled to the side and she was upright again.

Connor turned and called over his shoulder. "That's called an Immelmann. And this is called a split-S."

He flipped the plane upside down again and rolled it into a tight half loop that righted it and reversed their direction.

Allie laughed with the pure joy and freedom of the moment. All her problems and hurts seemed a million miles away, part of a different, earth-bound world. "This is great! I never want to land!"

"You like it?"

She laughed again. "I love it! This is better than a roller coaster with no rails!" It was even better because it was with him.

The next hour went by in a blur. They slalomed through wisps of cloud at 300 miles an hour. They dove down and roared over pastures just above the treetops, so low that Allie could see the faces of the cows looking up as they passed. They made slow passes through the steep-walled canyons Connor had hiked and camped in as a boy.

And then it was over. The red light of sunset turned the runway deep crimson as Connor brought the plane in for a feather-light landing. He taxied over to the hangar and then killed the engine.

The silence rang in Allie's ears. Connor slid back the canopy and a warm evening breeze wafted into the cockpit, carrying the faint scent of gasoline and hot asphalt. The dirty, painful, complicated earth-bound world swallowed her up again. She sighed, unbuckled herself, and searched for some way to lever herself out of the snug seat.

"Getting out of there can be a bit of a trick."

She looked up and saw Connor already out of the cockpit and standing on the wing. He smiled and reached out to help her. She took his hand. It was warm and strong and she didn't want to let it go. He pulled her to her feet in a smooth, strong motion.

She stood on the wing, still holding his hand. They were so close that his face filled her vision and the scent of his Armani cologne surrounded her. She looked up into his eyes and for a moment she was flying again.

But the moment passed. He stepped back and released her hand. "Everyone gets stuck the first time."

"Thanks." Too bad there wouldn't be a second time.

33

MITCH AND ED LEANED AGAINST THE RAIL AT the stern of the *Grasp II*. The ship's diesel engines chugged below them. Despite a breeze, the air smelled of exhaust fumes. It wasn't a pleasant place, which explained why Mitch and Ed had it to themselves.

"So why'd you drag me up here?" asked Ed, raising his voice to be heard over the engines. He took a sip from his mug and made a sour face. "This is a Sumatran blend with complex and delicate flavors—and this stink makes it taste like I stirred it with a tailpipe."

Mitch was in no mood to trade pleasantries. "I wanted to go someplace we could talk privately. You see what I saw?"

"Where?"

Mitch pointed at the churning ocean below them. "Down there. That submarine. Don't tell me you thought it was a Nazi wreck."

Ed looked into his cup and swirled its contents. "What'd you think it was?"

Mitch looked around quickly to make absolutely sure no one was nearby. Then he leaned close to Ed. "Russian nuclear missile sub," he hissed in Ed's ear. "Typhoon class. And I don't think, I know."

Mitch leaned back and watched his friend's

reaction. Ed nodded slightly and took another sip of his coffee. "Yep, that's what I saw too."

Mitch leaned in to whisper again, but Ed shoved him away with his shoulder. "Would you quit that? No one can hear us out here, but they can see. They're going to think we're up to something. Or that you're going Brokeback on me."

Mitch shoved him back. "Okay, fine. I was just going to say that Lee and Cho didn't look surprised. I'll bet they knew there was a Russian sub down there."

"Really? I'll go you one better and bet the sun will come up tomorrow. Of course they knew. It all fits together, don't you see?"

Mitch thought for a moment. "You mean like Lee and Cho and, uh . . ."

"I mean like everything." Ed held up thick hairy fingers and started counting off points. "One: the nonferrous metal detectors for Eileen. They're looking for uranium or plutonium, not gold. Two: the Nazi treasure sub cover story they fed Jenkins."

"And Jenkins fed you," Mitch interjected.

"Yeah, exactly. Think it's a coincidence that setting up Eileen to look for gold also sets her up to look for a nuclear sub? Three: the Koreans. They're obviously military. I wondered why a military unit would go treasure hunting. Nuclear missile hunting, though—that makes sense."

Mitch's stomach dropped and he felt sweat prickling his scalp. The dark portholes of the bulkhead opposite him suddenly looked threatening. "What do you think they're gonna do?"

"To us? Nothing. At least not 'til they've got the bombs or whatever it is they want from that sub. After that?" He shrugged.

Mitch swallowed hard and clenched his fists on the railing. He didn't want to believe it, but he couldn't find a way not to. It all made too much sense in a brutal way. He'd been in plenty of fights and thought of himself as a pretty tough guy, but he suddenly realized he was soft next to Lee and Cho. There was a hardness in their way of thinking that Mitch had never come up against in any barroom brawl. *I'm going to have to start thinking like that.* He set his jaw. "So what are *we* gonna do?"

34

CONNOR ENJOYED WATCHING ALLIE ENJOY Wente. She oohed over the view from the patio and aahed over the crab cakes. He had eaten here a hundred times, so the restaurant held few surprises. For him, coming here was like visiting a good friend—one who could cook. But for Allie it had the special savor of a new discovery. Sitting across from her was almost like experiencing it again for the first time. It was beautiful; she was beautiful.

She took a sip of Chardonnay and the corners of her lips curved up slightly in a smile that he was not quite sure how to read. "Mind if I ask a personal question?"

His antennae went up. "Fire away."

"Your family is rich, right? I mean really rich—buy-your-own-island rich."

He laughed. "Depends on the island."

"But you never really had to work, right? You could just do what you wanted to do and there'd always be someone to pay the bills. Just call up Citibank or Bank of America and it's taken care of." She snapped her fingers.

"Morgan Stanley, actually."

"But you didn't have to work, right?"

"Wellll . . ." He drew out the word to stall. Talking about the Norman-Lamont fortune always made him uncomfortable. He didn't like how he sounded when he spoke of it—he could hear himself veering among arrogance, false modesty, and evasion. He also didn't like the envy and gold-digging it brought out in too many listeners. He hoped the evening wasn't about to start sliding downhill.

Allie rolled her eyes. "Oh, cut it out. True or false: you could do whatever you wanted with your life."

He squirmed and looked at the table. So this is

what it felt like to be cross-examined. He'd have more sympathy for his next witness. "True."

"So how did you decide?"

"You mean why did I become a lawyer?"

"Sure, let's start there."

Connor swirled the merlot in his glass as he formed an answer. "In college, I wanted to be a senator like my father. The straightest road to the Senate runs through law school, so I went to law school. Then while I was there, there was a scandal in Washington. It had to do with defense contracts and campaign contributions. It was complicated, but the bottom line was that Dad was innocent. But a lot of his friends were guilty and Dad had known what was going on.

"I asked him about it, and he just said, 'That's how Washington works. You don't have to be dirty, but you have to put up with dirt in other people if you want to get anything done.' I wasn't willing to do that, so I gave up on the Senate."

"But you were already in law school."

"And loving it." He took a sip of wine. "I was a round peg in a round hole. It was great. So I went through on cruise control, happy as a shark in a school of tuna. Then I graduated and took a job with a big firm because that's what you do when you graduate from Harvard Law and you've got good grades."

"And here you are today."

He nodded. "And here I am today." He lifted his

glass. "To Harvard Law and Doyle & Brown."

She lifted her glass and clinked it against his. "Would you change anything? If you could start all over with a fresh slate, what would you do?"

"Put more money in Google and less in GM and AIG."

She laughed. "But other than that, you'd do it all again. Harvard Law, Doyle & Brown—all that?"

"Sure. Why not?"

She shrugged. "Well, it just seems like you took kind of a step down. You know, from a senator who's helping shape the course of the country—the world—to a lawyer who sues people. No offense."

"None taken. Actually, I think it's a step up."

"Really? Why's that?"

"I get to work with people like you."

She blinked and looked down. "You don't mean that."

"Oh, I most definitely mean it. Dad had to make deals with criminals. His proudest achievements were—at best—compromises. I don't have to make deals with criminals, I take them down. No compromises, no dirty friends. I get to spend my days representing people who put themselves on the line to clean up the system. People like you, Allie. I'm honored to be your lawyer."

She kept her eyes down and studied her wine intently. "You don't know me."

He searched her for any hint of false modesty, but found none. A warm glow came over him. He wanted to know her. He needed to know her. "So tell me about yourself. You asked how I wound up where I am. Now it's your turn. How did you wind up being a professional whistleblower?"

She shrugged one shoulder. "I didn't really plan on it. I had my CPA certificate but no job. So I started temping. One of my jobs was at NorCal Corporate Trust, remember them?"

"Oh, yeah. The bank that kept making errors in their favor when they managed state bonds. Our first case together."

"And the rest is history. Simple as that."

Connor regarded her for a moment. "Is it really as simple as that? I know what you've done, but not why. Is it just to make money so you and your boyfriend can live the sweet life and go snowboarding? Or is there something more?"

"He's my ex-boyfriend, but other than that, yeah, basically." She smiled sheepishly. "Sorry to be so shallow."

An uneasy thrill swept through him. A gate had just vanished from a path he didn't dare take. "Ex-boyfriend?"

She nodded and sighed. "As of today."

"I'm sorry to hear that," he lied. "Are you okay?"

"I am now. Thanks for taking me out. I'm having a great time."

"Me too." He looked into her eyes. Her beautiful face was right there—he could reach out and touch her cheek, caress her skin. He was exhilarated and unsettled by what he saw there—and what she probably saw in his face. He wasn't ready to cross this line. She was an important client and a friend—what would happen if she became more? He'd lose his job and all he had worked for. Worse, Devil to Pay would be compromised and she'd never blow another whistle. He couldn't do that to her.

He broke away from her gaze. "So, why do you keep transferring hundreds of thousands to an account in Elmhurst, Illinois? I don't think the slopes there are all that good."

Her eyebrows went up. "Didn't think you read Devil to Pay's bank statements that closely."

"Hey, I'm the general counsel. I've got a duty to read them. You own all the stock, so you can do what you want with the money. I'm just curious why you want to send it to Elmhurst."

She sighed and a look of pain clouded her face. "That's where my mom lives with my sister and her kids. They're on their own, so I help them out."

Connor smiled with satisfaction. "See? I knew there was more to it than having a good time."

The clouds thickened. "Yeah, well I wish there weren't. Trust me—sending money doesn't make me a hero."

"So why do you do it?"

"Because of my dad." Her answer was quick, almost automatic. Her eyes widened a split second after the words came out. "I mean, I . . . it . . ." Her voice trailed off and she drained the last of her wine. "I mean I owe my parents, you know, for raising me and everything. So, I guess I'll always be in their debt." She glanced quickly at him and then looked out into the night crouching beyond the reach of the patio lights.

"What did you mean before you meant that?"

She gave a short laugh and looked back at him, her eyes bright with unshed tears. "Man, you're good."

She dabbed her eyes with her napkin and took a deep breath. He watched her in silence, waiting until she was ready to go on. His heart raced. He knew she was opening the door to a private room. A room that had been locked for years. He felt like he was watching a butterfly come out of its chrysalis.

She took another deep breath and looked him in the eyes. "Cone of silence?"

He smiled. "I'm your lawyer and your friend. How many secrets am I already keeping for you?"

"This is different."

"Okay. Cone of silence."

"I'm the reason they're on their own. I killed my dad." Her voice shook and she paused for a moment. She swallowed and went on. "I was home from college for summer break. I needed to get some software for one of my classes and the school bookstore was out, so I decided to go to Best Buy. Of course, Dad had to come if someone was going to Best Buy." She sniffed and took a sip of water. "Anyway, we went together. It was raining pretty hard and Mom said, 'Pete, you should drive.'

"I said, 'No, it's my car. I'm driving.'

"So we started arguing. She trotted out all her favorite lines. 'Dad's a safer driver.' 'You drive too fast.' On and on. I got mad and started yelling back at her about how I'm just as good a driver, how I'm an adult and she shouldn't treat me like a child.

"Eventually Dad just says, 'All right, I'm going by myself.'

"I went after him and said, 'Hey, my car has antilock brakes. Let's take it.'

"He said, 'Fine. Give me the keys.'

"I said, 'Daddy, it's my car. I know how to drive it. Don't you trust me?'"

She bent her head and pressed her napkin to her eyes.

Connor wanted to reach out to her. "And you drove."

She nodded. "I drove. I drove too fast. And we hydroplaned—*I* hydroplaned—on the slick highway. The car flipped over and landed on the passenger side. I had a broken nose and some cuts, but Dad—" she broke off and buried her face in her napkin, sobbing uncontrollably now.

A few diners and restaurant staff cast curious glances their way, but Connor couldn't care less. Against his better judgment, he reached across the table and took her hand. "Oh, Allie. I'm so sorry."

Her face was blotchy and her makeup was a mess when she looked up again. "The last thing he said was, 'Mom won't understand. Say I was driving.' He made me promise to tell Mom and everyone that he was driving, so I did."

"And you've kept the truth bottled up all these years."

She nodded. "I promised I would. He was right too—Mom wouldn't understand. She'd still love me, but she'd never get past the fact that she told me not to drive and I drove anyway and Dad died."

Now he understood. "And you send money to take care of her because your dad can't."

"I can never pay her back. I can't bring Dad back. I can't fill that hole in her life. In all our lives. All I can do is take care of them like he would have."

"You're a good woman, Allie."

She shook her head and gave a smile that completely took his breath away. She was a mess—red eyes, smeared make up, blotchy cheeks—but she was more beautiful than he had ever seen her. Her face held a sweet, natural openness he had never seen in it before. "You just won't see through me, will you?"

He chuckled. "I think I just did."

"No, you're too good a man to." She squeezed his hand and released it. She opened her mouth, but then paused for an instant—as if she was revising what she had been about to say. "Thank you, Connor. For tonight. For being my lawyer and my friend. For listening and keeping my secrets. For everything."

She got up suddenly and walked around the table. He started to rise, but she was standing over him and leaning down. She kissed him, and her hair cascaded around their faces, shielding them from the world. Her lips lingered on his for a long moment, soft and insistent. She smelled of sun and Chardonnay and flowers.

She pulled back and smiled. "Good-bye."

Then she turned and walked away. The night swallowed her, and she was gone.

35

FIRST MATE JENKINS STOOD AS CHO AND MR. Lee entered Captain Wither's stateroom. "So that's what you were after." He whistled and shook his head. "What's down there is worth more than ten Nazi subs full of gold."

Mr. Lee took a seat across from the captain. Cho stood behind him, hands in the pockets of his jacket. Neither hand was empty. One gripped a pistol and the other a Taser.

Mr. Lee inclined his head. "Yes, it is quite valuable. I apologize for misleading you. If the wrong people had learned that we were looking for a Soviet submarine, there would have been serious problems."

Jenkins folded his arms. "Not just any Soviet submarine. That's a Soviet missile submarine."

"It is indeed." He and Jenkins regarded each other silently for several seconds. "What do you think of that, Mr. Jenkins? Captain Wither?"

Jenkins scratched his beard. "It was a surprise. Big surprise."

"Yes. Yes, it was," echoed the captain.

Mr. Lee leaned forward and rested his elbows on the small table. "Does it bother you?"

Jenkins shrugged. "That depends."

"On what?"

"Let's start with your plans. What are you going to do next? Salvage the missiles?"

Mr. Lee nodded. "Two of them should be sufficient."

"For what?"

Mr. Lee's face hardened. "That's not your concern."

"Really? Then why are you here talking to us?"

Mr. Lee said nothing. Cho tightened his grip on

his weapons and visualized what he would do. Sidestep and draw in one motion. Take down Jenkins first, then turn to the captain. If he was a threat, take him down too.

Jenkins suddenly grinned and chortled. "See, I'm thinking that you're planning to take these things back to Oakland. Go anywhere else and you'll get searched by customs and port security. But not in Oakland. We won't get searched there because the *Grasp II* didn't make port in another country and because they know the ship, the captain, and me. But if the captain and me aren't on board or we don't cooperate, then all bets are off. So you need us."

Mr. Lee nodded slightly. "You are a perceptive man, Mr. Jenkins. Please go on."

Jenkins's grin broadened. "Maybe you're terrorists and you're going to try to set off a couple of nuclear bombs in San Francisco."

Cho looked at Mr. Lee, but his face remained impassive.

"But I'm guessing you're not," Jenkins continued. "You don't seem like the terrorist types. And anyway, those warheads have been underwater for years, so they'd need a lot of work before they'd go off."

Mr. Lee smiled, and Cho could tell he was enjoying this. "So what do we plan to do with them?"

Jenkins knit his brows together for a moment.

Then he snapped thick fingers. "You're going to use them to make blueprints and sell those, like that Indian guy—what's his name?"

"I believe you are referring to the Pakistani scientist A. Q. Khan."

"That's the one. You'll also probably sell the plutonium from the warheads, but the real money will be in the blueprints." He paused and spread his hands. "Am I right?"

"Bravo, Mr. Jenkins! Excellent thinking. You've solved the puzzle."

Jenkins's face took on a sly look. "There's just one problem left."

"What is that?"

"You're the ones making all the money."

"Ah, that is a problem that can be solved. You will receive a one-million-dollar bonus for your services."

"Ten million."

"Three."

"Five." He nodded to Captain Wither. "And five for the cap'n, of course."

Mr. Lee turned to the captain. "Is that acceptable to you?"

Wither looked up at his first mate. "I . . . I suppose I can trust Randy's judgment on this."

"Excellent. Half of those amounts will be sent to you tomorrow, and the remaining half will come after our, ah, business is at an end. Please give wire instructions to Mr. Cho."

"Of course," replied Jenkins, who was now grinning from ear to ear.

Mr. Lee frowned. "We have not discussed Granger and Daniels. What about them?"

Jenkins made a dismissive gesture with his right hand. "Don't worry about those two. I'll take care of them."

36

CONNOR COULDN'T FOCUS. HE HADN'T been able to focus all morning. The only thing he remembered from the 8:30 Doyle & Brown partner meeting was that the breakfast spread had included Nantucket Nectars juices. And he only remembered that because he still had a half-empty bottle of orange juice on his desk.

After the meeting, Tom Concannon had stopped by Connor's office to chat about golf and firm politics. Connor had just smiled and nodded, waiting for his friend to leave.

When Tom was gone, Connor started writing a routine letter to opposing counsel in one of his cases. After forty-five minutes, all he had was "Dear Fred."

He knew exactly what the problem was, of course. Allie. He had hardly been able to think of anything else since their evening together yesterday.

Lying awake last night, he had given free rein to

his fantasies. He allowed himself to imagine showing off his favorite chalet in the French Alps. She'd be amazed at the snow and the manicured slopes. He'd ski and she'd snowboard, and they would see each other in flashes as they sped down the mountains.

Afterward, they would go to a little restaurant he knew that specialized in wild game. They'd get the table by the old stone fireplace and the owner would come out with two glasses of Beaujolais as soon as they were seated, like he did for all his regulars. Allie would sip her wine and look beautiful in the firelight. They'd have pheasant—no, venison—and Allie would make jokes about Bambi and Rudolph and they'd both laugh. Then they'd walk back to the chalet with the moonlight silvering the mountain and the narrow brick road before them. It would be cold and she would snuggle up against him and say how happy she was.

When he woke in the morning, he remembered why that was a fantasy. Doyle & Brown had a policy against lawyers dating clients, and they did not make exceptions. Five years ago, a former corporate client had sued, claiming that a D&B lawyer had seduced their general counsel in order to keep her from moving the company's multi-million-dollar legal budget to another law firm. D&B paid six million to settle the case and lost millions more when several big clients took their business elsewhere "to avoid even the appearance of impropriety," as they put it.

And a romance with Allie wouldn't just mess up his career, it would ruin hers. Too many people wanted to know who was behind Devil to Pay, Inc. Even if they were discreet, it wouldn't take long for someone to see them together. Then someone would put one and one together and guess what the two of them were up to. And then Allie would be nothing but an unemployed accountant with a string of bad references.

So what was he going to do when she called? He glanced at the clock. 11:15. Okay, fifteen minutes to figure out what he was going to say. Pretend last night never happened? No, that never worked. Besides, he didn't want to find a way to go back to the way things were—he wanted to find a way forward where they could be together painlessly. He was good at that—always had been. There was always someone he could call or a bank account he could draw on somewhere. Things could always be fixed. He just had to find the right lever to pull.

But how was he going to fix this? He bit his lip and stared out the window, hardly seeing the fog-covered bay outside. He could switch firms—but that would only solve his problem, but not hers.

Maybe he could arrange a high-paid accounting job for her at one of the companies where Mom and Dad were directors. No, that would take her away from the fraud-fighting work she loved. Plus, it would look like he was buying her.

He picked up a model P-51 from his desk (a gift from a former secretary) and spun the propeller. He waited for inspiration to come, but the only thing he felt inspired to do was get out of the office and take the *White Knight* up for an hour or two.

He looked at the clock again. 11:30. He sighed and put the plane down. He'd just have to fudge his way through the call and think some more. There was a solution there someplace. He just had to find it.

At least Max had given them plenty to talk about. DOJ had never turned down one of their cases before. Once Max filed a "declination to intervene" as it was formally called, the case would come out from under seal and litigation would begin in earnest. And so would the bills. If Max was right that the ceiling on their recovery was only about sixty thousand, they really had no business going much further. D&B's legal bills alone would probably cost over sixty thousand. *Per month.*

Connor was entitled to his attorney fees under the California False Claims Act, even if they far exceeded the actual amount of the judgment. But he'd have to fight for them, and the judge would likely slice a big chunk off of whatever bill Connor submitted. Overall, it just wasn't worth it.

He hadn't asked the Executive Committee for permission to continue with the case despite DOJ's decision, but he had a pretty good idea what they'd say.

He'd recommend to Allie that they fire off a massive wave of discovery as soon as the seal lifted, then offer to settle. The discovery would be cheap to prepare, but expensive for Deep Seven to answer. Presumably, they'd be willing to pay something to make the case go away at that point. Even if they weren't, the case would still go away. Or at least Connor would.

Allie would understand. She was a smart businesswoman, and she'd be able to see that going forward with the case would be stupid. In fact, as soon as she called, he would—

He looked at the clock in the corner of his computer screen. It showed 11:35.

Weird. She was always punctual, and they had specifically decided that she would call him because she didn't know whether she'd be home this morning.

11:37.

Maybe they'd had a misunderstanding and she was expecting him to call after all. He dialed her cell phone. It rang three times and went to voicemail. He left a message.

11:40.

He called her apartment. The phone rang once. Then a woman's voice said, "The number you are trying to reach is no longer in service. Please hang up, check the number, and dial again."

Connor hung up, checked the number, and dialed again. Same message.

He hung up again and stared at the phone, mind whirling.

37

MITCH PEERED DOWN THE HALL. NO ONE there. He walked up to Mr. Lee's cabin and took a deep breath. This had seemed like a much better idea when Ed suggested it two days ago. He'd give Mitch a skeleton key he "happened to have" and distract the Koreans while Mitch did a little sleuthing. Sure, it was a little risky, but life was full of risks, right? Besides, they really needed to know more before they could decide what to do.

Another quick glance down the hall. Still clear. He pulled a pair of canvas work gloves from his pocket and slipped them on. "Okay, Mitch," he said under his breath. "Here we go."

He pulled out the key and walked to the door of Mr. Lee's cabin. The key fit into the lock on the doorknob but didn't turn. Mitch's heart stopped and he silently raged at Ed, who had promised this would work.

He jiggled the knob and tried again. No dice. The key bent, but didn't turn. He could feel himself sweating.

In desperation, he tried turning the knob hard. Maybe he could pop the lock. The knob turned smoothly.

So it hadn't been locked after all. He pushed inside and shut the door behind him.

Gray half-light leaked into the cabin through two shaded windows, casting thick black shadows that seemed to reach for him. The room would be a small and Spartan hotel room on land, but it was luxurious by the standards of a working ship. The cabin had a bed, a small chest of drawers and a desk. All were bolted to the floor to prevent damage or injuries during rough seas. A half-open door led to a tiny private bathroom.

Everything was as neat as if Mr. Lee expected an inspection. Bed made, no drawers hanging open, no dirty laundry scattered on the bathroom floor or shoved in a corner. Mitch pulled open the top drawer and found crisply folded undershirts and socks.

He felt around in the drawer, careful not to disturb its contents. Nothing. He shut it and tried the next drawer. It contained only pants and a coiled belt. The third drawer held shirts. Extra bed linens filled the bottom drawer.

He turned to the rest of the room. Quick glances around the bathroom and under the bed revealed nothing unusual. Same thing for the closet.

He turned to the desk. Nothing on the desktop

except a leather blotter. It had one drawer—which had a lock. He winced. *Nuts! Why didn't we think of that?* He tried it—and to his surprise it opened.

Inside lay a stack of documents written in something that looked vaguely like Chinese or Japanese. They had an official looking letterhead that included a blue and red striped flag emblazoned with a wreathed red star in the center and "4.25" near the upper left corner.

He took the papers out and flipped through them, looking for pictures or anything that might give him a hint what he was looking at. He reached for his cell phone to take pictures for later review—and then remembered that he'd had to give it up when he boarded the ship.

He heard a noise in the hall and froze. Footsteps. He dropped the papers back into the drawer and shut it. He looked around for someplace to hide and his eyes lit on the half-open bathroom door. He tiptoed over and stood inside, holding the door almost shut and watching the hall door through a crack.

The footsteps grew louder. Shadows moved in the sliver of light under the door leading to the corridor. They paused. Mitch held his breath.

The shadows vanished. The footsteps passed and faded into silence. Mitch exhaled and opened the bathroom door. Time to get out of here.

He took one last look around the room. He put

his ear to the door and listened. He heard nothing except the faint sound of the printer humming and clicking at the end of the hall.

He opened the door a crack and peered out. The hall was empty. He jerked the door the rest of the way open, stepped into the corridor, and yanked the door shut behind him. He looked both ways. Still clear.

Giddy laughter welled up inside him as he walked down the hall. He'd done it! He had penetrated the inner sanctum of the boss of the Korean commandos!

He took off the work gloves and shoved them in his pocket as he skipped down the steps to the lounge, where Ed was playing Super Mario Bros. with some of the Koreans as a distraction. Ed was teaching Cho how to play the game when Mitch walked in and poured himself a cup of coffee.

A moment later, Ed clapped Cho on the back. "Okay, I think you've got it now." He walked over to Mitch. "Hey, could you give me a hand? Let's see if we can fix that forward thruster."

Mitch followed him to the ROV. The two of them crouched down in front of the damaged thruster. One of the propeller blades was bent and the shaft was slightly out of true. "All right, let's get that thing out of its housing and see what we can do," Ed announced loudly. He looked around, then said more softly, "So, did you get in?"

"Yep. No thanks to you—that key didn't work."

Ed stopped working. "The door was unlocked?"
Mitch nodded.

Ed went back to taking apart the damaged motor. "Huh. Not sure what to make of that. So, what did you find?"

Mitch described the documents in the desk. "They had this red and blue flag on them. I hadn't seen it before. It had some numbers too."

Ed picked up a socket wrench and started removing bolts. "Numbers? What kind of numbers?"

"Like a price—four point something."

Ed put down the wrench. "Four point two five?"

"Yeah, that was it."

Ed looked up at Mitch, his face pale beneath the grime. "Mitch, that's the flag of the North Korean Army!"

38

"**I** HOPE YOUR COMPANY LETS YOU VISIT their investment every now and then, Jenny." The real estate agent winked at Allie, who had left her name in California and was going by Jenny Jackson here in San Salvador, Bahamas. The realtor was about sixty, very tan, and seemed to always unbutton his shirt one button too far. He probably considered himself a roguish flirt, and he may even have been one twenty years ago.

"San Salvador is a beautiful island."

"You'll fit right in." Another wink. "It's known for its beautiful women."

She smiled. She hardly felt beautiful. As part of a comprehensive effort to change her appearance, she had cut her hair short, dyed it red, and gotten rid of her cat tat (which had hurt way more than the tattoo removal place had promised). She felt like she should be driving a minivan to soccer practice.

"Well, here you go." He handed Allie the keys to the small, white beach bungalow in front of them.

"Thanks." Allie took the keys and weighed them in her hand. She wondered how long she'd be living in the Bahamas. A year? Ten years? Forever? How long would it take for Blue Sea and the Kansas police to forget about her? She suddenly felt an overwhelming desire to be alone.

She shook his hand quickly and grabbed the handle of the larger of her two rolling suitcases. "Goodbye, Mr. Thornton."

He took the handle of the other suitcase and began to follow her. "Not so fast, Jenny. Let me help you get these inside." He grinned. "Also, I left a little house-warming gift in the refrigerator. What do you say we open it and toast your first night in your new home?"

Allie retrieved her other suitcase from the arthritic lothario. "Thank you, Mr. Thornton, but I'd like to be alone. Besides, it's the company's house, not mine."

He shook his head. "There's nothing sadder than a pretty woman drinking champagne by herself."

Allie could think of a lot of sadder things. Drinking champagne with him, for example. "Goodbye, Mr. Thornton," she repeated.

She opened the door and walked in, pulling the bigger suitcase over the threshold after her.

Mr. Thornton didn't follow her, but he also didn't walk away. "Well, you know you'll never need to buy a drink when you're in Nassau, Jenny."

"Thanks, I'll keep that in mind." She pulled in the second suitcase. "Goodbye, Mr. Thornton," she said a third time.

She shut the door and took a deep breath. A window was open and she could hear Mr. Thornton's footsteps finally retreating toward his rental car.

The last time she had seen the bungalow, it looked like the set of an early 1960s period movie. Wicker furniture, a fondue set, framed Mondrian prints, black rotary dial phone, the works. It even had a record player and a stack of dusty jazz albums. She could almost smell the Brylcreem.

Now it was bare and empty, except for a few major appliances that she insisted stay behind. She walked over to the fridge and opened it. As promised, it held a bottle of champagne. Good stuff too—Taittinger. It had probably set Mr. Thornton back forty dollars. She felt a little bad about not letting him come in for a glass. Not bad enough that she actually regretted her decision, though. Not even vintage Dom Perignon would have done that.

She looked around for a glass and saw two plastic champagne flutes on the counter. She popped the cork and filled one. She took a sip and the taste suddenly and powerfully evoked the memory of the last time she had tasted wine. At Wente. With Connor.

She closed her eyes and saw him at the airport—bright white shirt and smile, oh-so-professional brown hair mussed by the wind, intelligent gold-flecked brown eyes lingering on her. She remembered the feel of his hand in hers as he helped her out of the plane and the smell of Armani mingled with old leather when she stood next to him on the plane's wing.

The scene in her mind switched to dinner—his easy grace, how he lit up when she liked an appetizer or a wine he'd ordered, the candlelight reflected in his eyes. She'd never thought of him as stunningly good-looking, particularly not compared to Erik. She would have put him against George Clooney that night, though. And not just his looks—he was the whole package in a way no other guy she'd dated had ever been.

And then she remembered the surprised look on

his face when she kissed him. Well, that had surprised her too.

The plan had been to have a fun evening, nothing more. They'd go flying, go to dinner, and maybe flirt a little, but that was it. A nice last memory for both of them.

But then the thrill of flying—really flying, not just sitting in an airborne bus—got into her blood, coloring the rest of the evening with a sort of reckless exhilaration. Then she'd had a little too much wine because he kept insisting that she taste this or that reserve vintage.

After that, she'd found herself telling him her deepest, darkest secret. She hadn't realized how much she wanted to let it out—how much she needed to. Confessing it had been such a relief. She'd never been able to before, but the wine and the fact that it was her last night brought the words gushing out.

Then when she'd finished, he told her she was a good woman. Just like that.

All of a sudden, she had been on the cusp of telling him everything. Erik's drug dealing and her complicity in it. The dead boy in Kansas. Blue Sea's blackmail. Even the fake invoices she had planted at Deep Seven to buy time while she planned her escape strategy.

Fortunately, she had stopped herself. Once he knew, he'd never let her disappear to the Bahamas. He'd insist on doing all sorts of impossible things: fighting the good fight against Blue Sea, talking to the Kansas police, and confessing her fraud on Deep Seven.

She smiled and shook her head. Then she lifted her flute. "To Connor. You're too good for my good."

She drained her glass and refilled it. The bungalow suddenly felt stuffy and dead, so she walked to the sliding glass door that opened onto a spectacular beach. She slid it back and stepped out into paradise.

She slipped off her shoes and socks on the small wooden deck behind the house and walked down to the ocean. The wet sand was cool and fresh on the soles of her feet and between her toes. A breeze blew in over the pale blue sea, bringing a wild salty scent and scraps of conversation and laughter from a boat of tourists in snorkeling gear about a hundred yards offshore. "This is heaven. I love being here," she insisted to herself.

39

CONNOR TOOK A SIP OF HIS COFFEE AND tried to ignore the emotions roiling inside him. He set the mug down onto the black granite conference room table with a dull thunk. He was alone, but that would change soon.

A plate of saucer-sized gourmet cookies sat in the middle of the table and an assortment of drinks rested on the credenza, courtesy of Doyle & Brown's omnipresent office services. He realized that he'd skipped lunch and picked up a chocolate-macadamia nut confection. Then he changed his mind and dropped it onto a napkin beside his coffee.

He could have waited for his guest in his office, but he wanted to be away from his phone and e-mail for a few minutes. He needed to think, to sort things out some before the meeting started.

Allie had disappeared on purpose. That much was clear, at least. Her phone was disconnected, all the corporate bank accounts had been drained in the past twenty-four hours, and her landlord said she had canceled her lease.

She hadn't told him where she was going. No address, no phone number, not even an e-mail address. She wasn't just hiding from the world, she was hiding from him.

That hurt. They had worked together closely for three years. They had been more than business colleagues, they had been friends who trusted and respected each other. Then last night they had opened the door to becoming much more.

And today she was gone without a word. She kissed him, said good-bye, and walked away.

He got up and looked out of the window. The fog was flowing in through the Golden Gate, cloaking the bay and shoreline with dank chill. He'd been on the water once when the fog rolled in. The sun vanished, the temperature dropped twenty degrees in less than a minute, and every boat near him vanished. A gray and lonely cocoon surrounded him. That's how he felt now.

"Do I even want to find her?" he murmured to the empty room. "What would I find?"

A dark possibility began to take form in his mind: Allie disappeared because she had been setting up a scam and she had just pulled it off. From whom? Him? His family? His firm?

He remembered her probing for financial information last night. Did his family have accounts at Citi or B of A? Nope, he had told her, just Morgan Stanley.

Cold knifed through him. He grabbed his Blackberry and dialed the family's private banker. "Joel, it's Connor Norman. I need you to run an emergency check on all our assets. Look for any unusual activity, especially large withdrawals in the last forty-eight hours."

"I'm on it. One sec." Connor could hear typing in the background. "Nothing big in any of the main cash accounts. Just some autopayments. It'll take a little longer to check the other assets, especially the stuff with outside investment managers. What's going on? Anything in particular I should look for?"

Connor relaxed, but only a little. "One of my . . . colleagues disappeared suddenly, and I want to make sure she didn't take anything with her.

Check my portfolio first, then the family's, and then the foundation's. Liquid assets, then illiquid."

"Understood. And don't worry—we'll be very discreet."

Connor reddened. "She's a *professional* colleague. I'm about to go into a meeting. Text me the results."

He hung up and shook his head. His stomach felt like it was full of cold gravel.

The phone on the credenza rang. The caller ID showed the reception desk. "Hi, Janet."

"Hi, Connor. There's a Mr. Clayton here to see you."

"On my way."

Connor walked out of the conference room and down the long hallway to the reception area. He walked fast and the air seemed to clear as he went.

It would be good to talk to Julian Clayton. He was a good detective and a good friend. He also went to Connor's church and shared his interest in World War II planes, which didn't hurt.

Connor walked into the lobby and Julian rose to meet him. He always reminded Connor vaguely of Charles Barkley. He had the same intense eyes and perfectly spherical bald head. "Thanks for coming in on such short notice, Julian."

They shook hands warmly. "Not a problem, my friend. How are you?"

"Been better, been worse. How about you?"

"Same. So, what's the emergency?"

Connor took his friend by the elbow and guided him toward the conference room. "Let's save that for the meeting. How was the Giants game last weekend?"

They chatted about the game as they walked through the firm. Connor's mind was elsewhere, of course, but that hardly mattered. He had learned to make conversation at the same age that he learned to walk, and both skills were equally unconscious for him.

Connor closed the conference room door behind them and sat at the table. Julian poured himself a cup of coffee, picked up a cookie, and sat down opposite Connor. He pulled out a notepad and pen and looked up expectantly. "Well?"

"One of my clients just disappeared. I need you to help me find her."

Julian stopped in the process of breaking a piece from the cookie. "What's her name?"

"Allie Whitman. You did some work for her."

A frown tightened Julian's forehead, drawing his gleaming scalp taut. "I remember. What happened? Is there a police report?"

Connor pressed his lips together and shook his head. "Not yet. Probably not ever."

"Why not?"

"No crime. They'll probably conclude that she

disappeared voluntarily—at least that's what I see happening based on what I know."

The detective nodded and popped a piece of cookie into his mouth. He brushed crumbs off of his notepad and jotted something down.

"You don't seem surprised."

He shook his head as he chewed. "I'm not," he said around a mouthful of oatmeal and chocolate chips. He swallowed. "Disappointed maybe, but not surprised."

The shadow on Connor's heart deepened. He waited for a moment, but Julian didn't elaborate. "Can you tell me why you're disappointed?"

Julian shook his head. "Sorry, I can't say anything more than that. Client confidentiality. You understand."

Connor nodded. "I understand." He very much wanted to know why Allie had vanished, of course, but he appreciated Julian's scrupulous ethics. The two of them shared the same uncompromising moral compass, and it was one of the reasons they worked well together.

But client confidentiality surely didn't cover everything. "Any idea where she is?"

"None."

"Do you know whether she engaged in any . . . financial crimes before she left?"

Julian's eyebrows went up. "No idea. Do you want me to look into that?"

Connor nodded. "It's . . . Well, it's possible that

she might have taken money from accounts belonging to me or my family. Not certain, you understand. But possible."

The detective shook his head slowly. "I'm sorry, man. Truly sorry."

"Don't be. Not yet. We don't know whether she stole a dime."

"You used to trust this girl, didn't you?"

Connor looked down at the table. An inscrutable black reflection looked back. "Yeah, I did. We worked together pretty closely."

"And then she pulls a Houdini on you and leaves you wondering whether you've been grifted." He shook his head again and looked Connor in the eyes. "That's what I'm sorry about."

"Yeah, thanks." Connor took a deep breath, leaned back, and crossed his arms. "All right, so our private banker is looking into it too. I'll put you in touch with him."

Julian looked at him silently for a moment, then nodded. "Got it. Anything else?"

There was one more question gnawing at the back of Connor's mind. "Just one more thing—do you know whether she's safe?"

Julian thought for a moment. "No."

40

Mitch stood in front of Eileen, a hammer in one hand and a pair of wirecutters in the other. In two minutes, he could turn her into a worthless hunk of metal. If he cut the right wires and smashed the camera lenses and key circuitry, the ROV would be nothing but scrap.

No one would stop him. He and Ed had been tinkering with Eileen off and on the entire trip, so the North Koreans wouldn't think twice if they saw him "working" on her now. Once he was done, it would be impossible to retrieve missiles—or anything else—from the sea floor.

What would the North Koreans do when they found out? And almost as frightening, what would *Ed* do?

"What's on your mind, Mitch?"

Mitch turned and saw Ed, a coffee mug in his hand and a suspicious look on his face.

"I was just wondering what we're gonna do now."

"And you were thinking of trashing Eileen."

Mitch shrugged and looked past Ed's shoulder. "I—"

"Don't worry about it. I was thinking the same thing."

Mitch blinked. "You were?"

"Yeah, but—" He patted the ROV. "I've got a soft spot for hard women."

"I know. I met your ex-wife."

Ed relaxed and his face split into a gargoyle grin. "I remember. She thought you were cute. Should've known right then that she was a nut job."

"You should've known that when she said she'd marry you."

Ed barked a laugh and punched Mitch in the shoulder. "Seriously, don't talk about scrapping Eileen. At least not in front of her."

Mitch wasn't sure whether that was a joke, so he changed the subject. "So, what are you thinking we should do?"

Ed scratched his stubbly jaw. "Here's the thing: let's say Eileen had a cable break underwater or something. What are we after she's gone?"

"Uh, an ROV pilot and co-pilot without an ROV?"

Ed nodded. "And that's just a long way of saying 'dead weight,' isn't it? You know what else we are? Witnesses."

A chill went through Mitch. "I hadn't thought of that."

"I kinda guessed."

"Would it be so, you know, awful if they just got the missiles or whatever it is they want from down there? I mean, North Korea already has nukes, right?"

"Yeah, but not in America."

"Couldn't they just put one on a missile?"

"You don't read the news much, do you?"

Mitch's face got hot. "Not as much as you, but—"

"Two things. One, they haven't been able to build a missile that's anywhere near able to get across the Pacific, and they've been trying for years. Two, we've got all sorts of defenses in Hawaii in case they ever manage to build a decent rocket."

"Okay, so—"

"And here's the other thing: let's say they manage to shoot a missile at America and it gets past Hawaii and blows up L.A. or something, what happens then?"

"Um, there's a war?"

"Yeah, for as long as it takes for our missiles to reach North Korea. Then there's a big, glassy crater where their country used to be."

Mitch pondered that for a moment. "Okay, so if they've already got nukes and they don't want to blow up L.A., why are we out here?"

Ed nodded and glanced over one of his lumpy shoulders, as if he felt eyes on his back. "Yeah, I was wondering the same thing. Here's what I think: firing a missile starts a war, which they lose. But things might turn out different if they just happened to know of a couple bombs already hidden in the U.S.—not that they planted them or anything, but they know who did. They know some terrorists who know some terrorists who managed to get some bombs into the country.

Something like that. And if America does them a favor or two, they'll let Washington know where the bombs are. Maybe they even have a bomb go off first to get the country's attention, so the U.S. will be willing to do pretty much anything to keep another one from going off."

"Oh." Mitch thought through Ed's theory. It made sense. Too much sense. Then a new fear hit him. His stomach muscles suddenly tightened and the hairs on the back of his neck went up. "That plan doesn't work so well if we're still around, does it?"

Ed shook his head and took a swig of his coffee.

The cold realization sank into the pit of Mitch's stomach. They weren't just in danger once they stopped being necessary for the ROV. They were dead men walking. "So why not just wreck Eileen and at least keep them from getting the bombs? We're dead either way."

Ed's eyebrows went up, making his narrow forehead nearly vanish. "Don't be so sure about that."

A spark of hope lit in Mitch's chest. "Really? Why not?"

"If we can get a call out to the Navy, they can save our behinds and take care of our Korean friends."

"But how do we make a call? They've got people in the radio room 24/7, and we don't have an excuse to go in there."

"We don't." Ed drained his mug. "But an officer does. I've seen Jenkins head up there every couple of days. I'll bet he's making regular reports to the company."

"But if one of the North Koreans is always in there with him—"

"Let's say there was a disturbance while Jenkins was in there—a fire or a fight right outside the door. I'm thinking there's a good chance the Korean would leave, at least for a minute."

Mitch felt like laughing with relief. "You know, that could work!"

Ed grinned. "Yeah, I *do* know—that's why I suggested it. We'll talk to Jenkins tonight."

41

TOM CONCANNON WALKED INTO CONNOR'S office and closed the door behind him. "Connor, we need to talk right now."

Connor was on an international conference call, but one look at Tom's face convinced him to end it immediately. He made his apologies and said good-bye. Tom seated himself in one of Connor's guest chairs and watched with a stone-faced expression. Whatever was coming, it was bad.

Connor hung up the phone. "What's up, Tom?"

"Carlos Alvarez called. He's suing the firm and one of your clients, Devil to Pay, Inc."

"Suing us? Why?"

"Abuse of process. He claims that you and Devil to Pay intentionally filed a false complaint against a company called Deep Seven. He says you fabricated evidence and lied to the Department of Justice in order to extort a settlement from Deep Seven."

"That's nuts! That's absolutely stark raving insane!" Connor jabbed the air with his finger. "We'll file a motion for summary judgment right off the bat. He'll have to show his evidence—which he won't have. Then we'll get him and his firm sanctioned for filing this kind of crap."

Tom's expression didn't change. "Connor, I've known Carlos Alvarez for nearly twenty years. He is many things, but he is not a liar."

Connor stared at his friend. "Are you saying I am?"

"Of course not, but this situation is . . ." He frowned and shook his head. "Well, it's perplexing."

"So let's get it resolved quickly. Let's file that summary judgment motion."

Tom looked skeptical. "What will DOJ say? Will they back you up?"

"I'm sure they will."

"Have you asked?"

"No. I didn't have any reason to until about two minutes ago. Why?"

"Carlos says they won't."

Would Max really leave him hanging like that? He couldn't believe it. But then a few days ago he would never have believed that Allie would betray him either. "I find that very hard to believe, but I'll let you know what they say."

A slight frown creased Tom's forehead and the corners of his mouth. "I'd like to be on that call."

That hit Connor like a kidney punch. "Of course." He sat back in his chair and looked out the window. "You need an independent witness on the line."

"It's not that we don't trust you, Connor. I—"

"Don't lie to me, Tom." He turned and looked his friend—no, the office managing partner—in the eyes. "I thought you were better than that."

Tom reddened. "Don't push it, Connor."

"Just play it straight with me."

Tom took a deep breath and blew it out. "You want it straight? All right, I'll give it to you. The Executive Committee held an emergency meeting over lunch to talk about this. They're taking it very seriously, and they voted to put me in charge of the firm's internal investigation. I'll make my preliminary report in two days. Whatever I say, you've got a problem."

"Even if you say that I'm telling the truth? That doesn't make any sense."

"Oh, it makes sense, Connor. You may not think it's fair, but it makes perfect sense. Let's say I tell ExComm that you're clean as a surgeon's scalpel. The bottom line is still that you got us sued. The firm still has to report this to our malpractice carrier, still has to deal with the bad PR, and still has to spend time and money investigating you."

Connor shook his head in disbelief. "But that could happen to anyone, Tom. Besides, shouldn't that be weighed against everything I've done for the firm?"

"Like refusing to represent an important client you didn't think was up to your moral standards?" Tom's face was hard and unforgiving. "They took their business to another firm. Did you know that?"

So that's what this was about. Now he understood why the Executive Committee was looking for an excuse to punish him. "I didn't. I'm sorry to hear about it."

"Are you sorry that you refused to represent them?"

Connor chose his words carefully. "I'm sorry that my refusal to represent them hurt the firm."

"So am I. So is ExComm." He took a deep breath and let it out slowly. "All right, are you ready to call DOJ?"

Connor felt cold and numb. "Sure. The guy you'll want to hear from is Deputy Attorney General Max Volusca. Let's give him a call. I'll put it on speakerphone."

Connor pushed the speakerphone button and a

jarringly loud dial tone filled his office. Connor hurried to turn down the volume. "Sorry."

He pushed the speed dial button for Max Volusca, and a few seconds later the deputy attorney general's deep voice boomed from the phone. "Department of Justice, Max Volusca speaking."

"Max, it's Connor. I'm here with one of my partners, Tom Concannon. Do you have a minute?"

"Sure."

Tom leaned forward. "Thank you, Max. We'd like to talk to you confidentially about a company called Deep Seven. You're familiar with them, I take it?"

"We investigated them not too long ago. Connor can tell you all about it."

"Actually, I'd like to ask you a few questions about that investigation."

"We don't normally reveal what happens during investigations, but you're welcome to ask. Fire away."

"Do you know a lawyer named Carlos Alvarez?"

Max's chuckle rumbled through the speaker. "Oh, yeah. I know Carlos Alvarez."

"Did he ever make any allegations to you about the, ah, candor of this firm and one of its clients?"

Max's voice turned serious. "Why do you ask?"

"Because he made such allegations to me, and

they touch on this firm's relationship with the Department of Justice."

Long seconds ticked by. "I'd rather not get involved in this."

There was a roaring in Connor's ears. Tom shot him an accusatory look. "I'm sorry, Mr. Volusca, but this is a very important matter. Deep Seven has threatened litigation and we need to be able to accurately evaluate their claims."

"I'll tell you what I told the other side: we don't comment on the reasons why we don't intervene in cases."

"I'm sorry?"

"Carlos seems to think that we turned down the Deep Seven case because we decided that the disclosure statement and complaint we received were full of lies. He called me up and wanted me to confirm that to him. I told him to go pound sand."

The tight lines on Tom's face began to smooth. "So you didn't decide that our submissions were fraudulent?"

"Look, I just said that we don't disclose why we make our decisions. Maybe we declined to intervene because we didn't think there was much money involved. Maybe we thought you guys could handle the case fine without us. Maybe it was a Monday and we didn't feel like taking on another new case. Or maybe we decided your client was lying to us."

Connor leaned forward and cleared his throat. "Max, you told me that your investigation only found three fraudulent invoices from Deep Seven and that they only totaled around twenty thousand. That's not a lot of money, is it?"

Max grunted and Connor heard his office chair creak. "It's smaller than your other cases, I'll give you that. A lot smaller."

The knots in Connor's stomach started to untie themselves. He glanced at Tom, who looked almost friendly again.

Connor looked at the phone and debated what to do next. Quit now? His friendly cross-examination of Max had probably scored enough points to slow down ExComm's witch hunt. But Connor's gut told him he could get more. "Max, you performed an in-depth investigation into the allegations in the complaint and disclosure statement, didn't you?"

"Of course. The Government Code requires us to."

"And if Carlos Alvarez was right, if we really had told a bunch of lies to DOJ, your investigation probably would have uncovered that, right?"

Another silence long enough to make Connor sweat. But then Max said, "Yeah, probably."

"Thanks, Max. That's all I wanted to know. Tom, did you have anything else you wanted to ask?"

He shook his head. "No, that covers it. Thanks for your time."

Connor pressed the "Call End" button on his phone and the light for the line they had been using went out. "So, are you satisfied?"

Tom shrugged and examined his Montblanc pen. "He didn't exactly back you up."

Connor slapped his desk. "Oh, come on! You heard him. If we had lied to him, he'd know it. And if that was the case, would he have made it sound like they declined because the case was worth peanuts?"

"Relax, Connor. No, he didn't *sound* like he thought you'd been lying to him, but that's not quite the same thing as *saying* you hadn't." He held up his hand to forestall Connor's objection. "I heard what he said about DOJ policy. I know he can't proclaim your innocence. Maybe he would if he could. Off the record, I'm guessing he'd probably like to. That's all good. All I'm saying is that it's not enough. And as long as there's still a lawsuit pending against you and the firm, it can't be enough. You understand that, don't you?"

Connor could feel the dynamic changing. Tom was mollifying him now, explaining why the firm really had no choice. The accusatory, look-what-you've-gotten-yourself-into tone was gone. Good.

Connor decided to press his luck. "I understand,

but . . ." He sighed and shook his head. "I don't know. This conversation makes me wonder whether I really fit in here. You basically told me that ExComm is uncomfortable with the way I practice law. And just between you and me, that makes me uncomfortable with practicing here. Maybe I should go someplace else."

Tom instantly went into damage control mode. "Whoa. Slow down, Connor. You're completely misreading the situation. The firm isn't happy about this lawsuit Carlos Alvarez is threatening, but let's keep things in perspective. We value you. A lot. Yes, your principles sometimes, ah, create complications, but we know it's an important part of you, and you're an important part of us. You're a tremendous asset to the firm, Connor. We'd hate to lose you."

Translation: as long as he was profitable for the firm, he was safe. ExComm thought he needed to learn a lesson about being a team player, but they weren't going to let that come between the firm and the money he brought in. As long as Alvarez's lawsuit ultimately failed, no one would be pushing him toward the door. How nice.

Connor gave a knowing smile and nodded. "Thanks, Tom. I appreciate that. If you'll excuse me, I've got some calls I need to make."

"No problem." Tom stood and smoothed his slacks. "Not to any of our competitors, I hope."

He grinned and chuckled, as if he was making a little joke.

Connor grinned back. "Keep me in the loop on your investigation, okay? I'd rather not get surprised again."

"Sure thing," he said as he sauntered toward the door. "Say, are we still on for golf on Saturday at the Marin CC?"

"Absolutely. Say, could you shut the door on your way out?"

Tom's smile wavered for an instant as he stepped out into the hallway, as if he was wondering whether Connor really was about to call the hiring partner at a competing firm. Well, let him wonder. The door clicked shut behind him.

Connor chuckled, but not for long. The whole thing bothered him. He'd won a round, but he never thought he'd be fighting against his own firm. Maybe he really should start looking someplace else.

He picked up the phone and dialed. "Department of Justice, Max Volusca speaking."

"Hey, Max. It's Connor. Thanks for helping me out."

"Do you know how much I helped you out?"

"Uh, what do you mean?"

"So you don't know?"

Connor's spine tingled and he lowered his voice even though the door was shut. "Max, you're starting to scare me."

"That's what I figured." He dropped his voice to a gravelly whisper. "I'm about to go off the reservation, so keep this strictly to yourself. Understood?"

"Understood."

"All right. I sort of implied that we declined because there's not much money in this case. That's true, but there's more. You know those invoices you sent us? The ones Allie swore she downloaded from Deep Seven's computers?"

"Sure. Of course."

"Fakes."

Connor closed his eyes and slumped in his chair. "You're sure? How do you know?"

"Sorry, I can't open the kimono that far. All I can say is that after you and I talked, I had our auditors and our IT people look at this again to see if they could figure out whether there was anything illegal going on at Deep Seven. So they went over the package Allie gave us—and they're 99.99 percent sure those aren't real invoices. Somebody—and I think we both know who—fabricated all three and uploaded them into Deep Seven's system."

Connor's stomach revolted and he swallowed back bitter bile. "I had no idea, Max. None at all."

"I believe you. If I didn't . . . you know how I feel about liars."

"I do." The image of him and Allie in handcuffs flashed into his mind. "Is there going to be a criminal referral?"

"Sorry, I can't comment."

Connor took a deep breath and stared out the window. Brilliant white gulls rode the breeze between the azure dome of the sky and the deep blue floor of the bay. A line from *Forrest Gump* appeared in his mind: *Dear God, make me a bird so I can fly far—far, far away from here.*

"Connor, are you okay?"

"No."

42

A FAMILIAR KNOCK AT THE STATEROOM DOOR woke Cho. He exchanged a glance with his roommate, a hulking noncommissioned officer with a large collection of violent tattoos. On this trip, his name was Kang.

A second, more urgent knock sounded just as Cho opened the door. Mr. Lee stood outside, dressed in pants and a wrinkled t-shirt. "Sorry, sir. We were asleep."

"Both of you come to my room now." He turned on his heel and was gone.

Cho and Kang quickly pulled on some clothes. Sixty seconds later, they walked into Mr. Lee's stateroom. Cho stopped in the doorway in surprise.

Jenkins sat in the room's only chair, which folded out of the wall near a collapsible desk. He looked both nervous and pleased with himself.

Mr. Lee sat on his bed and nodded to Jenkins. "Go on, Mr. Jenkins."

"I just talked to Granger and Daniels."

"Yes, you said you would take care of them. This happened?"

The big American's eyes flicked back and forth between Kang and Cho. "Not yet. They're not as, um, reasonable as I am."

Cho rubbed his eyes. Was there no end to the greed of these filthy capitalists? "How much do they want?"

"It's not really a problem of . . . of numbers. They're convinced that you're going to try to blow up Los Angeles or something. I tried to talk sense into them, but it didn't work. Granger can be an idiot sometimes, and Daniels believes whatever Granger tells him."

So Granger and Daniels were potential allies. Best to stop this conversation now and continue it outside the presence of Mr. Lee and Kang. "Thank you for informing to us, Mr. Jenkins." He turned to Mr. Lee. "Sir, would you like me to take care of this?"

Mr. Lee nodded.

"Mr. Jenkins, there is no need to keep these men awake. You and I can talk outside."

Cho started to open the door, but Jenkins held up his hand. "Hold on, hold on. I haven't told you everything yet. They're planning something."

Mr. Lee leaned forward. "What?"

"They want me to send a message to the Navy the next time I'm in the radio room. They're going to try to set off a bomb as a distraction."

Mr. Lee's face hardened into a stern frown. "I see. Mr. Cho, Mr. Kang—please do what is necessary. Mr. Jenkins, have you ever operated an ROV?"

"Not this one. Granger won't let anyone touch it, except him and Daniels."

"You must operate it for the rest of the voyage."

Jenkins's eyes widened and he jerked upright. "I can't do that! That's why we've got Granger and Daniels, remember?"

"We will not have Granger and Daniels any longer. You will learn to operate this ROV or you will lose the remaining $2.5 million." Jenkins opened his mouth to protest, but Mr. Lee cut him off. "And if you are not cautious, you will lose much more."

43

ALLIE LET GO OF THE LADDER AT THE END OF her dock and slipped into another world. The sound of wind and gull vanished, replaced by the wide silence of the ocean. The only noise was the intermittent gurgle of bubbles escaping her regulator and floating up to the surface.

She kicked her feet and glided several meters from the dock. She had the shallow cove to herself today, except for a handful of semitame groupers that swam up to her in the hope that she (like many tourists) would feed them. Scuba diving alone is a big no-no for the safety conscious, but Allie had never fallen into that category.

The bottom slipped beneath her, a warm tapestry of sand, rock, shell, and darting fish. As she moved farther from shore, the water grew gradually deeper and the profusion of life increased. Brilliant blue and yellow angel fish appeared, darting in and out of the coral. Urchins and starfish hunted among the crannies and hills of the coral landscape.

She imagined bringing Mom, Sam, and the girls here. They'd love it. Mom would sit on the deck wearing lots of sunscreen and a big floppy hat while she drank iced tea and watched her daughters and granddaughters have fun—which was her favorite pastime. The girls would snorkel in the shallows and squeal every time they saw a fish or "Auntie Allie" came up underneath them and blew bubbles. Sam would wear a one-piece suit to hide her stretch marks and would spend most of her time making sure her daughters were safe.

A weightless joy welled up in Allie's heart. She reveled in the moment, unburdened by memory or worry. Part of her mind knew that she was still hiding, of course, but she had left that fact back at the dock—just like she had left the things she was hiding from back in California. For now, she could live in a warm and brightly lit future.

The heedless excitement she felt as she slid through the water was like snowboarding. Or no, it was more like what she felt that day in Connor's plane. She reached an open sandy stretch, empty of fish and coral. The water stretched to a hazy sky-blue horizon in front of her. She put her arms out to the side and pretended she was flying. Such a little kid thing to do, but fun. Her nieces would approve.

She smiled and rolled over on her back. The sun shone down on her through the liquid glass surface. So beautiful. So peaceful.

Her family faded from her thoughts, and she imagined Connor swimming beside her. The marine sunlight dappled his lean, muscular body, and his brown hair waved rhythmically as he swam. She'd notice something funny—fat tourists wading hippolike in search of shells—and point it out to him. They'd share a silent laugh. Maybe they'd hold hands as they swam, like the honeymooning couple who rented the bungalow on the other side of the cove last week.

She realized that she hadn't checked her dive computer in a while and glanced at it. Time to head back.

She kicked back across the cove, her daydreams trailing after her. She rose gradually as she swam, and the blue light grew brighter and lighter. Soon the dock loomed ahead of her, a shadowed grove of weedy pillars in the haze of the marine world. She slowed, letting her gaze drift from the dock down to a school of flashing shad below her.

In a few minutes, she'd be on the hard, hot wood of the dock, stripping off her diving gear while simultaneously trying to avoid splinters. Then she'd rinse at the little shower on her deck, get ready, make herself some toast and tea, and then . . . what?

Good question. There wasn't all that much to do on San Salvador beyond diving, fishing, and lying on the beach. Fishing had never appealed to her, and she had already spent more time on the beach than she should. Diving was always fun, but it wasn't cheap. She'd already hit all the tourist attractions, so her only other options were biking around the island again or getting hit on at one of the Club Med bars.

She'd hinted to a few inquisitive locals that she was a budding author working on the Great American Novel. Maybe she could start hanging out at the tiny local library in Cockburn Town with her laptop. She shuddered. The thought of sitting by herself and writing (or pretending to write anyway) for hours on end struck her as incredibly sad. Better to risk skin cancer and wrinkles down at the beach.

She reached the ladder on the dock and held

onto the bottom rung with one hand while she pulled off her flippers with the other. She tossed them up onto the dock and reluctantly pulled herself out of the water. Gravity reasserted itself and the tank and weight belt dragged at her shoulders and hips.

She stopped at the top of the ladder and stared in open-mouthed shock. There he was. "Connor!"

He didn't greet her or even smile. "Let's go inside, Allie."

Without waiting for a response, he turned and walked toward her bungalow.

Allie hurried after him, dripping her way across the deck and the lawn. She was acutely aware of the fact that she was wearing a bikini and no makeup. And she hadn't brushed her teeth after eating a can of tuna for breakfast.

She caught up with him at the sliding glass door. "Wow, what a surprise!" She laughed, then winced at the shrill nervous sound that came out of her mouth. "So, when did you get in? Where are you staying?"

He turned to her, his face an expressionless mask. "I'm not staying. I flew in this morning, and I'm flying out tonight. There's a car waiting for me outside right now."

Her mouth opened and shut, but her brain had no words to give it.

"I'm here for two reasons. First, I hereby inform you that Doyle & Brown is withdrawing from representing you." His voice was polite and cold as a lonely winter night. "We can no longer ethically continue as your lawyers in light of your repeated misrepresentations to the firm and to me personally."

"You—you came all this way just to tell me that?"

"A letter sent by process server would have been enough, but I wanted to tell you personally. I wanted you to know exactly what your lies have done—what happened because I was stupid enough to trust you. Deep Seven sued Doyle & Brown and has filed an ethics complaint against me personally. The firm is investigating me and is likely to expel me if they think I had the slightest hint of what was going on. Oh, and we'll never know what Deep Seven is up to. Max shut down his investigation as soon as he discovered that Deep Seven really hadn't stolen any state money after all. And, of course, he's not going to make a criminal referral. Not for them anyway—you and I may be a different story."

He stopped and his mouth quivered slightly, but when he went on his words were as hard and polished as before. They were like well-aimed stones, chosen with care and hurled at her with all his strength. "So I wanted to tell you that in person. That's the first reason I'm here. The second is that I wanted to ask why you did it—

why you decided to lie to me, to lie to the courts and the Department of Justice, to ruin everything we built together, and then to run away and leave me holding the bag."

Her throat seemed swollen shut and her tongue felt like a giant sausage in her mouth. She stared at his shoes. Expensive-looking Cordovan leather lace-ups. Perfectly shined, of course.

"Well? Why did you do it?"

She felt the tears coming, but pushed them back. She wasn't going to cry her way to forgiveness, and she didn't want him to think she was trying to. "I'm sorry, Connor," she said to his shoes. "I'm so, so, so sorry. I just . . . I didn't mean to hurt you or the firm or any of that." She shook her head. "It's just that they were blackmailing me. So I . . . I did something stupid and wrong and I'm really, really sorry."

"Who was blackmailing you?"

What could it hurt to tell him the truth now? Every bridge she had ever crossed with him now lay smoldering behind her. "It was Blue Sea—the place I worked before I went to Deep Seven. They told me that if I didn't go to work at Deep Seven and find fraud there, they'd tell everyone I was behind Devil to Pay and—" Might as well let it all out. "Well, you know Erik smoked meth, right? He also sold some. One night while we were on the road with his band, he sold to a teenager." Her throat constricted again as she remembered Jason Tompkins's face smiling at her from his yearbook picture.

"He died," she forced out. "I broke up with Erik after I found out about that, but Blue Sea wouldn't leave me alone. They said if I didn't find a way to sue Deep Seven for government fraud, they'd tell the cops and I'd go to jail. I didn't want to go to jail, so I—" She shrugged. "You know the rest."

"Why didn't you say anything?" It was an accusation more than a question. "I could have helped you!"

Sudden anger burned in her chest and she glared at him. "Helped me what? Go to jail for the rest of my life?"

Righteous indignation turned to confusion in his eyes. "What are you talking about?"

"Don't you remember? 'If you commit a crime, you should pay the price. Every. Single. Time. No excuses, no compromises.' You expect me to trust the man who said that? To come to him when I'm in trouble?"

Something cracked in his face, but then it hardened again. "Maybe you didn't trust me, but I trusted you. My mistake."

His expression made her feel like an insect. The kind you squash with an old newspaper because you don't want it on your shoe. She couldn't bear that look. It was worse than anything he could have said.

"I didn't have any choice!" she insisted.

He shook his head in disgust. "You always have choices, Allie. What you really mean is that the right choice was hard, so you want to pretend it didn't exist. Well, it did and you blew it. You blew everything. And now I'm going to have to go back and pay the price."

He turned and walked toward the door.

The tears came now, flooding down her face as great gasping sobs choked her. She buried her face in her hands and wished she could die, that she'd never lived.

The door opened and shut, and she was alone with her agony.

44

CONNOR SAT IN A WINDOW SEAT IN THE FIRST class section of a US Airways Airbus A319, watching Lynden Pindling International Airport slip away beneath him. For a moment they were over the sun-drenched suburbs of Nassau. The beach flashed past and then the light blue coastal waters, dotted with pleasure boats. Then the blue darkened as the water deepened, and a featureless navy carpet stretched to the horizon.

He turned away from the window as the flight attendant walked by. He stopped her and asked for a glass of cabernet sauvignon. She returned with it a moment later, smiling the entire time.

He took a sip. Cheap stuff and too warm, but he wasn't in a discriminating mood. He drained the glass in three large swallows and ordered another. The smiling attendant refilled his glass and he downed that as well.

He hadn't eaten anything since a croissant at breakfast, and he felt the wine in a hot pool in his stomach. The alcohol reached his brain after a few minutes. He started on a third glass and drank it more slowly.

He usually didn't drink when he was flying. No point in pouring mediocre booze down his throat just to make the trip go faster. He could do that by working or watching a movie. But he needed a drink today. He needed to wash away the taste of what he had said to Allie.

She deserved it, of course. And more. What she had done to him and the firm was bad enough, but that was nothing compared to what she told him today. He could hardly believe it. Looking the other way when her boyfriend sold drugs was bad, but looking the other way when he sold to *children?* And then not even turning him in when one of those children died? He shook his head and made a mental note to have Julian look into it. That kid deserved justice. As for Allie—well, whatever happened to her, she had it coming. And to think she'd tried to pin some of the blame on him, claiming she couldn't trust him to help her. That was as low as it got.

And yet . . .

He remembered his last image of her, glimpsed as he looked back before walking out the door. Her scuba tank was still ridiculously strapped to her back. Seawater dripped from her lank wet hair, forming little puddles around her feet on the tile floor. Her head was bowed, her face in her hands, her bare shoulders shaking.

He took another sip of his wine. She had made her choices, and those choices had painful consequences. It was hard for him to see her like that, but she had brought it on herself.

He thought back over their conversation again. Had he really said that thing about everyone who commits any crime going to jail every single time? It sounded a little like him. It also sounded a little like a fascist Pharisee, if there was such a thing. He shifted uncomfortably in his seat.

Best not to dwell on it. He would keep Allie in his prayers, of course, but otherwise do what he could to put her out of his mind.

It was time to look to the future, to think of the road ahead. The first step on that road was obvious: formally withdraw from representing Devil to Pay. He already had a draft motion ready to file. It recited the applicable ethics rules prohibiting lawyers from representing clients who bring lawsuits "without probable cause and for the purpose of harassing or maliciously injuring any person." It stated in general terms that he had just discovered that his client was doing exactly that. The court probably wouldn't insist on details, so Connor hadn't included them.

The whole humiliating story would come out soon enough, though. He'd get deposed in Deep Seven's lawsuit against the firm, and then he'd have to testify at trial if the case got that far. Tom Concannon and ExComm had already decided what their defense would be: he and the firm were innocent because they had acted reasonably and were pursuing what they thought was a legitimate lawsuit. "Improper motive," an essential element of a lawsuit for abuse of process, simply didn't exist. If they could prove that Connor had thought Deep Seven really had violated the California False Claims Act, that would be a complete defense. So Connor would have to testify about how he had worked closely with Allie for years, how he had come to trust her, how she had lied to him this time, and how he had believed her.

It would probably work. The firm would beat Deep Seven's lawsuit. Connor's career would survive. Sure, he'd take some punches along the way. Deep Seven would ask insinuating questions about his relationship with his pretty client and he'd have to tell the truth, the whole truth, and nothing but the truth. The truth wasn't that bad: one evening together, one kiss, their corny tradition of telephonic victory dinners, a dozen or so meetings, and hundreds of basically professional e-mails and calls. Talking about it would be awkward, and the legal newspapers might even take an interest. But then it would be over. He'd be embarrassed, but undamaged—or at least that's how he hoped it would turn out.

He took another sip from his glass and pushed his thoughts beyond the unpleasant aftermath of his entanglement with Allie. Tom had a big case going to trial next spring, and he had talked about possibly bringing on Connor as colead. That would be fun. The two of them hadn't handled a case together since Connor was a junior associate, and he relished the idea of working with his mentor as an equal. It sounded like a fun case too—interesting legal issues, high stakes, a client who cared more about good work than low bills, and most important, he would get to wear the white hat. No everyone-is-entitled-to-a-defense rationalizations.

Even if that didn't work out, there would be other options, other ways to cleanse his mental palate. He might even join Max at DOJ. He imagined what it would be like to work next door to Max and then found himself wondering how thick the office walls in the State building are. He also remembered Max complaining because he couldn't get reimbursed for an $89 room at a Holiday Inn Express, which the accounting office thought was too expensive. Connor had difficulty picturing himself lasting long in a world where a night in a Holiday Inn Express was a forbidden luxury.

Okay, maybe the California Department of Justice wouldn't be such a good fit. The U.S. Attorney's Office might be fun. Or maybe the SEC. Even if they all had Dilbertesque accounting trolls, they had one big advantage over private practice: no clients. He could choose his own cases, do the investigations himself, and only sue the defendants who deserved suing. He'd only have to trust himself.

He held his wine glass in the shaft of fading sunlight that slanted in through his window. Sullen reds glinted in its depths like coals of a dying fire. He drained his glass and closed his eyes.

45

"WAKE UP!" A VOICE HISSED IN MITCH'S EAR. Someone shook his shoulder. "You must wake up!"

He opened his eyes and saw a blurry face beside him. It was very dark in the bunkroom, and he couldn't make out the features. He pushed himself up on one elbow, his mind not yet functioning. "Wha's goin' on?" he asked in a loud slur.

A hand covered his mouth. He struck out clumsily, but another hand soon pinned his wrist. He thrashed in a vain attempt to get free.

"Wake up!" the voice repeated in an urgent whisper. "You must get up now."

He heard movement in the bunk below him, followed by Ed's gravelly whisper. "I'm up. What are you talking about, Cho?"

Mitch stopped struggling and Cho released him.

"You must go to the radio room right now," Cho said in the darkness. "There will be one man there, but you can surprise him. Lock the door and call your navy. I talk to men outside so they don't kill you."

"Hold on a sec," said Ed. "What's going on? What are you talking about?"

"There is no time! All are your enemies. They come for you soon. Go, do your plan now!"

A quick movement in the darkness and Cho was gone. The door clicked shut behind him.

Now wide awake, Mitch pulled himself out of bed and dropped to the floor. He had no idea what to make of what just happened. Ed was sitting on his bunk, pulling on pants.

Mitch took his clothes off a hook in the wall and followed Ed's example. "Are we gonna do what he said?" he asked as he pulled a sweatshirt over his head.

"Still sortin' that out." Ed grunted as he bent over to tie his shoes. "I don't trust him, but what could he be up to? And we've gotta do somethin'—he knew what we said to Jenkins, which is very bad news." He stood up and took a deep breath. "Okay, let's go."

They opened the bunkroom door and slipped out into the empty hallway. It was narrow, dark, and full of places where someone could be hiding. Plus, what if there were other bugs or cameras around—like the one that must have captured their conversation with Jenkins? Mitch hoped that Cho had warned the first mate too.

"Let's go out on deck," Mitch whispered.

Ed nodded and opened an exterior door. A gust of chill air and rain blew in. Mitch shivered, but at least they would almost certainly have the deck to themselves.

A wet wind blew in Mitch's face, and he had to shield his eyes to keep from being blinded. Not that it really mattered—the deck was pitch black except for the ship's running lights and occasional puddles of warm glow coming from the windows of lit rooms.

They stumbled along the rain-slicked deck, holding onto the railing to keep their balance. Mitch banged his shin hard and stifled a curse.

A doorway loomed out of the rainy darkness and Ed motioned for him to stop. They had gone as far as they could outside. They were only about 10 or 15 yards from the radio room, but the rest of the way would be inside and would take them past half a dozen occupied staterooms.

Ed disappeared into the darkness for a moment,

then reappeared carrying a wrench and a hammer. He handed the wrench to Mitch. "Let's go."

Back inside, a listening quiet seemed to enfold them after the windy night outside. Even the tiny squeaks from their shoes seemed to echo. Mitch tried to breathe quietly.

Light showed under the doors of two staterooms, but the rest were dark. To Mitch's relief, Jenkins still had his light on. Good— hopefully he'd be ready to join them. Then it would be three against one in the radio room. Mitch liked those odds, even if the Koreans were all kung-fu experts or something.

Ed pointed to Jenkins's door and muttered something as they passed.

Mitch nodded and opened the door.

Ed grabbed at him frantically. "What are you doing?"

Mitch found himself face-to-face with a huge, tattooed Korean. Before he could react, the man hit him in the stomach. Mitch doubled over and staggered back into the wall on the other side of the hall. Something crashed into the back of his skull and he collapsed to the floor.

He lay there for several seconds, stunned and gasping for breath. Sounds of shouting and fighting filled the air above him.

Mitch pushed himself up onto his hands and knees. Black spots filled his vision and his head spun. But he had to get back up. He *had* to. It couldn't end like this.

He staggered to his feet and saw the big Korean wrestling with Ed. He picked up the hammer from the floor and lunged forward. The Korean's back was to him. One good blow from the hammer and—

Someone grabbed him from behind. A strong hand gripped his right wrist and smashed his hand against the wall. The hammer fell to the floor with a clang.

Mitch started to turn to face his attacker, but a huge fist smashed into his jaw. He fell again, his mouth full of jagged pain and blood.

A thick arm looped around his neck and squeezed. He twisted and fought, but it was no use. The black spots returned and grew. His strength faded.

The last thing he heard was Jenkins's voice in his ear. "Sorry, Mitch. Nothing personal."

Then it was over.

46

CONNOR SAT IN THE GALLERY OF DEPARTMENT 301 of the San Francisco Superior Court, the courtroom designated for hearing motions in odd-numbered cases. He was waiting for the court to call his motion for leave to withdraw, which was sixth on the day's docket. To his annoyance, Deep

Seven had decided to oppose it, and Carlos Alvarez had shown up to handle the hearing personally. He had pointedly ignored Connor when he walked into the courtroom and now sat two rows up on the other side of the gallery.

To make matters worse, the court had issued a tentative ruling denying the motion unless either new lawyers appeared to represent Devil to Pay or the company obtained a new registered corporate agent (Connor was the current agent). Both of those alternatives would take time and would involve further contact with Allie, which Connor would rather avoid.

The clerk called the fifth motion on the docket. Connor's heart rate picked up at the realization that he was next. He hadn't argued a contested motion in years. Most of his cases settled early, and DOJ always took the lead on those that didn't. He would help write the briefs, slip notes to Max during hearings, and so on, but he'd had the luxury of sitting back and watching the actual combat from a front-row seat. This time he was in the ring.

"Line number six, *State ex rel. Devil to Pay, Inc. v. Deep Seven Marine Technology*, case number 401775," the clerk announced.

Connor walked up to the plaintiff's table on the left side of the courtroom, and Alvarez took his place at the defendant's table on the right. "Connor Norman for movant Doyle & Brown."

"Carlos Alvarez for defendants."

The honorable Karen Bovarnick looked at them over her glasses. "All right, you're here on Doyle & Brown's motion to withdraw, right?"

Connor nodded. "That's correct, your honor."

"My tentative ruling is to deny the motion without prejudice. I assume you want to talk me out of that, Mr. Norman?"

"Yes, your honor. The ethical rule in question, Rule 3-200, makes it mandatory for an attorney to withdraw in these circumstances. We do not have a choice in this matter—and, I respectfully submit, neither does the court. I am not aware of any authority that allows a court to order an attorney or firm to continue representing a client when they are ethically required to withdraw."

The judge held up her hand. "Let me stop you for a second, counsel. Are you aware of authority allowing me to run my courtroom in an orderly and expeditious manner?"

"Yes, your honor, but—"

"And are you aware of any authority saying that I can't set reasonable conditions on your withdrawal, if that's necessary to make this case proceed smoothly?"

"I think the authorities are very clear that if an ethical rule requires a lawyer to withdraw, he or she must do so."

A line appeared between the judge's eyebrows as Connor spoke. She looked exactly like an exasperated schoolteacher in a black robe. "Yes, but you can't just leave an empty chair behind you when you go. For example, if I let you withdraw and Mr. Alvarez wants to file a summary judgment motion, who does he give notice to? The rules require him to serve it on Devil to Pay, right? But if you're gone, who does he notify?"

"He can send notice to the corporation's agent for service of process."

"Which is you."

"Yes, your honor."

"You don't find that the tiniest bit odd? You want to withdraw as their lawyer because they've caused you to violate ethical rules, but it's somehow okay for you to stay on as their agent? In fact, speaking of giving notice of motions— wait a second." She shuffled through the papers in front of her. She held one of them up, though it was too far away for Connor to see what it was. Her face wore an incredulous look. "The rules require you to serve notice of a motion to withdraw on your client, and according to this proof of service you served *yourself?*"

A snicker ran through the courtroom and Connor felt himself blushing. His secretary must have used an auto-fill form that plugged in the name of the corporate agent—and he stupidly hadn't looked at it before it was filed. Rookie mistake. "I'm sorry, your honor. That's a, uh, a typo. I can assure you that the client was notified that we planned to withdraw. I personally spoke with one of the corporate officers."

The judge smiled. "That conversation didn't happen to involve a mirror, did it?"

Louder laughs from the gallery.

Connor started to speak, but Judge Bovarnick held up her hand. "I'm sorry, Mr. Norman. I shouldn't have said that. But I have a low comfort level with what's happening here. I'm going to adopt my tentative ruling as my order with the following modification: any future motion to withdraw must be served on an officer of the company other than yourself—and I'll want that spelled out in detail both in the proof of service and in your declaration. I'll want to know exactly who you talked to, when you talked to them, and what you said. Do you understand?"

"Yes, your honor."

"Good. Mr. Alvarez, did you have anything you wanted to say?"

Connor looked over at his opponent, who was doing his best not to grin. "No, your honor has said it all."

47

ALLIE KEPT WAITING TO FEEL BETTER. AFTER Connor walked out the door, she wanted the echoes of his words to fade so she could get on with her long vacation. But they didn't. They rang true and loud, repeating themselves in the back of her mind in an endless loop. "You decided to lie to me, to ruin everything we built together, and then to run away and leave me holding the bag. What you really mean is that the right choice was hard, so you want to pretend it didn't exist. Well, it did and you blew it."

It was as if an invisible cloud of dirt, decay, and guilt surrounded her, penetrating to her very bones and clinging to her day after day. She called it "the Smell." The Smell followed her everywhere. It covered her bed like a fetid comforter. It greeted her anew when she stepped out of the shower, wrapping her in its slimy embrace. It corrupted her breakfast and tainted her coffee. It trailed after her as she walked out the door, and it polluted the cool morning breeze coming in from the sea.

And then there were the eyes. She saw them in her dreams and felt them watching her when she woke. Sometimes they were Connor's eyes, looking down on her with contempt and disgust. Sometimes they were her father's, their light fading as his blood spilled out onto the cold asphalt. Sometimes she saw Jason Tompkins's clear blue eyes, staring at her from his yearbook picture.

She did the things that made her happy. She took a shuttle flight to Nassau and spent the day impulse shopping and the night dancing at an exclusive club. She watched an entire season of *The Office*, one DVD after another. She went diving at the Wall, Treasure Reef, and other spectacular sites off Grand Bahama Island. She ate an entire two-pound box of Godiva chocolate. None of it worked.

The Smell grew stronger and fouler as the days passed. The gaze of the eyes weighed on her like a scarf of lead wrapped around her neck, choking her and pressing her down. She couldn't escape.

Even the hissing ocean and muttering breeze tortured her, whispering her crimes to each other. Their noise used to lull her to sleep. Now it grated on her nerves, and she had to close her windows at night to create a brittle silence in which she could slip into haunted dreams.

She couldn't even talk to anyone. The only one who knew what she was going through and why was Connor, and she couldn't call him, of course. Mom? She knew vaguely that Allie was hiding, but not why. Besides, they'd never had the sort of confessional relationship that some mothers and daughters did. Talking to her would do nothing to lift the black fog that filled Allie's soul. Trudi or one of her other friends? Right.

She was so alone. So utterly cut off from everyone she knew. So separated from the joys of the world around her. She walked through a sunlit paradise, sealed in her own private bubble of hell.

48

Tom Concannon poked his head into Connor's office. "Got a minute?"

Connor was trying to finish a letter before a meeting with Julian Clayton in twenty minutes, but he wasn't about to brush off his main defender at the firm. "Sure. I've got as many as you want."

Tom walked in and sat in one of Connor's guest chairs, resting his right ankle on his left knee. "I hear Judge Bovarnick gave you a hard time."

"Yeah, it wasn't much fun. But at the end of the hearing she basically just ordered me to do the proof of service differently if we want to file a new withdrawal motion."

Tom nodded sympathetically. "She likes to jerk big firm lawyers around. Don't let it get to you."

"Thanks."

"So, how does she want the proof done differently?"

"Well, that's the awkward part. She wants me to serve an officer of Devil to Pay. She also wants me to file a declaration saying who that is, when I talked to them about withdrawing, and what I said."

Tom shrugged. "Why is that awkward?"

"Because Allie is the only officer."

"So?"

"That would mean outing Allie. Her whistle-blowing career is probably over already, but if we connect her name to Devil to Pay, she'll have much bigger problems. There are lots of people who would love to make life hard for whoever is behind Devil to Pay. She'll have trouble ever getting a job again. She might even be in danger."

Tom sighed. "Connor, your loyalty to your client is admirable, but it's not mutual. Remember that. If Allie hadn't betrayed you, we wouldn't be in this situation. Besides, didn't she already go into hiding on some Caribbean island? Let her stay there."

Connor shifted in his seat and looked at his hands. "I still don't like it."

Tom uncrossed his legs and leaned forward. "Like it or not, we don't have a choice. We've got an ethical duty to withdraw, and we've been ordered to put Allie's name on the proof when we do—so that's exactly what we're going to do."

Connor's phone rang.

Tom glanced at it. "Do you need to get that?"

Connor looked at the caller ID screen. "It's reception. I think I've got someone waiting, but he's early. I can leave him in the lobby while we finish talking."

Tom got up. "We're finished. By the way, I'd like to look over the new withdrawal papers before they're filed. Could you shoot me a draft by the end of the week?"

So Tom was going to start reviewing his filings. Ouch. "No problem."

He turned and picked up the phone as Tom walked out. "Hello."

"Good afternoon, Mr. Norman. There's a Mr. Clayton here to see you."

"On my way."

Five minutes later, he and Julian were in one of the firm's small conference rooms, chatting about football. This was a business meeting, but Connor found himself reluctant to move past small talk and socializing. He hadn't realized how hungry he was for simple conversation with a friend he knew he could trust.

At last, Julian said, "We've already confirmed that Allie didn't steal from you or your family. Was there anything else you wanted me to do?"

"There is. I'd like you to look into whether Allie and her boyfriend may have been involved in the death of a kid who overdosed from meth. I'm sorry I can't give you more details, but—" Julian was nodding and his mouth was drawn tight. "What? You already know something about this?"

Julian sucked in a breath through his nostrils and let it out. "I do, and it's been bothering me for a while." He paused and looked at Connor for a long moment. "Can I ask your advice?"

"Sure. As a lawyer or a friend?"

"Both."

Connor felt queasy about where this was headed. "Okay, go ahead."

"I've always kept my investigations confidential, but I don't think I can keep sitting on this. When you referred Allie to me, she asked me to investigate the death of a teenage boy named Jason Tompkins. He died of a meth overdose in Salina, Kansas, on May third. Allie's boyfriend sold him the meth, and Allie was there when the meth sale happened."

"She told me basically the same thing, but without the details. What happened next?"

"I asked her to go to the police. A young man was dead and her boyfriend was still dealing."

"How did she respond?"

"She told me to mind my own business, and I told her I was going to give her a chance to do the right thing. The next thing I knew she'd run away to the Bahamas."

Connor smiled bitterly. The prospect of blowing her cover bothered him less than it had a few minutes ago. "Sounds like our girl. So, is that what you want advice on? Are you thinking of going to the police yourself?"

Julian nodded.

Connor stared out the window. It was hard to believe just how badly he had misread her. A month ago she had been Qui Tam Girl, the undercover fraud-fighting hero—and he had been her partner, Lawyer Boy. His face grew hot, and he clenched his jaws.

He forced himself to focus on Julian's question. "I don't know much about the law governing private detectives, but I'd be surprised if there's anything that forces you to keep your mouth shut if you come across evidence that could lead to the capture of a dangerous criminal." He paused, unsure of whether to go on. But anger and humiliation won out over caution. "And if you're uncomfortable telling the police yourself, I'll do it the second I'm not her lawyer."

The conference room phone rang before Julian could respond. It was reception again. Connor picked it up. "Hello, Connor Norman."

"Hi, Connor. There's a Ms. Allison Whitman here to see you."

49

ALLIE HAD BEEN IN THE DOYLE & BROWN lobby at least half a dozen times, but she had never before really looked at the portrait of Hamilton Doyle (whom she assumed was the firm's founder) that hung on the wall behind the receptionist. It was a serious, almost funereal picture—an unsmiling Doyle stood in front of a dark wood bookcase filled with grim-looking legal tomes. He wore a conservative gray suit and a burgundy tie, and he was looking slightly down, so that Allie had the uncomfortable sense that he was staring at her. The only bright color in the painting was the disconcertingly vibrant blue of Doyle's eyes, which looked a lot like Jason Tompkins's.

Allie was nearly as buttoned down as the picture. She wore her most professional outfit (navy suit with a cream blouse), her hair was freshly styled and dyed back to its original brown, and she had applied her makeup with careful minimalism. She needed to convince Connor and Doyle & Brown to take another chance on her. That meant convincing them that she wasn't—well, that she wasn't really the selfish, unreliable flake that she'd been acting like. So she did everything she could to look trustworthy and responsible. She would act it too. When Connor walked up, she would rise gracefully, smile, look him in the eye, and say—

"Hello, Allie," said Connor's voice behind her.

She stood quickly and turned to him—or tried to anyway. She caught a quick glimpse of his face, unsmiling and cold-eyed. Then her heel caught on the carpet and she fell. Flat on her face. She landed in push-up position as the contents of her purse scattered across the lobby floor. Of course her emergency tampon flew out even though it had been tucked away in a pocket. And of course it now lay exactly in the middle of the floor.

"Are you okay?" Connor asked as he helped her up.

"Yeah, fine." She lunged for the tampon, jammed it back into her purse and then started collecting the rest of her belongings. Her newly-styled hair now hung in her face. She tucked it behind her ears. "At least I still know how to make an entrance, huh?"

He smiled. "That you do. Sorry I startled you."

"At least if I'd broken my neck, I wouldn't have had trouble finding a lawyer." She forced a laugh and he chuckled politely. "So anyway, I'd like to talk to you."

"So I gathered. I'm actually in the middle of a meeting, but if you don't mind waiting for a few minutes, we can talk when I'm done."

"Sure, no problem."

As soon as he was gone, she went to the bathroom to do repair work on her face and hair. She noticed that her knee hurt and looked down to see a rug burn framed by two massive runs in her nylons. Oh, great. She did what she could and headed back to the lobby—nearly running into a man as she walked out of the bathroom door.

"Excuse me," she said automatically. A split second later, she recognized him. "Julian! What a surprise. What are you doing here?"

"Oh, I just finished a meeting about a couple of cases I'm investigating. I need to get back to my office now. See you later."

He stepped around her and strode quickly toward the elevator bank. As he walked away, she realized that he hadn't asked her why she was there. He also hadn't seemed surprised to see her. Her chest tightened as she realized that must mean that Julian and Connor had been meeting just now and they'd been talking about her.

Before she could start wondering about what they'd been saying, Connor materialized out of a side corridor. "Ah, there you are. Come with me."

She followed him into a small conference room with a round table topped with black granite and a matching credenza. An original oil painting of a French street hung on the wall. Connor already had a notepad and a mug at a spot opposite the door. She'd been in this room several times before and usually sat next to him so they could look at documents or a laptop screen together, but today she chose a chair facing him.

"I've got a few things to discuss with you," he said after they were both seated, "but why don't you go first since you've obviously got something to say to me."

"Yes, I do." Allie took a deep breath and began a speech she'd rehearsed at least ten times in the hotel mirror. "First of all, I'm sorry for showing up unannounced like this. I was afraid that you wouldn't be willing to see me if I tried to make an appointment." She watched him for a reaction, but he sat watching her impassively, his hands folded on the table in front of him.

"Second, I want to repeat what I said in the Bahamas. I'm very sorry for the mistakes I made and I take full responsibility for them. I screwed up and I admit it. I've put you and Doyle & Brown in a very bad position even though I owe you a lot. And I've done more than that. I've unintentionally helped cover up whatever is going on at Deep Seven. I also haven't done everything I could to help the Kansas police investigate the death of Jason Tompkins."

She paused and glanced at him. Still no reaction. He was as expressionless as a pro poker player.

"But I know being sorry isn't enough. It doesn't change anything. I've got to do what I can to make up for it. I've got to at least try to fix things. I've got some ideas on how to do that, but I'll need your help."

A tiny skeptical line appeared between his eyebrows. "What exactly are you planning on doing?"

Okay, he hadn't immediately forgiven her and agreed to help, but she hadn't expected that. She moved to her to-do list, leading with the item that should interest him most. "For starters, I'll help you sort out whatever trouble I've caused for you and the firm. I'll tell whoever wants to listen that you didn't know anything about the invoices at Deep Seven. That was all me. I'll also talk to the Kansas police."

His cool professional mask cracked and his eyebrows went up. "Good. That's . . . that will certainly help. Hold on just a minute and I'll get a videographer in here so we can get this on tape before you leave." He turned toward the phone on the credenza.

"Um, I can't do it right away. Or at least not if you're going to use it anytime soon."

He turned back to her, his face hardened by skepticism. "Why not?"

"Because there's something I need to do first. I'm going back to Deep Seven. I'm going to find out what they're hiding if it kills me."

He stared at her. "It just might kill you. Remember what happened to Sam Stimson."

The respect in his eyes and voice was like a fresh spring breeze cutting through the foul Smell that hung around her. She smiled. "Only if they catch me. Don't you have any faith in me anymore?" Oops, dumb question. "I mean—"

But he was already frowning and shaking his head. "No, that won't work."

"Why not?"

"Because we're withdrawing from representing you and Devil to Pay, and I've been ordered to put the name of a Devil to Pay officer—and you're the only one—in the withdrawal papers. So your name is going to come out anyway and . . . Well, that was a nice idea you had, but let's just stick with you testifying for us and talking to the Kansas police."

She couldn't believe what she was hearing. She had finally worked up the courage and resolve to do what she knew in her very marrow was the right thing and Connor was trying to talk her out of it? This was the guy who never met a dirty company he didn't want to spank with a battle-ax. And now he was telling her to walk away from what could be the dirtiest company she had ever found. Who slipped the wimp pills into his coffee this morning? "Are you serious? What about Deep Seven? Didn't you beat my head in about two weeks ago because I'd screwed up any chance that DOJ would investigate them? Well, *I* want to investigate them now."

He gave a small shrug. "I'm sorry, but that's the firm's decision. I don't have any choice."

"I thought you said we always have choices, but they're not always easy."

He flushed and shifted in his chair. "That's true, but this isn't really my choice. It's the firm's."

"But don't they usually let you make decisions about your own cases?"

"Yeah, but I don't exactly have a lot of clout with management right now—and I think you know why."

That shot went home, but she didn't give up. "Can't you at least talk to them?"

He sighed and rubbed his eyes. Long seconds ticked by. "I'll talk to them. I haven't decided what I'm going to say, but I'll talk to them."

50

CHO DID HIS BEST TO HIDE HIS TENSION AS HE and Mr. Lee watched Jenkins and Kang at the ROV controls. Seeing them in Granger's and Daniels's places was a daily reminder of the failure of his last tactic—and of how close he was to losing the war all together. But that was not why he was tense.

He cleared his mind and focused on what was happening in front of him. Jenkins was "flying" and Kang controlled the manipulator arm and other devices in the "tool sled." The manipulator arm held a slender, but very strong, loop of cable. The other end of the cable was attached to the *Grasp II*'s powerful crane.

The plan was for Jenkins to fly the ROV down to one of the missile tubes that lay on the sea floor in the wreckage of the submarine. Each tube contained a massive R-39 missile. An R-39 weighed ninety tons, which was too heavy for the ship's crane to lift. Kang would use the ROV's hydraulic grinder to detach the missile's MIRV housing (which contained its ten warheads) from the rest of the rocket. Kang would then slip the cable around the warheads and secure it with clamps. Other team members would reel in their prize while the ROV monitored its trip to the surface for any problems.

To Cho's surprise, Jenkins and Kang had actually made good progress. After several days of tedious work, they had managed to slice through the missile tubing and the missile itself. Now the MIRV housing lay on the ocean bottom, wires and tubing dangling from an uneven cut. It was a little over two meters wide and four meters long, and it looked vaguely like the severed head of a giant robot.

Today would be the day of truth. They would hook the cable to the MIRV housing and bring it back from its watery grave to the sunlit world.

In preparation for this crucial moment, they had done two practice lifts with pieces of scrap metal lying on the bottom. Every inch of the lift cable had been inspected twice. So had the crane.

The ROV cable, however, had not.

Jenkins took a deep breath and rubbed his hands together. "All right, here we go. Ready?"

"Ready," replied Kang.

The dark water on the video screens gave way to images of the wrecked sub as the ROV closed in on its target. "I'm going to set her down in the debris field one meter in front of the MIRV housing," Jenkins announced.

Cho felt his hands perspiring and put them in his pockets. Just a tug, that's all he needed. If only the cable looping up from the ROV would catch for a moment—a slight snag on a rock or some wreckage, even a strong current. The cable would snap and the ROV would become a permanent part of the wreckage on the bottom.

A small cloud of silt flew up as Jenkins landed the ROV on the sea floor. It floated away, giving a clear view of the dark metal cylinder in front of them.

Kang moved the manipulator arm slowly out and pushed the lift cable underneath the MIRV housing. It was slow, painstaking work. Kang hunched over the controls and sweat began to bead on his forehead.

After half an hour of trying to get the cable in exactly the right position, he leaned back and stretched. His tattoos danced as the muscles writhed beneath his skin. "It is stuck. Please to move ROV to left side."

Jenkins lifted the ROV off the bottom and flew it around the side of the missile section. The ROV was quite close to the side of the missile. With any luck, the cable would be pulled against the corner for an instant and—

The video screens all turned to static. Kang cursed in Korean and Jenkins shouted inarticulately.

Mr. Lee stepped forward. "What happened? Tell me!"

Jenkins's head swiveled from side to side as he looked at different monitors and tried various controls. "We've lost contact with the ROV. It suddenly went dead."

"What? How did this happen?"

Jenkins gave up and turned around. "I don't know what to tell you. We'd better bring it back up."

The four men went up to the deck and watched as the ROV's crane reeled in meters of dripping cable. Then suddenly the cable ended in a frayed wisp of wire and plastic.

Jenkins and Kang cursed anew. Cho slammed his fist into his hand and exulted silently. Mr. Lee merely looked at the ragged end of the cable in silence. Then he expelled a sharp breath through his mouth and shook his head once. "Bring up the lift cable."

Jenkins and Kang hurried to carry out the order. The crane came to life and the ship shifted slightly as the lift cable started coming up. Mr. Lee walked over to the railing and leaned over, his eyes intent on the cable coming out of the dark water. Cho joined him and the two men stared in silence as long minutes dragged past.

A shadow appeared in the depths. Cho held his breath. He could feel Mr. Lee's arm beside him, taut and quivering.

A form slowly materialized in the water, growing more distinct as it came closer to the surface. It was a dark cylinder, about two meters in diameter and four meters long, hanging at an angle where it had snagged on the loop of lift cable.

Mr. Lee laughed and embraced Cho. "At last, at last! We hold victory in the palm of our hand!"

51

"YOU WANTED TO TALK TO ME ABOUT something confidential before Monday's ExComm meeting?" Tom Concannon leaned his elbows on his antique mahogany desk and steepled his fingers. "What's up?"

"It's about Allie Whitman and Devil to Pay," Connor replied.

Tom frowned. "I was afraid you were going to say that. There's nothing to talk about. We're withdrawing."

"I know that's the plan. You convinced me it's the right one too. But there have been some new developments." He related Allie's plan to go back into Deep Seven. "So I'm wondering if maybe we should reconsider."

Tom shook his head vigorously. "No. Absolutely not. Think about how bad that would be for us, Connor." He started ticking off points on his fingers, which he usually only did when talking to mentally challenged junior associates or paralegals. "One, we're litigating against Deep

Seven. Two, she's talking about snooping around in their files. Three, you're talking about representing her while she does it. Don't you realize how incredibly stupid that would be? How many rules we'd break if we sent our client—who, by the way, we've already admitted we can't ethically represent—on an end run around their lawyers to do some freelance discovery? We'd be lucky to keep our bar licenses."

"But she wouldn't be doing freelance discovery. She'd be looking into something completely separate from Deep Seven's case against us, and—"

"You really think Judge Bovarnick would believe that? She would crucify you, Connor. And she'd crucify every member of this firm right beside you. Our next partnership meeting would look like the last scene from *Spartacus*. And you know what? We'd deserve it."

Connor nodded. "I understand where you're coming from, Tom. I really do. Protecting the firm is important to me too, but it's not the only thing that's important. We've got a client who's trying to do something that—in my very strong opinion—needs doing. Do I completely trust her? No, I don't. But that doesn't mean we shouldn't at least look at ways we can help her."

"Just because something needs doing doesn't mean we have to put our necks on the line to make sure it gets done. I appreciate your moral stance. You're the conscience of the firm in some ways. But we have to pick our fights. We have to practice the art of the possible. This just isn't possible, Connor." He paused and smiled paternally. "Now go and find something that needs doing and won't give ExComm or our malpractice insurer heartburn."

"That sounds like something my father would say."

Tom nodded in acknowledgment. "Thanks, I've always admired the Senator."

Connor sat at a table by the window of his church's cafe, taking in the view of the parking structure. He drummed the fingers of his left hand spasmodically on the window sill until a woman at the next table glanced over to see what was making the noise. He stretched his face into an apologetic smile. "Sorry, I should have quit after the second espresso."

He dropped his hand beneath the table and turned back to the window, his chin cupped in his right hand. His left hand curled into a fist in his lap. He didn't like the idea of walking away from Allie when she needed to be helped. And he really didn't like the idea of walking away from Deep Seven when they needed to be hurt.

On the other hand, if he *didn't* walk away from them, he'd be in for a world of hurt himself. He'd be forced out of the firm as soon as ExComm could arrange a meeting. After that, things could get really ugly. He couldn't ethically keep representing her now that he knew the lawsuit was a fraud. And Tom was right about how Judge Bovarnick would react if Deep Seven caught Allie. The judge would refer him to the state bar, and he'd probably get disciplined. Maybe even disbarred. There would probably even be some sneering press coverage—his father's old political enemies would see to that.

Then it would be over and his legal career would be history. He'd have to pick up the pieces and find something else to do with his life. He had a vision of himself as a parasite living off the Lamont-Norman family fortune and telling half-lies at cocktail parties: "I'm a philanthropist" or "I'm a writer" or "I do charity work." The sorts of things rich failures say. His stomach churned.

Julian Clayton walked through the cafe door and looked around. He spotted Connor and walked over. "Sorry I'm late. Pastor Dan wanted to talk about the Guatemala mission trip. Want me to get you anything?"

"I'm good, thanks."

Five minutes later, Julian sat across from him, stirring too much sugar into his coffee. "So, what are we going to do with our mutual client?" Even though there was no reason to believe that anyone was eavesdropping, he avoided using names in public—a habit common to both lawyers and detectives.

"Good question. I can't keep representing her and I can't stop representing her. So I'm pretty much stuck. How about you?"

He took a sip of his coffee. "I'm taking your advice. I'm going to call her tomorrow morning and tell her I'm going to the police. If she wants me to wait so she can go back into that other company, I'm going to tell her I want a videotaped statement now."

"Good idea. Give her the chance to do the right thing, but don't trust her."

Julian tore open yet another sugar packet and emptied it into his cup. "You can't do the same thing? Kick the can down the road far enough to give her some time to do whatever she's going to do?"

"Nope. That's what's bugging me. I can't stay in a case where I've got an ethical duty to withdraw, and I can't withdraw without announcing that she's connected to Devil to Pay."

"Why not?"

"Because the judge has told me that I have to talk to an officer of the company before I can withdraw, and she's the only officer."

"Can't you just make someone else an officer?"

Connor shook his head. "No one knows about Devil to Pay except her, me, and a few lawyers at my firm and the Department of Justice." Julian opened his mouth, but Connor quickly added, "And no, I can't make myself an officer."

"Oh, well never mind then." He tipped back his coffee cup and shrugged, his hairless forehead wrinkled in sympathetic confusion. "Well, if there's anything I can do to help, let me know."

An idea kindled in Connor's brain and he grinned. "Dangerous words, my friend."

52

"LINE 3, *STATE EX REL. DEVIL TO PAY, INC. V. Deep Seven*," announced Judge Bovarnick's clerk.

Carlos Alvarez and Connor walked up to the counsel tables and took their places. "Okay, this is Doyle & Brown's renewed motion to withdraw, correct?" asked the judge as the lawyers situated themselves.

Connor stepped up to the podium. "Yes, your honor."

"I've looked at your declaration and proof, and I'm satisfied that you've given proper notice this time." She looked around the courtroom. "Is there a representative of Devil to Pay here today?"

"There is, your honor." Connor turned to see Julian rising from one of the benches, wearing a twenty-year-old gray suit and looking distinctly unhappy. "Julian Clayton, the company's vice president is in the courtroom."

"Mr. Clayton, do you have any objection to Doyle & Brown withdrawing as your counsel?"

"No, your honor."

"Do you have new attorneys?"

"We do not, your honor. We would like sixty days to find some."

The judge drummed her fingers on her chin. "Thirty days."

Julian shifted his weight from foot to foot. "Could we, um, could we have forty-five?"

She laughed and tossed up her hands. "Okay, fine. Forty-five, but that's it—unless you have an objection, counsel?"

Connor turned to see Carlos Alvarez rising from his seat. "Yes, your honor. Forty-five days is much, much too long. The plaintiff has already had well over a month since Mr. Norman filed his initial motion to withdraw. The Court should not countenance further delay. Ten days should be more than sufficient."

Connor wondered what he was up to. Delay is a defendant's best friend, so why was he trying to make the case move faster?

The judge apparently was wondering the same thing. "Counsel, how will your client be prejudiced if I give them forty-five days instead of ten?"

"Well, your honor, the interests of justice will be prejudiced because the resolution of this matter will be postponed, which will waste valuable time and judicial resources."

The judge shook her head. "All you're saying is that *I'll* be prejudiced, not that *your client* will be. I can live with whatever waste of judicial resources comes from giving them thirty-five extra days. Anything else?"

"Yes. Not an objection strictly speaking, your honor, but I'm concerned that we know very little about this Mr. Clayton. Might I suggest that the Court question him further before simply accepting his representation that he can speak on behalf of Devil to Pay. When did he become an officer of the company? What are his responsibilities? What is his connection to the facts underlying this litigation?"

The judge's eyebrows slowly crawled up as Alvarez spoke. When he finished, she said, "Well, I'm touched by your concern, counsel. I'm sure the plaintiff is too, but I don't see how any of that matters." She turned to Julian. "Mr. Clayton, you are vice president of Devil to Pay, Inc. and you have authority to act on behalf of the company here today, correct?"

"Yes, your honor."

She looked at Connor. "And you—speaking as an officer of the court—you have no reason to doubt that, correct?"

Connor shook his head. "No, your honor. Quite the contrary—I have good reason to believe that Mr. Clayton is telling the truth. And since we're expressing our concerns here today, let me just say that I'm concerned about what Mr. Alvarez is suggesting. He apparently wants to turn this hearing into an improper surprise deposition of my client—er, former client."

"I guess I'm the only one here who's not concerned about anything," said Judge Bovarnick. She looked down and started writing. "I'm going to sign your proposed order, Mr. Norman. Doyle & Brown has leave to withdraw. Plaintiff has forty-five days to obtain new counsel. If they don't, I will entertain a motion to dismiss this case for lack of prosecution." She stopped writing and looked up. "Everybody clear?"

"Yes, your honor," said Connor, Julian, and Alvarez in unison.

Once they were outside the courthouse and walking beneath the gilded dome of San Francisco City Hall, Julian turned to Connor. "You didn't warn me that I might have to testify today! That could have gotten very dicey if I'd had to answer those questions he was asking."

"Well, the judge didn't go for it. I'm surprised that he even tried that stunt. He'll get to take your deposition soon enough."

"I got the impression that 'soon enough' wasn't soon enough for him. He seemed to be in a big hurry."

Connor nodded slowly as he thought that through. "He was. Which is odd. He'll be able to schedule your deposition in a month and a half and the case is basically on ice until then, so why does he care?"

"Even if the case is on ice, I'm guessing that something else isn't."

"Yeah, that could be. Maybe they've got something going on right now, something that won't wait until they can take your deposition in two or three months. They think we may know about it, so it's probably related to the lawsuit somehow." He grimaced in frustration. "I knew we hit a nerve at Deep Seven. I just don't know which nerve. If only Allie hadn't—" He bit off the rest of the sentence.

Julian nodded. "But she has. At least she's trying to undo some of the damage."

"So she says. I'm not completely sure this whole thing isn't some new scam I haven't figured out yet."

"I hear you. I don't trust her either."

"Best to make sure we don't have to. I'm going to make a point of staying out of situations where I have to rely on her."

"We should let her know about today, though."

"You mean that Alvarez wanted to cross-examine you in the middle of the hearing? I'll tell her to keep her eyes open, that there might be a confidential project that's going to be active in the next sixty days. Something like that. Something she might have stumbled across the last time she was there without knowing it." He paused. "I wonder if Samuel Stimson came across the same thing."

53

ALLIE WORMED HER WAY THROUGH HER NEW apartment, navigating the maze of boxes that held her life. She was surrounded by cryptically marked packages that she needed to unpack. Until she did, they loomed around her in guilt-inducing piles, forcing her into narrow, complicated paths and threatening to topple and make ugly messes if she didn't tread carefully.

This place was smaller than her old apartment. Shabbier too. Painted-over cracks marred the off-white plaster walls. Holes left by long-gone carpet nails lined the edges of the hardwood floors. But this place had two big advantages over her last address. The first was that it had the best security she'd ever seen at an apartment building. The second was that it was half a block away from Tang Dynasty's San Francisco restaurant.

After three hours of unpacking (which had not visibly reduced the number of boxes), her leaden arms and rubbery legs told her it was time for a break. And her guilty conscience told her it was time to do what she had come back to do.

She picked up the phone and dialed a familiar number. Half a minute later, Trudi's voice came through the phone. "Hello, TempForce. Trudi Wexler speaking."

"Hi, Trudi."

"Hey, Al! It's great to hear from you. Where have you been? I haven't been able to get hold of you for months. Where are you?"

Allie sat down on the only chair in the apartment not occupied by a box. "I'm back in the city. I've got a new place down south of Market. It's all full of boxes right now, but it'll be something once I've unpacked. I love the neighborhood."

"Very cool! Welcome back."

"Thanks. Say, all this moving has me starved. What do you say to an early dinner at Tang Dynasty?"

"I'd love to, but I need to get home. Our nanny gets off at six, and Dave and I were both late yesterday. Not good. We should get together for coffee or something. I can't wait to hear what you've been up to, what's going on with you and Erik, and all that stuff."

"Erik and I aren't together anymore."

"Oooh! Okay, maybe I've got time for a quick cup of tea or something. I'll charge it to employee relations. Speaking of which, are you looking for work?"

Allie licked her lips nervously and her heartbeat

quickened. "Yeah, as a matter of fact I am. I really liked the last place I was—Deep Seven. I was, um, wondering whether you knew if they were hiring."

Trudi's clear laugh rang through the phone. "What a coincidence! They're hiring, and they're looking for people exactly like you. Apparently some big government investigation totally messed up their files and computer system, and they need it fixed like yesterday. It was all over the news a while back. Did you hear about it?"

Allie stood and began pacing in the five feet of free space by the chair. "I, um, might have seen something about it on TV."

"Well, they'll be pumped to hear that you're available. I'll call them right now. See you at Tang Dynasty at five?"

"At five."

Tang Dynasty was an Asian fusion restaurant with great food and an off-beat menu that Allie enjoyed. How many places offered deep-fried tripe? Or "exploding turkey" sandwiches (so named because a cook once failed to thaw a turkey before deep-frying it, leading to a spectacular fireball in the kitchen)?

Trudi arrived thirty seconds after Allie, and they were seated at a little table in an alcove upholstered with red leather. Trudi looked just the same as she had the last time Allie saw her—the perfect picture of a stylish professional woman who also happened to be a mom. Allie used to think that was sad, proof that Trudi had become boring. Now she felt a little twinge of envy.

"So, what happened with Erik? Where have you been? Tell me about it!"

Allie split her chopsticks apart and rubbed them against each other as she spoke, giving her something to do with her hands and eyes. "There's not that much to tell really." Or at least not much that could be told. "The whole meth thing finally got to be too much for me, so I told him to hit the road. Then I did the same thing—hit the road, I mean. I just had to escape from everything for a while."

"Where'd you go?"

"Bahamas. I just rented a little place on the beach and hung out. Did some diving, did some biking, tried to give myself skin cancer. That kind of thing."

Trudi grimaced in mock agony. "Ah, stop! I'm already too jealous! I wish Dave and I could get away for just one or two days like that. It sounds wonderful."

That stung. Trudi hadn't meant to hurt her, of course. But Allie couldn't help picturing her happily married friend laughing on the beach or snorkeling in the coves of San Salvador—and contrasting that image to the lonely agony of her time there.

The waitress came up and took their orders. Allie ordered quickly. She had several minutes to collect her thoughts while Trudi first repeatedly tried to pronounce chawanmushi and then asked detailed and slightly suspicious questions about what it contained. She ultimately went with a chicken won ton salad.

"You know, I'm a little jealous of you too, Trude. You've got your own kind of wonderful going on right here."

Trudi gave Allie an appraising look. "Wow, you are a changed woman, Al. Well, good for you. I can tell you firsthand that there's life after the party ends. I'm still having fun, and I can't remember the last time I had a hangover."

"I feel a sudden urge to buy some sensible shoes and a minivan."

Trudi laughed. "And pick up some Spanx while you're at it. I can't tell you how fast my fat jeans became my skinny jeans after I started having kids."

Allie held up her hand. "Not so fast! That's still a looong way in the future for me. But speaking of the future, what can I expect tomorrow morning at Deep Seven?"

"I'm not really sure. All they said was that you should show up at 8:30 tomorrow and ask for Franklin Roh. They probably just want you to do whatever you did last time."

Which, of course, was exactly what she intended to do. But without the fake invoices this time.

54

ALLIE PULLED INTO THE EMPLOYEE PARKING lot at Deep Seven and found a space. She parked her car and looked up at the building. It crouched in front of her, looking like a malevolent giant lizard made of black glass and steel. The outsized lobby was its head, the double doors its mouth, and the curving limestone path its pale and poisonous tongue.

She suddenly wanted to run again, to flee back to the Bahamas or to some unfindable place in South America or Asia. Anything to avoid going back into that place. How had she ever thought that she could do this? It was one thing to look around in the billing files of unsuspecting companies while doing their accounting work. She knew exactly what to look for, and she had a near perfect cover: how many people would raise an eyebrow at an accounting temp looking at accounting files?

But even that hadn't been easy enough for her. She'd blown it at Blue Sea. And Blue Sea had been child's play compared to what she was about to try now. If she couldn't look at some invoices on unsecured servers without getting caught, what made her think she could penetrate the strongest defenses of a company like Deep Seven? Even if she did, she had no idea what to look for, and she doubted that they had a file labeled "Secret Evil Plan."

Even if she somehow managed to get past their security, find whatever they were hiding, and get back out, what then? Her likely prize would be the opportunity to spend a lot of quality time in a Kansas prison. And if she didn't win that, her consolation prize would be sitting in court and testifying against Erik. She remembered his voice on her answering machine as she played his last message over and over to torture herself. He had said he loved her, needed her. She imagined the look on his face as he watched her betray him on the witness stand.

She vaguely remembered reading a poem in college about a poet who discovered the road to truth. It appeared to be overgrown with grass, but as the poet took his first step on it, he discovered that each blade of grass was actually an exquisitely sharp knife. So he turned back and took another path.

But there was no other path for her. She knew that. Her last weeks in the Bahamas were still fresh in her mind. She vividly remembered the scent of hell surrounding her wherever she went, the perpetually judging eyes watching her. If she ran again, she knew it would be worse. Ten times worse. She couldn't bear that.

Staying in her car forever wasn't really an option, unfortunately. She looked at her watch.

8:28. She took a deep breath, opened her car door, and stepped out onto the knife-filled path in front of her.

Deep Seven buzzed with activity. Hurrying workers filled the halls, and temps (several of whom Allie recognized from prior jobs) hammered at the keyboards of hastily installed computer terminals in every conference room she passed. Even the break areas were busy, having been converted into impromptu conference rooms.

As Franklin Roh guided her through the office, her despair grew. She was sure he'd stick her in a room with twenty other people, which would pretty much eliminate any chance to do some quiet espionage. But he took her right past all the hubbub and deposited her in an isolated cubicle in a quiet corner of the IT department's area. A fake ficus tree loomed over her, further shielding her from the rest of the office.

Mr. Roh (he had never invited her to call him Franklin) told her about her assignment, speaking quickly. "The government seized Deep Seven's servers and held them for nearly a month. We were forced to rent replacement equipment and operate off of back-up tapes for that whole time."

Allie made careful expressions of shock and sympathy.

He nodded impassively and continued. "When

the government finally returned our equipment, we had to migrate all our data back onto the original servers. Not everything made it, however. A number of files were corrupted in the transition or disappeared entirely."

Allie shook her head and clicked her tongue.

"You don't need to figure out what went wrong—Deep Seven's IT staff is handling that—but I will need you to find how many problem files we have.

"Unfortunately, I won't be able to give you the supervision this project deserves because I'll be busy on the Golden Gate turbine project. We won the bid, and the project is sucking up every minute of my time. Sorting out the problems with their servers will have to be left to temps, but TempForce said a lot of good things about you, so I assume you'll be able to work very independently."

She assured him that she could handle the job on her own.

He glanced at his watch and asked whether she had any questions, clearly indicating that it would be best if she didn't.

She gave the right answer, and he turned and hurried away like a parochial school nun who fears that somewhere children are having fun.

She watched his retreating back, marveling at her good fortune. She would be working on her own and out of the way. And her job was to poke around in the servers looking for anything problematic—what better cover for a little fishing expedition?

She'd have to be careful about what she did electronically, of course. She wouldn't copy, print, or even open a single suspicious file. Instead, she'd simply note where a hard copy of it was physically filed and then she'd go look at it.

Deep Seven kept pretty much everything in a central file room. It had security cameras at the doors, but not inside. If she had an excuse to go in and out carrying files, she'd be golden. And getting that excuse should be easy. She would mention to Mr. Roh that she needed to check a random sample of electronic documents against hard copies to make sure the files hadn't become corrupted during the server transfers. He wouldn't have any reason to object, and no one would think twice about seeing her take piles of files back to her cube. Once she was safely behind the dingy gray fabric walls of her workspace, she could read at her leisure and use her cell phone to take pictures of anything interesting.

Perfect. She couldn't imagine a better setup. The icy gray hopelessness that gripped her half an hour ago melted away as she made her plans. She could do this! It really was possible. A wave of elation swept over her and she discovered that she was smiling so hard her cheeks hurt.

She got to work on her sampling protocol and made quick progress. After an hour, she had a set of rules that should take her into likely areas for prospecting—and which she could easily explain to Mr. Roh if he asked what she was doing. She was just selecting her first set of documents when she heard footsteps behind her.

She instinctively popped up the company's internal e-mail program to hide what she had been doing and turned. She saw a balding South Asian man of about her age walking toward her. A chunky gold watch adorned his wrist, and he wore a red polo shirt that was a little tight across his stomach. "Hello, my name is Rajiv," he said with a musical accent. "Welcome to Deep Seven."

"Thanks. I'm Allie Whitman. And it's actually welcome back. I'm a temp, and I worked here a couple of months ago."

He shook his head and smiled. "No, you didn't. I would have remembered you."

She glanced at his left hand and saw that he wasn't wearing a wedding ring. Rajiv was hardly her type, but . . . well, she needed information. She braced herself and giggled demurely. "Why, thanks. I was down in accounting the last time I was here."

"Ah, that explains it. I hardly ever get out of IT. I have many important projects to manage here."

"I'll bet you do, especially now." She nodded

toward the steady bustle of workers hurrying along an arterial hall a few yards away. "It's gotten a lot busier since the last time I was here."

"Yes, Deep Seven has definitely become very active. Just today I had to set up twelve new workstations. I also have my regular work, of course." His eyes darted toward the plastic tree by her desk. "Franklin keeps me busy. He gives me lots of, ah, fascinating projects."

"Wow, what does he have you working on now? I know about the Golden Gate turbine project and I'm working on the remigration project, but I was thinking there must be some other stuff going on with all these people."

He rubbed the bushy mustache that graced his upper lip. "Oh, I'm working on lots of things, but I don't want to take up your time during the work day. Shall we have lunch? There is an excellent Chinese place just down the street. It is called Asian Express."

She had been to Asian Express three times during her last stint at Deep Seven, and it was no Tang Dynasty. In fact, she had eaten better frozen Chinese food. "That would be great. When do you want to go?"

"Shall we say 12:15? I would not want to keep you away from your desk for too long on your first day."

How thoughtful of him. "Sure. I'll meet you in the lobby."

Rajiv left, and Allie went back to work. She picked her first sample and started pulling documents in groups of ten. The first five groups held nothing interesting, but the sixth time was the charm: her net caught a juicy-looking memo titled "Resolution of *Grasp II* Problem."

She went to the file room and pulled the hard copy of the memo, which bore the legend "CONFIDENTIAL: LIMITED DISTRIBUTION." She stuck it into a stack of random documents and hurried back to her desk, trying hard not to look like she was hurrying.

Five minutes later, she was hunched below the protective walls of her cubicle, her shaking fingers paging through the memo. It was about one of Deep Seven's ships, the *Grasp II*. About a year ago, the company discovered that it had been writing off the value of a bunch of equipment on the ship at too high a rate. That meant they had been claiming too much in deductions. And that meant they owed a bunch of back taxes and penalties to the IRS.

Her heart slowed down as she read. This wasn't exactly a good document for Deep Seven, but it didn't look like the sort of thing that would get anyone killed. Not even an annoying IT geek. She'd seen this sort of thing at plenty of companies—some bookkeeper messes up, the firm spots the problem later, and they've got to figure out how to tell the feds. They might have to pay some penalties and someone might get fired, but it shouldn't be a big deal. But, on the other hand, maybe there was more to this than a single bad tax return. Maybe this was the tip of some iceberg that she didn't see yet.

Allie flipped through the memo again and decided it was a keeper.

She poked her head up and scanned the surrounding area. No one around except the never-ending foot traffic in the hall.

She pulled her cell phone out of her purse and was about to take a picture of the first page when she noticed the time on her phone's display: 12:20.

Nuts! Nuts! Nuts!

She stood up quickly and hit her head on the branches of the fake tree. It shook violently—and something fell out of it. She looked down at the off-white Berber carpet. There it was: a small black object no larger than a pen cap. She bent over and looked at it. It was a tiny video camera.

The floor suddenly felt uneven beneath her feet and she almost staggered. It all made perfect, sickening sense. The isolated cubicle, him telling her to work independently, the project she had been given. Everything. It was all a trap. They would bait her into doing something to confirm that she was a spy. Then snap!—the jaws would spring shut. She'd disappear just like Samuel Stimson, erased from the face of the Earth.

55

CONNOR'S COMPUTER CHIMED SOFTLY, announcing that he had a new e-mail. His leather chair creaked as he swiveled from his desk to his computer stand and pulled up his in-box. The message was from "Bahama Girl" and was marked urgent. The subject line said "Call this number now." He opened the e-mail, which contained a phone number he didn't recognize and the message, "Use a pay phone."

He grabbed a pen and a pad of Post-Its from his desk and wrote down the number. But then he stopped. He stared at the e-mail, beating a rapid tattoo on the arm of his chair with his pen.

The firm had given him clear instructions: once he withdrew from representing Devil to Pay, he was to have no further contact with Allie. He would be the key witness in the Deep Seven's case against Doyle & Brown, and he could *not* do anything that might undermine the firm's defense. That, of course, included staying in contact with the very client that he claimed had betrayed him.

He had explained all that to Allie. And to make sure she understood, he had even given her a description of the line of cross-examination questions he would get if he *didn't* stay clear of her. It would go something like this:

—Mr. Norman, you claim that Devil to Pay lied to you, correct?

—You claim that you had no idea that Ms. Whitman was using your services to pursue a fraudulent lawsuit against Deep Seven, isn't that right?

—In fact, you say were shocked—shocked!—to discover that she had planted falsified invoices at Deep Seven, right?

—So, of course, you refused to have anything to do with her once you discovered her betrayal, correct?

—Oh, so you kept in touch with her?

—You even continued to help her?

—Are you familiar with the expression 'actions speak louder than words,' Mr. Norman?

He slowly pulled the Post-It off the pad, crumpled it in a ball, and threw it in the wastebasket.

He turned back to his desk and stared down at the brief in front of him, but he couldn't focus on the words on the page. Allie knew he couldn't talk to her, but she wanted him to call anyway. What if she had found what she was looking for? What if she had the goods on Deep Seven and was on the run now? What if she was in danger?

He grimaced and looked back at her e-mail. Call this number now. Use a pay phone. Urgent.

"This had better be good," he warned the computer. He fished the Post-It out of the trash and shoved it in his pocket. There was a pay phone down by one of the neighborhood Starbucks.

Pulling his coat on as he walked out of his office, he called to his secretary. "Going out for a cup of coffee, Lucy. Want anything?"

"A raise."

He grinned. Some variation of this dialogue was part of their daily routine. He'd miss it if he ever left. "If they're out of those, how about a maple-nut scone?"

"That'd be great. Thanks, Connor."

Ten minutes later, Connor was standing at the pay phone, sipping black Italian roast and waiting for Allie to pick up. The phone rang four times. Five. Six. Seven.

What would he say if Tom Concannon walked up and asked whom he was calling and why he wasn't using his office phone? Chill sweat prickled his forehead and he looked up and down the street, wishing he'd picked a phone that was less conspicuous or further from the office.

Eight rings.

Enough. He put his finger on the receiver cradle and was about to press down when he heard a clattering sound followed by Allie's voice. "Connor?"

"Yes. What's up? Why did you e-mail me?"

"I almost got caught!" Her voice was a hoarse whisper, full of quavers. "They're watching me.

My boss, Franklin Roh—he hid a tiny spy camera over my desk. I was *this* close to taking some pictures of a document with my cell phone. If I hadn't found out before I started snapping away—I don't want to think about it."

"So you've got evidence? You know what they're hiding?"

"Well, not really. All I found so far is that they had a tax issue. But I can't go back in there! What if they know?"

"That's too bad, Allie, but there's not much I can do about it. And I thought we agreed that you were on your own, that you wouldn't contact me. Were you not clear on that?"

"I'm sorry. I didn't think about that. I just . . . I'm scared and I needed to talk to someone."

"Talk to someone else next time. Call Julian."

"Okay, I will. I'm really sorry. But since I've already got you on the line—"

Connor felt his blood pressure rising. "Listen, if they knew about you, they never would have brought you back into the company. That would be incredibly dumb. Maybe Roh suspects, but that's it. He knows Devil to Pay had an inside source at their company. He knows it's not Julian because he never worked there. He might think it was you. Or he might just like to spy on female temps."

"But I can't go back to Deep Seven, can I?"

Now he realized what was going on. She

wanted him to give her a pass, to tell her she could give up. An angry breath hissed out through his teeth. "Well, that's for you to decide, isn't it?"

Pause. "I was just hoping—"

Connor heard a familiar voice and turned to see two Doyle & Brown paralegals emerging from Starbucks. He could see them through the open glass and brass doors, but they hadn't noticed him yet.

"Sorry, gotta go." He hung up the phone and ducked around the corner. No one called his name. At least he wouldn't have to come up with an explanation on the spot.

As he walked backed to the office, Connor's irritation grew. There had been absolutely no reason for Allie to do that to him. None. She knew a lot better than he whether she was in serious danger and ought to bail. She knew contacting him would hurt him. But she did it anyway. Why? So that she could feel better about herself when she did what she had already decided to do. How incredibly selfish.

His steps slowed as he remembered the fear in her voice. The pleading. His anger began to leak away. He pictured the sweaty, bland Franklin Roh watching Allie on a hidden camera as he licked his lips with that bright red tongue.

That bothered him. He stopped and drained the rest of his lukewarm coffee, then wadded the cup into a tight ball and threw it hard into a nearby trashcan. Well, whether it bothered him or not, there was nothing he could do about it. It was up to Allie now.

Allie stood a few feet from the pay phone, sucking on a cigarette and trying not to choke. She didn't smoke, but there was a pay phone at a convenience store ten yards from the smoking area outside Deep Seven. And it was out of view from the Deep Seven building.

The smoke stung her eyes and tasted awful, but she made the cigarette last as long as possible. Maybe Connor would call her back. Probably not, but maybe.

Minutes crawled by as the acrid blue smoke curled around her and the cancer stick slowly burned down to its filter. The phone stubbornly refused to ring.

Why had she e-mailed him in the first place? Because she started panicking and stopped thinking. She had fired off the message with nothing more than a half-formed idea that he'd get her out of this horrible box she was in. She would tell him about the camera and he would immediately suggest—no, demand—that she get out of Deep Seven. He would somehow take over the situation or get the government involved or something.

Stupid. Painfully, utterly, indescribably stupid. She had screwed up yet again. All she had managed to do was get Connor to yell at her again. And she had deserved it.

Her hope turned to ash with the cigarette, leaving an empty, sour feeling in her stomach. She stubbed out the butt and walked back toward the mouthlike front doors of Deep Seven, which gaped open to swallow her.

56

CONNOR GOT OFF THE ELEVATOR AND walked across Doyle & Brown's lobby as he did every morning, briefcase in one hand and fresh black coffee from the Starbucks downstairs in the other. His mind was wrapped up in an important appellate brief that was due the next day, and he didn't notice anything—or anyone—in the lobby.

"Good morning, Connor."

Connor turned and saw Julian rising from a chair in the far corner of the room. "Hey, Julian. It's good to see you. A surprise, though. What's up?"

"Someone broke into my car last night." His voice was level and matter of fact, as if he were reporting what he had for breakfast. "Yours too, probably."

A chill swept over Connor and the brief tumbled completely out of his thoughts. "I didn't notice anything this morning."

"You wouldn't."

"But I park in a private garage. With security guards."

"Did you drive to work?"

"Yes."

"Okay, let's have a look at your car."

Connor led Julian down to the building garage. His silver Bentley convertible was right where he left it. As he approached, he looked for scratches around the lock or anything else that would show forced entry. But the car looked as pristine as if it were on a dealer's showroom floor.

Julian bent down for a cursory look at the driver's door and ran his fingers along the weather stripping at the base of the door windows. "Unlock it."

Connor clicked his key and the car chirped. Julian opened the door and got down on his knees. He looked under the driver's seat, then the passenger's.

"Here we are." He sat back on his heels and held up a small black box with a pencil-like antenna. "Standard GPS vehicle tracker." He grinned and winked. "I assume this isn't yours."

Connor shook his head slowly. "That could have been a bomb."

"But it wasn't. Look on the bright side—they don't want us dead. At least not yet." He leaned back into the car and put the box back under the passenger seat.

"Hold on a sec," Connor protested. "What are you doing?"

"If you take out this one, the next one will just be harder to find. Or they'll decide that it's too risky to track you and the next one *will* be a bomb."

"Oh, I hadn't thought of that." Adrenaline clouded his mind and he shook his head to clear it. "This is all new to me. I've had PIs follow me a few times. One guy even went through my trash." He nodded toward the open car door. "But that's a first."

"Welcome to my world." Julian got up and clapped Connor on the shoulder. "This was pretty typical when I worked on the organized crime task force. You're taking it better than I did the first time it happened to me. I couldn't sleep for almost a week."

Connor shut the Bentley's door. "Your phone is bugged too. That's why you drove down here instead of calling."

"You're catching on."

Connor looked at his reflection in the dark window glass, thinking hard. "They don't want us dead," he echoed. "But they do want to keep tabs on us. Now why is that?"

"That's how these people operate. Back when I worked with the task force, the mob was always trying to figure out what we were up to. They'd follow us into the john if they could."

"Yeah, but they know what we're up to." Connor turned and leaned against his car so that he was facing his friend. "We're withdrawing. We're bailing out. We're not a problem anymore. So why break into our cars and put trackers in them now?"

Julian shrugged. "Tough to say. Didn't you have a PI following you after some other case was finished?"

"That was the garbage guy. But he was probably doing it because his client wanted to know who was behind Devil to Pay even though the lawsuit had settled. That would be valuable info in certain circles."

"But now the whole world knows who Devil to Pay is, right?" Julian pointed to himself. "Wasn't that the whole point of that little charade last week?"

Connor jerked to his feet as the puzzle pieces fell into place. "No, they don't. Not entirely, anyway. I'm guessing that those fake invoices Allie put into their system could only be uploaded from inside the company."

"Makes sense."

"And they know you never worked for them. Maybe you broke into their offices, hacked into their system, and uploaded the invoices—but that's pretty unlikely."

Julian tugged at his beard thoughtfully. "They've guessed we have an inside source and they're waiting for us to lead them to her."

The unpleasant image of Franklin Roh watching Allie on a video monitor appeared in Connor's head again. "That could be dangerous for Allie, don't you think? She's already contacted me once. She was careful about it, but still."

"Yeah, we should warn her."

"How?"

They looked at each other in silence for almost a minute.

Julian shoved his hands into his coat pockets and fidgeted with something. "Can't think of anything," he confessed. "You have any ideas?"

"Uh-uh. I—" Connor froze with his mouth open, and then his face broke into a wide smile. "Actually, I do."

At 6:30 that evening, Connor pulled out of the garage and drove his Bentley across the Bay Bridge to the slightly seedy area of Oakland where Clayton Investigations had an office on the fifth floor of a red wooden building that needed to be repainted. There were empty parking spaces along the street, but there was no way Connor was parking his Bentley there.

He found a secure lot with a valet and five minutes later he was walking down the hallway toward Julian's office. Julian met him outside the door and handed him a note that said "Office and phone both bugged."

Connor nodded and followed him in. They walked through a glass door emblazoned with "Clayton Investigations" in dull gold letters. "So, do you want to try his office number first?" Connor asked in clear voice.

"Okay," replied Julian just as clearly.

They reached his office and moved the speakerphone to the middle of the desk. Julian punched in a number from a green Post-It stuck to the phone. It rang three times and then went to voicemail. He hung up without leaving a message. "That's weird," he announced. "He said he'd be there."

He repeated the process three more times over the next five minutes, letting the phone ring until voicemail picked up, then hanging up.

"Let's try his cell phone now," said Connor.

Julian looked at the Post-It again and dialed again.

"Hello?" said a bland male voice with the hint of an Asian accent.

Connor leaned over the desk. "Franklin, where are you? We tried calling you at Deep Seven, but you didn't pick up."

"What is . . . 'Clayton Invest?'" Connor pictured him looking at the caller ID display on his phone. "Who is this?"

"You know perfectly well who this is. We need those documents you promised, and we need them *now*."

"What are you talking about?" Connor could almost see him starting to sweat and lick his lips, as he had during his interview at DOJ. "I demand to know who you are!"

"Don't play games, Franklin! Devil to Pay gave you a lot of money and all you gave us were some fake invoices. Then you promised us something really big if we gave you a second chance. Well, that second chance is just about up, buddy. You give us the info on that big secret project in twenty-four hours or there really will be the Devil to pay! I've just about—"

"Shut up! Shut up! Shut up!"

"Don't you talk to me that—"

"SHUT UP!" He was half way between screaming and crying now. "Please, I don't know who you are and—"

"Wait! Are you saying this phone isn't safe? That it might be bugged? Nuts! Look, we'll touch base later."

"I—"

"But get us those documents!"

Connor pressed the "Call End" button.

57

THE NEXT DAY STARTED LIKE EVERY DAY AT Deep Seven. Allie walked in with the morning crowd of temporary and permanent employees hurrying across the lobby with a cup of something hot and caffeinated in one hand and a magnetic key card in the other.

Her first clue that today would be different came when she passed Franklin Roh's office on the way to her cubicle. The lights didn't seem to be on, which was odd—he was usually at his desk by 8:30. Curious, she slowed as she passed it and looked in through the window.

She stopped and stared. The office had been stripped bare. The computer was gone, the desk was completely clear, and the drawers of his file cabinet hung open and empty. Even his nameplate had disappeared from its slot beside the door.

"Strange, isn't it?" The voice made her jump. She turned and saw Rajiv walking up behind her. "I apologize for startling you."

"Oh, and I'm sorry for standing you up at lunch. I, um, got sick suddenly."

He stepped back. "Nothing contagious, I hope."

"No, no. Just a, ah, severe stomach ache. All better now."

He smiled sympathetically and patted his lower stomach. "Ah, yes. I know that can happen to women. No need to apologize."

She felt a sudden temptation to make it happen to him, but resisted. "What happened to Franklin Roh? Did he move offices?"

"I wondered the same thing when I walked in this morning. It is possible, but I would have expected an e-mail from him or something—

'Rajiv, come see my new pad' or 'Hey, Rajiv, now I've got a view of the health club pool next door.' But I have heard nothing from him." He paused and looked her in the eye before going on in a lower voice. "Do you think perhaps something happened to him?"

She realized that her subconscious had been thinking exactly that for the last couple of minutes. "Like what?"

"I don't know. Perhaps he was punished for—" He shrugged his round shoulders. "For something."

"Like what?" she repeated.

Rajiv leaned in close, and for a horrifying moment Allie was afraid he would try to kiss her. But he went for her ear rather than her mouth.

"He was watching you." She felt his breath on her ear. "Franklin was watching you."

"What . . . what are you talking about?"

"There is a tiny camera in that tree beside your cubicle. I saw him put it there last week."

Her eyes went round and her mouth dropped open. "Really?"

He nodded. "I said nothing because I did not know why he was putting the camera there, and we have had security problems in the past. But perhaps it was not the only camera." He grinned and winked. "Maybe you were not the only pretty young woman he was watching. Maybe one of the other ones caught him."

"That must be it." She started walking back to her desk. "See you later."

"Lunch perhaps? If you are feeling better."

"Thanks. I'll let you know."

He plucked a Post-It off a pad on a nearby desk and scribbled something on it. "My cell phone number. I do not usually give it out, but I will make an exception for you."

"Thanks." Allie shoved it into the bottom of her purse and did her best to forget it was there.

Allie began to feel better as she walked to her cubicle. The fear she had felt since discovering the camera lifted. Rajiv was probably right—Roh was just a weird guy who liked to spy on women. He'd gotten caught, and they fired him on the spot. It all made sense. And with him gone, she could go back to trolling for good documents and not worry about having someone literally watching over her shoulder. She would make a show of looking in the tree, but she had no doubt that the camera would be gone. Roh probably moved it as soon as she left her desk yesterday.

When Allie reached her cubicle, she found a Post-It on her computer screen that read "Please report to Randy in Accounts Payable, 4th fl. East."

She went up to the fourth floor and found a harried-looking man standing outside an office on the east side of the building. The nameplate beside the door said "Randy Johnson." He was having conversations with two people at the same time, and she could hear the phone ringing in the office behind him.

"Randy?"

He held up a hand to the person who was talking and looked over. "What?"

"I'm Allie Whitman. I'm supposed to report to you."

"You the CPA temp?" She nodded.

"All right, I need you to do an expense allocation for each of our ships based on when they went on the Golden Gate project—fuel, maintenance, crew wages, everything. I want it on a daily, weekly and monthly basis. Oh, and make sure it's in an Excel spreadsheet. I hate the reports that other computer program spits out."

That would keep her busy for a while. "Um, okay. Where's the data?"

"I don't know. Go talk to Robin. Conference room at the end of the hall." He turned away from her, signaling that she had been dismissed.

The conference room he sent her to was just like the others she had seen—crammed full of people, paper, and computer terminals. She stood uncertainly in the doorway for several seconds, waiting for someone to notice her. When no one did, she called out, "I'm looking for Robin."

A large African American woman on the far side of the room motioned her over. "What is it, dear?"

"Randy Johnson sent me to you to get the data on costs for the company's ships. Do you have it?"

"Oh, he found someone to do the allocations!" She clapped her hands. "Good, good, good. Here, sit down beside me." She patted the seat next to her and pointed to a vacant computer terminal.

There went any chance of doing some subtle poking around, at least until she finished this project. Oh well, better get it over with fast.

As she sat down, however, a new idea occurred to her: maybe she could get something useful out of Robin. In Allie's experience, what companies regarded as tightly held secrets were often semiopen knowledge among employees. You just had to find the right person to chat up.

Chatting up Robin turned out not to be very difficult. If anything, it was far too easy. Within half an hour, Allie knew that Robin had three children, six grandchildren, and a wide assortment of nieces and nephews. One of her nephews was about Allie's age, handsome, single, and "has a good job with the Navy in San Jose." Maybe Allie would like to meet him? No? Well, Robin hoped he met the right girl soon. He never brought girlfriends to family gatherings, and "some people" were beginning to wonder whether he might be gay.

By lunch, even Rajiv would have been a relief. But duty called. Allie picked up a wilted Caesar salad and a bottle of Honest Tea at the cafeteria and sat down next to Robin at a table with two other women who had an equal capacity for conversation. Eventually, Allie managed to turn the torrent of conversation from their families and homes to their workplace.

Finally, after nearly an hour of work, the moment was ripe. Allie leaned forward. "So, what deep, dark secrets does the company have? What's with all the security cameras and stuff?"

The women looked at each other. "I never really thought about the cameras," said one with flaming red hair. "Are there more here than other places?"

Robin snorted. "More than any place I've worked. Even more than a Walmart. I wouldn't be surprised if they've got them in the bathrooms."

"They can't do that," objected the redhead. "It's not legal."

The other women laughed and rolled their eyes.

"Yeah, right," said a skinny young blond woman with teased hair.

"Like that would stop them," put in the redhead.

"But why would they need them?" persisted Allie. "Is it all just to keep people from stealing staplers and pens?"

"I'll bet it's because of those guys from the ships," said the big-haired blonde. "Like that ROV guy from the *Grasp II*. The ugly one."

"Ed?" suggested both Robin and the redhead.

"Yeah, that's the one. He always takes big handfuls of M&Ms from my bowl and dumps out all the coffee in the coffeemaker so he can make it his own way. I've complained about him like five times."

The redhead snorted. "You think they put in security cameras to protect the coffeemaker and your M&Ms?"

The blonde crossed her arms. "Well, it's a problem, isn't it? They should fire him."

"Maybe it's got something to do with those security guards up on the executive floor," said Robin. "They've got just tons of guns and stuff up there."

The blonde shook her head. "Not anymore. There's only one guy up there now. The rest of them all left yesterday."

Allie's ears perked up. "Where did they go?"

"I don't know."

"Training," Robin said authoritatively.

The blonde frowned, a tiny line forming between her perfectly shaped eyebrows. "Luis didn't say anything to me."

"I processed the invoices," Robin replied. "They're staying over at the docks in Oakland. We rented trailers, ordered catering, brought in a bunch of guys from some Korean security company."

The redhead nodded. "Sounds like a training exercise to me."

"But Luis would have told me," the blonde insisted. "He tells me everything."

Robin laughed. "Just like you tell him everything, right?"

58

MITCH COULDN'T SEE ED IN THE COMPLETE darkness of the *Grasp II*'s storage compartment, but he could smell him. Mitch didn't know how many days they'd gone without a shower or change of clothes, but it was a lot. Both of them were very nasty, but Ed's stink had to be inhaled to be believed. Even the outhouse aroma of the 20-gallon bucket they'd been given smelled better. Mitch could even tell roughly where in the compartment Ed was by the smell. He'd heard that whales and dolphins could use their ears for "echolocation." He could use his nose for Edolocation.

So when his nose detected a strengthening in the Ed aroma, he knew his friend was near and started breathing through his mouth. A second later, he felt a hand on his shoulder and heard Ed's voice in his ear. "You feel that? Wave action is different."

Mitch paused and concentrated on the rhythm of the ship. "Yeah, you're right. The engines are slower too."

"We're in port. You know what that means."

"They'll kill us?"

"Think, Mitch. If they'd wanted to kill us, wouldn't they do it before now? It's a lot easier to get rid of a body in the middle of the ocean, don't you think? Just dump us overboard and say we must've fallen. No witnesses, no evidence. Harder to do that now."

"So what's going to happen now that we're in port?"

"Not sure. But whatever it is, it's going to happen." He slapped something, probably the bulkhead beside them. "We're going to get out of this place. No more waiting."

As it turned out, they weren't quite done waiting. More hours passed as they sat in the blackness, listening to changes in the little mechanical noises of the ship and wondering what they meant. Then came a faint but solid "thump" and the thrumming of the engines stopped completely. Mitch didn't need to be told that they had just tied up at a dock.

Still nothing happened. He heard a faint liquid rumbling and Ed grunted. "Dinnertime."

The word was hardly out of his mouth when the door clanged open and a wedge of bright light poured into the room. It was only the light bulb in the hall, but it blinded Mitch and he shaded his eyes and squeezed them shut. In a few seconds, the door would slam and they would feel their way to it, where they would find food and an empty latrine bucket.

But the door didn't shut immediately. Mitch heard quick footsteps crossing the room and tried to force his eyes open. He saw a blurry figure silhouetted by blinding glare. It thrust something into his hands and spoke with Cho's voice. "The door will be unlocked when I leave," it said, speaking so rapidly and softly that Mitch had trouble catching the words despite the near silence. "The stairs will not be watched for the next ten minutes. The gangway is guarded, but the ladder on the stern is not. Go quickly and silently, and give this package to the FBI or CIA. It is important that they receive it soon. Very important."

The door shut and the darkness returned, leaving Mitch's eyes and mind dazzled by the last few seconds. His hands held something small and heavily wrapped in what felt like plastic. He shook it and felt it cautiously, trying to decide what it was.

His investigation was interrupted when Ed's hand grabbed his shirt and pulled him toward the door. "Come on!" he hissed.

Mitch shoved the package into his pants pocket. "Don't—don't you think it's a trap?"

Ed continued to pull him along. "We're *already* trapped, moron. I don't know what Cho is up to, but anything that gets us out of here is a step in the right direction." Ed released him and he heard the door's latch turning slowly. A halo of light appeared around the jamb. Ed's lumpy profile thrust itself against the glow. "Looks clear." He paused. "Don't hear anything either. Okay, on three. One . . . two . . . three!"

The door flew open and Ed stumbled out, followed by Mitch. As promised the hallway was empty. They half-ran and half-staggered toward the narrow staircase at the end of the hall. They were clumsy and nearly blind from their captivity, and they banged into pipes and walls as they stumbled forward.

They were on the stairs. They pulled themselves up as quietly as they could, but Mitch was painfully aware of the clanging their feet made on the slatted steel steps. But he saw no one and heard no sounds of pursuit.

They stopped again at the door at the top of the steps. Ed cracked the door and peered out for a few seconds. It was dark, and a cold night breeze leaked in. Ed motioned for Mitch to follow and yanked the door open.

They were out on the deck now, running hunched over through the chilly air. Still no one stopped them and no shots or yells came from behind. The only sounds Mitch heard were his rasping breath and the sounds of his and Ed's feet slapping against the deck as they sprinted from the door to the cover provided by the winch machinery, and then on to the top of the stern ladder.

Mitch took a quick look around, recognizing the Port of Oakland in an instant. There were the giant cranes that looked like the Imperial Walkers in the *Star Wars* movies, and there were the Deep Seven buildings. If he could just get past the North Koreans, he'd be practically home. It was so close!

They started down the ladder, Ed first and Mitch following him. A cold gust caught Mitch and he shivered. It couldn't be above forty, and the water wouldn't be much warmer. How far were they going to be able to swim in that? They would need to get around the end of the dock and all the way down the next one over to have any chance of getting far enough away from the ship to avoid being seen. That would be at least a hundred yards. A long way in cold water. A very long way.

59

ALLIE CROUCHED BETWEEN TWO OIL DRUMS, looking through a pair of expensive night vision binoculars she had picked up at a sporting goods store at the mall after work. She was in a dark corner of Deep Seven's lot at the Port of Oakland, hiding in what seemed to be a junk storage area between the water and the wall of a warehouse.

She saw five white housing trailers lined up on

a parking lot next to a small administrative building and what looked like a garage or machine shop. A ship—the *Grasp II* she had remembered from the tax memo—lay tethered to the dock, rising and falling slightly with the waves. A large tractor-trailer waited on the shore next to the ship. A high fence surrounded the whole compound like a steel hedge.

She'd been there for over an hour, and the initial adrenaline rush of sneaking into the dock had worn off. Petroleum fumes from the barrels gave her a headache. She was cold. Her legs and back were stiff, and the grime all around her had already stained her new jeans and the sleeve of her jacket.

So far nothing interesting had happened. The ship had arrived and tied up at the big concrete dock. They set up a gangway. A bunch of Asian guys came off, some carrying boxes or bags on hand trucks. Maybe they were carrying nuclear bomb parts or smuggled diamonds, but she kind of doubted it.

Other people went on the ship. Some other Asians wearing body armor and carrying assault rifles milled around, talking to each other and looking bored. Big deal. She saw that in the parking lot every morning at Deep Seven.

She put down the binoculars and rubbed her eyes. At least she hadn't called Connor or Julian to tell them about her new lead. That would have been painful. No one knew she made this little recon trip, and no one would unless and until she found something.

She sighed. It would be a lot easier to find something if she had some idea what she was looking for.

Oh, well. Back to work the next morning. Maybe she'd find something good before her assignment ended. She looked at her blackened knees. Maybe those stains would even come out. Miracles were possible.

She took one last look at the ship, and a movement in the shadows at its back—stern?—caught her eye. She lifted the binoculars to her eyes and the world turned from night to green-tinged twilight.

Two figures were climbing down to the water. They paused for a minute and then dropped into the dirty water of the harbor, making hardly a ripple.

They didn't swim directly for shore, but moved in a wide crescent that kept them in the shadows and out of view from the dock. She leaned forward, forgetting her dirty knees and aching back. "Now we're talking."

The swimmers made slow progress, disappearing under water and then popping their heads up for a few seconds ten yards away for a breath and a quick look around before disappearing again. They turned toward shore, following a line of pilings that gave them some cover. With a start, Allie realized that they would reach the cement seawall just a few yards from her.

Excitement and fear twisted her insides. Should she run? Stay put and see what happened? Go to meet them?

Inertia won out. She moved back further into the shadows and watched as they came closer and closer. They seemed to be having some trouble—they came to the surface more often, staying up longer. Then they stopped going down at all. They swam with slow, uneven strokes. One of them lagged behind, and the other went back and began half-towing him.

Allie looked around, but didn't see anything resembling a life preserver. So there really wasn't anything she could do to help, was there?

The swimmers continued to make gradual progress. Eventually they disappeared from view beneath the edge of the wall. Long minutes ticked by. Allie looked at the glowing face of her watch and wondered how long the men had been out of sight.

Finally, she decided to go over to the wall and look down. But as she started to rise, she heard grunting and a hand appeared over the top of the wall. She crouched back between the barrels and watched as a man pulled himself over and collapsed to the ground.

He lurched to his feet and called down in a rough, shaking whisper. "Hold on, Ed!"

He staggered toward the random piles of junk as if looking for something. His hands shivered badly as he fumbled among the trash. After half a minute, he found a heavy chain with a hook on one end and started dragging it over to the seawall. But the chain suddenly went taut, jerking the man to a halt. He yanked on it without result, then stumbled back and began shoving a large piece of scrap metal that was apparently pinning the chain down.

Allie couldn't bear it any longer. Against her better judgment, she pushed herself to her feet and ran over.

The man was intent on his task and didn't see her until she set her shoulder beside his. He looked up, surprise on his dripping face. He grunted his thanks and pushed harder.

The metal groaned and scraped forward, releasing the chain. The man grabbed it and ran back to the low wall, Allie a step behind him.

She looked down and saw dark waves rolling up against slimy green cement ten feet below. Rusty D-shaped loops of rebar stuck out from the wall, forming a rough ladder. A semi-conscious man hung from the bottom, his right arm wedged through a rung to keep him from slipping under.

The man beside Allie let the hook down. It thumped against the wall with a dull clank. The man at the bottom lifted his head and reached for the chain with his left hand, but he couldn't seem to catch it. His other arm slipped out of the rung and he flailed wildly for a few seconds before grabbing the rung again. He clung to it with both hands.

"I'll go down." Allie's voice surprised her, but she found herself stepping over the top of the seawall and gripping the top rung. It was rough and very cold in her hand. Then she was climbing down, and a few seconds later she had almost reached the bottom.

A shockingly cold wave rose out of the dark and slapped her. Her foot slipped off a slimy rung, and she barely avoided falling. Wet and shivering, she cowered against the hard wall, wondering what she was doing. She should be in her apartment right now, or at Tang Dynasty or Starbucks with Trudi, or planning her next move at Deep Seven. Somewhere—anywhere—other than hanging from a cold and unforgiving cement slab over inky waters, trying to save some man she'd never met.

She looked down. The man was looking at her. He shook uncontrollably. His face was pale and slack, his eyes half-glazed.

Another wave rolled toward her and she tensed as it splashed against the wall, soaking her a second time. The man below her hardly seemed to notice.

She climbed down the final few rungs and grabbed the chain that hung beside her. She tried to hand it to the man, but he shook his head. "B-belt."

"What? Oh, the hook."

He nodded.

Allie stepped down into the frigid water and felt the man's waist. There it was. It felt thick—hopefully thick enough to support him. She attached the hook and gave the chain a jerk.

The man at the top of the wall pulled and the chain went taut. With Allie pushing the second man's dripping and copious backside, he rose out of the water, pawing weakly at the ladder as he went up.

His legs disappeared over the top, and Allie heaved herself over right behind him. He had curled into a shivering ball, but he nodded to her with a quick jerk of his head. "Th-thanks."

Allie nodded back. She was wet and freezing, but a sunny glow spread through her. She knew she didn't look her best, but she wished Connor could see her now.

The man she had just saved grunted something.

"What was that?"

"Phone," he repeated, his voice slurred and shaking. "You gotta phone?"

Fortunately, it was in her purse, which was still back by the oil barrels. She retrieved it and returned a few seconds later. "I'll call you an ambulance."

She started to dial 911, but he shook his head. "No! Cops first. There's n-nukes on that ship. Buncha North Korean commandos too."

60

CHO STOOD ON THE FORWARD DECK, watching and waiting. It was a starless and peaceful night. The only sounds were the soft rhythmic splash of the waves and indistinct murmur of conversation on shore. But he doubted the quiet would last. His turn on guard duty was scheduled to last until midnight, though he suspected there would be no need for a watchman by that time.

His eyes swept back and forth over the dock, the warehouses, the bright white trailers for the American security guards. While he helped unload trash and restock provisions, he had heard the Americans complain about their quarters, comparing them to prison cells. Curious, he had looked inside one of the trailers. It was warm, well lit, had six soft-looking beds with blankets and pillows, a bathroom, and even a small kitchen with a coffeemaker and a basket of plastic-wrapped snacks. If American prisons were really like that, they were more comfortable than most apartments he had been in. No wonder so many poor Americans chose to go to jail.

Then he heard it—the high ululating sound he had listened for ever since he freed Granger and Daniels. The American police car siren sounded exactly like the ones in the grainy black-market movies he watched to practice his English.

He stared at a dark stretch of pavement about a kilometer away: the spot where the entrance road appeared between two low buildings and turned toward the dock. The siren grew louder. The dark pavement suddenly glowed. Then a car with flashing blue and red lights burst into view and turned toward the dock.

Only one police car. No military. Odd. The information on the drive he had given to Daniels should have called for a much stronger response.

He turned and ran for the bridge. He yanked open the door and jumped down a narrow flight of stairs. He raced down the corridor to Mr. Lee's quarters and jerked open the door without knocking. The room was dark, so he pulled to a halt and stood at attention in the doorway. "Apologies, sir! A police car approaches!"

He saw a stir by Mr. Lee's bed, but kept his eyes straight ahead. A few heartbeats later, Mr. Lee appeared in the light. He was still pulling on an undershirt and jeans. Red lines from pillow creases marked the left side of his face, but his eyes were bright and fully alert. "Have you spoken to the Americans?"

"No, sir. I came directly to you."

Mr. Lee nodded crisply and walked out.

They met Captain Wither in the hallway. He was still fully dressed, but his shirt was half unbuttoned. His face was flushed and his eyes were wide and bloodshot. "The cops are coming!" A pungent scent of alcohol wafted over them as he spoke.

Mr. Lee drew his brows together in a disapproving frown. "Yes, we know. Mr. Park will talk to them, yes? We paid extra for him for just this reason."

The captain looked away. "Yeah, I'm sure he will." He returned his gaze to them and pulled the corners of his mouth up in a smile. "Nothing to worry about."

Mr. Lee regarded him silently for several seconds, then nodded. "Very good."

They left the captain and continued down the corridor toward the bridge. Without turning his head, the general spoke softly in Korean. "Assemble the men around the MIRV housing. Kill anyone who enters. I will stay with the captain to make sure he does not betray us."

Cho nodded and turned to the men's quarters.

Three minutes later, they were all awake and in the large storage room with the MIRV housing. Two men aimed pistols at the door while the others took positions around the door and waited and listened.

Unidentified creakings and grumblings from the depths of the ship. Footsteps on the deck above grew louder, then fainter, and then disappeared. More footsteps—clanging on the metal stairs this time.

The men tensed and readied themselves. The electricity of imminent violence charged the air.

Footsteps outside and faint conversation. The voices were indistinct but sounded jovial and relaxed.

The footsteps stopped at the door. It opened. The captain and First Mate Jenkins began to step in but jerked back at the sight of the men ready in ambush.

The captain put a hand to his chest.

The first mate swore, then guffawed. "I almost peed my pants!"

No one else laughed.

Jenkins's smile faded. "Anyway, you'll be happy to hear that the cops are gone. So you can all relax and go back to bed."

The captain looked at Cho. "Except you. Mr. Lee would like to talk to you in his stateroom."

Cho nodded and followed the captain upstairs.

Mr. Lee sat facing the door. He did not look happy. "The police said someone rang them and said there were nuclear weapons on this ship—nuclear weapons from a sunken Soviet submarine. Fortunately, Mr. Park was able to persuade them that this was a misunderstanding."

Cho gasped and widened his eyes in what he hoped looked like shock. "Who rang the police?"

The captain cleared his throat and clasped his hands behind his back. "First Mate Jenkins discovered that Granger and Daniels managed to escape."

Cho stared at the man. "Escaped? How?"

The captain shifted his weight from foot to foot. "We're not sure. Jenkins found the door unlocked."

Cho continued to hold the captain with his gaze. "Jenkins and Granger were friends, yes?"

The captain looked down. "They did drink together sometimes."

Cho turned back to Mr. Lee. "Sir, may I suggest that Mr. Jenkins stay in a locked room until we are done. May I also suggest that," he glanced at the captain for a split-second, "that he be guarded by one of our men."

The alcohol-fueled flush on the captain's face deepened, but he did not speak.

Mr. Lee nodded. "Yes, I thought the same. It is being done."

"Sir, do you wish for me to arrange a search for Granger and Daniels? Perhaps they are still nearby."

"They will have difficulty escaping now. There is a fence around the docks, and it was lit and electrified as soon as the escape was discovered. Mr. Kang is already leading a search squad. If Granger and Daniels are still there, he will find them. I need you to supervise removing the warheads from the MIRV housing and loading them onto the truck on shore. We need to move them as quickly as possible. This place is not safe."

"Yes, sir. Anything else?"

Mr. Lee pursed his lips and folded his arms, as he often did when he was about to speak of something he found distasteful. "I am told there is a well-equipped interrogation room on shore. Go inspect it."

"Yes, sir."

"And please do supervise Kang," Mr. Lee continued in Korean. "He is a good interrogator, but he enjoys it a bit too much. It impairs his results."

61

CONNOR'S CELL PHONE BUZZED AGAIN. HE discreetly slipped it out of his pocket and glanced at the screen. Allie. Again.

He suppressed his irritation and returned it to his pocket. Even if he wanted to talk to Allie, this was a particularly bad time. He was sitting next to Tom Concannon on one side of a table at Slanted Door, a fashionable Vietnamese restaurant on San Francisco's waterfront. On the other side sat Bill

Fisher, head of D&B's litigation department. And next to Bill was Frank Garibaldi, general counsel of Phoebus Partners—a wealthy and highly litigious investment group in San Francisco.

Years ago, Frank had worked on the staff of a congressional committee headed by Connor's father. A couple of weeks ago, Frank and Connor had sat at the same table at a black-tie charity dinner. Frank had mentioned that Phoebus wasn't happy with their current outside counsel. Connor had suggested that Doyle & Brown might be a good fit and had offered to arrange dinner with some D&B partners. Frank had accepted, and here they were.

Frank noticed the phone call. "You're a popular guy tonight, Connor." Genial male laughter. "Do you need to get that?"

Connor looked back at his companions and dropped the phone back into his pocket. "No, no. I'm sure it's nothing. Sorry, Frank, I didn't mean to interrupt your story. So, you were in New Orleans for the Vikings-Saints playoff game and you met Zygi Wilf in a karaoke bar on Bourbon Street."

"Right. He'd obviously had a few and he was singing 'Born to Run' as loud as he possibly could." Connor nodded and laughed as his guest told a rambling ten-minute anecdote, the main point of which appeared to be that he knew the owner of the Minnesota Vikings.

Connor didn't mind. Phoebus was a plum client, with billings worth millions per year. If he could land them, he could write himself a one-way, non-stop ticket from the firm's doghouse to its penthouse. Nothing encourages law firm forgiveness quite like a fat book of business. Profitability is next to godliness in the Big Law world. Actually, it beats godliness cold—as Connor knew through personal experience.

Connor's phone buzzed again. Frank and Bill discovered that they shared a love of Buster Keaton movies and were busy quoting favorite scenes to each other, so Connor risked a quick look at his phone. A new text message from Allie. He opened it and read, "trapped @ dp 7 dock. help!!"

He glanced up quickly. Frank and Bill hadn't noticed, but Tom was looking at him. Connor showed him the message below table level. Tom frowned and shook his head slightly.

Connor messaged back, "Call 911."

Bill had steered Frank away from movie trivia and back to business. ". . . and our financial litigation group has had quite a run of success in recent years. We're also open to alternative billing models, as Connor may already have explained to you."

Frank's eyebrows went up and his martini glass stopped halfway to his lips. He looked at Connor. "Why, no. I'd be very interested in hearing about that."

Connor put his elbows on the table and put on his most winning smile. "And I'd be very interested in telling you about it. We—" His pocket buzzed again. "I'm very sorry. I've just learned that we have a minor emergency brewing. Could you excuse me for just a moment?"

Frank swept his martini toward the door, spilling a drop on the table. "Of course."

Connor rose and hurried an exit, opening the new message as he went. "already called cops. they stopped @ gate, talked to grds & left. dont know what to do now. bad stuff going on-nkoreans w/ nukes! im scared."

"Allie again?"

Connor turned and saw that Tom had followed him out and was standing behind him on the walkway between the restaurant and the water.

Connor handed the phone to his friend. "So, what do we do?"

Tom glanced at the message. His jaw tightened and his eyes narrowed. "What do we do? Nothing! Not one blessed thing, you understand?" He shook the cell phone in Connor's face. "She is trespassing on Deep Seven property and you're giving her advice! And you're doing it on your cell phone by text message so that they'll get every word when they subpoena the phone company!"

"I'm sorry, Tom, but I didn't have much choice. She might be in real danger and—"

326

Tom bared his teeth and cocked his arm. For a frozen instant, Connor thought he was going to throw a punch. But he pivoted and hurled Connor's cell phone far out to sea. "Don't you lie to me! You had a choice and you made it! You chose to shaft me and the firm so that you could keep helping that cute, lying little—" He bit off the last word and took a few seconds to master himself. "Look, you know how bad this'll look in Deep Seven's suit against the firm, right? Didn't we talk about exactly that? And didn't you agree that you wouldn't have any contact with her? You're already hanging by a thread, Connor. You know that. Why are you trying to cut it? If you can't shut up and do exactly what you're told, *you . . . are . . . dead.*" He shook his head and rubbed his eyes, then nodded toward the door. "All right, let's go back in there and have dinner. If you can land Phoebus, maybe ExComm will let this go. Maybe."

He turned and walked back in. Connor followed him in a daze. Tom had never acted like that toward him. No one had. Or at least no one who inhabited his world. Every now and then, he'd run into a loudmouth at a baseball game or a bar, but you couldn't expect class from people like that. But from Tom Concannon?

They crossed the restaurant and found their meals waiting for them. Tom flashed a grin at

Frank. "Emergency resolved! Did Bill fill you in on our alternative billing models?"

"I gave him an overview, but I thought I'd let Connor tell him about a couple of cases where our partial-contingency fee system turned out to be a real win-win for us and our clients."

Tom took his seat. "And a lose-lose for our opponents."

"That's how our cases tend to turn out." Bill picked up his chopsticks and winked at Connor. "Now you talk while I work on this delicious-looking branzino."

Connor stood looking down at the table, every detail crowding in on his senses. He saw the exquisitely presented Dungeness crab and cellophane noodles on his plate and the dew-beaded glass of Chardonnay next to it. The click of Bill's chopsticks and the pleasant murmur of a dozen conversations around them blended into a wistful music in his ears. The bouquet of fresh gourmet food and a hint of sea tang filled his nose with a tempting perfume. He felt three pairs of eyes looking up at him expectantly.

"Aren't you going to sit down," Bill asked.

He almost did. He put his hand on the gray leather chair and started to pull it out. The invitation lay right there in front of him, waiting for him to accept. He would sit down and make his sales pitch to Frank, who would probably accept it. Phoebus would become a Doyle &

Brown client, and Connor's future road with the firm would be wide and smooth.

But he stopped. Allie had told him once that she couldn't trust him. It was time to prove her wrong. And to follow his own advice about hard choices.

For a few seconds, he prayed for the strength to say the necessary words. Then he looked up and smiled. "I'm sorry, but I'm going to have to bid you all good night. There's a pressing matter I have to attend to."

Tom's face turned deep red and the muscles of his neck stood out. "What are you doing, Connor?"

"I'm making a choice. You were right, Tom. It's wrong for me to endanger the firm's finances or reputation by my actions. I am therefore resigning my partnership, effective immediately."

62

ALLIE AND THE TWO SWIMMERS (WHOM SHE had learned were named Mitch and Ed) huddled behind a stack of crates in a warehouse beside Deep Seven's dock. They had run into the warehouse when brilliant lights came on a few minutes after the two men called the police on Allie's cell phone. The lights topped lamp posts built into a tall security fence that completely surrounded Deep Seven's dock and a collection of dockside buildings. The fence looked like something from a maximum-security prison. It was at least ten feet high, topped with razor wire, and had signs inscribed with bright red lightning bolts and skulls.

The nearest gate—the one Allie had come through—was fifty yards away on the other side of a noon-bright obstacle course of rusted metal and sharp-edged shadows. Worse, the gate had clanged shut when the lights came on. There was a number pad next to the gate, but without the pass code, that wouldn't do them much good.

Allie thought about suggesting that they swim to safety as soon as Ed and Mitch had warmed up enough, but then she looked through her night-vision binoculars and saw two men on the ship sweeping the shore with similar binoculars.

Fear prickled down her back as she noticed something else: what looked like a SWAT team crossing the gangway from ship to shore. They carried assault rifles and wore bulky dark clothing that looked like it covered body armor. Their helmets had complicated eyepieces that she assumed were designed to help them see enemies in dark, cluttered places like the warehouse.

The helpless, unreasoning panic of a trapped animal seized her. *Do something! Do something!* it shouted. But what?

Maybe Connor or Julian had come up with

something. She took her cell phone out of her purse and checked her messages, cupping her hands around it to hide the light from the screen.

"Anything?" asked the taller man, whose name was Mitch.

She shook her head. "Not since my lawyer—ex-lawyer—told me to call 911. The detective isn't picking up at all. Don't know who else to try."

"Don't try anyone," whispered the short, squat man, whose name Allie had learned was Ed. "Your phone lights up like a little searchlight every time you touch it."

"I'm being careful."

"Not careful enough." He pointed to a tiny spot of light dancing on the warehouse wall next to them.

"It's not doing us any good anyway." She snapped her phone shut and shoved it to the bottom of her purse, under wads of receipts and notes, her lipstick, and her pepper spray.

Pepper spray. She took it out and looked at it in the near darkness. Was there anything she could do with this? She thought for a moment, then rolled her eyes. Yeah, she was going to mace half a dozen commandos. That would work. She'd be better off trying the lipstick. At least that had gotten her someplace with the last male Deep Seven employee she had met.

Her eyes went wide. *Rajiv!* Did she still have his cell phone number? She dug through her purse with frantic fingers. There! A crumpled Post-It matted with lint on the gummy strip.

A metallic screech echoed through the warehouse and a door at the far end opened. One figure peeked in. A second later six men ran through the door, each silhouetted for an instant against the cold merciless glare of the lights on the security fence. Then they vanished into the darkness inside.

Allie took out her phone and dialed fast, keeping the light as hidden as possible.

Ed tried to grab it from her. "What are you doing?" he hissed.

She batted away his hand. "Getting help!"

One ring and Rajiv's voice was in her ear. "Hello?"

"Rajiv, it's Allie Whitman," she whispered. "I really need your help."

"Ah, certainly, Allie. Of course. What seems to be the problem?"

"Long story, but I'm trapped in a warehouse on Deep Seven's dock in Oakland. I need the code for the gate in the security fence."

The phone was silent for several seconds. "All right . . . okay," he said at last. "I'm not in the office. Let me try accessing the system remotely. This may take a little while."

"Please hurry." She peeked between two crates and glimpsed a dark figure methodically checking possible hiding places about halfway across the warehouse. "I'm, uh, late for something. I'll be really, um, grateful if you can get me the code fast."

"My pleasure, I assure you. By the way, you wouldn't happen to be free for dinner tomorrow night?"

"Sure. My treat." She couldn't see the figure anymore. How soon before one of the searchers reached them? A minute? Five minutes?

"Nonsense! I insist on paying."

"Okay, fine. Do you have the code?"

"Do you mind if I put down the phone so I can type with both hands?"

"No, no. Please do."

"I don't wish to be rude."

Allie fought back the urge to scream. "Really, it's totally, completely fine. Put it down now."

There was a rattling noise as he put the phone on some hard surface, followed by the intermittent faint clatter of a computer keyboard. She could hear Rajiv muttering to himself and humming a Britney Spears tune.

Seconds dragged by, each weighted down with unbearable tension. If she knew how to pray, she would.

A scuffing noise and the sound of footsteps nearby. Ed leaned close to her other ear. "We gotta get outta here!"

She nodded. There was a door about twenty feet away that stood ajar. The three of them crept toward it, darting from the stack of crates to a row of barrels to a pile of pipe—whatever offered cover.

They were outside! They stood in the white glare of the naked high-wattage bulbs, exposed and blinded. Allie shielded her eyes and blinked until the painful brilliance began to resolve into recognizable shapes.

She grabbed Ed's arm and pointed toward the gate. They ran toward it, squinting and half stumbling.

She held the phone to her mouth. "Rajiv!" Nothing. They'd be spotted in seconds if she didn't get that code. *"Rajiv!"*

Clattering noise. "Yes, what is it, Allie?"

"Do you have the code?"

"Almost . . . one moment."

They were at the gate now. She stopped and looked back as Ed and Mitch caught up. No pursuit. Yet.

More humming and typing in her ear, then, "Ah, here we are. The code is 2583. Did you get that?"

"Yeah, 2583." She punched in the numbers as she spoke. "Thanks, Rajiv. I owe—"

A clanging alarm cut her off. It hammered in her ears and in her skull.

She yanked at the gate, but the rubber-coated handle wouldn't budge. She punched in the numbers again, hit the pound sign, and pulled the handle a second time.

Ed cursed and pointed back toward the warehouse. "Here they come!"

"Rajiv! The gate won't open! What do I do?"

He said something she couldn't hear over the alarm.

"What? I can't hear you!"

"You are going to die. Truly I am sorry."

An awful empty space opened in her stomach. "What do you mean?"

"You asked what happened to Franklin Roh. You're about to find out."

63

THE WORLD SEEMED SURREAL TO CONNOR AS he walked out of the Slanted Door. A casual observer might see a man walking out of a restaurant, but in reality he had just walked out of his life. Behind him lay the past seven years—no, more than that. It wasn't just the time; it was the career as a big firm lawyer, the mold he had chosen to pour himself into when he decided against politics. All that was gone, swept away by a few words spoken over Vietnamese food.

In front of him lay—what? He looked around at the uncertain night, full of bright, disjointed lights and domed by foreboding black. Streams of people and cars swept past, moving in unison, but not traveling together. They were autumn leaves, carried by a common wind and drifting together, but always separate and alone.

Where would he go now? What would he do? The future is always hidden in the hand of God, but sometimes that hand is more visible than others. Tonight it was utterly invisible to him.

He shook himself. His task for the immediate future was clear enough: find a payphone. Amazing how those had virtually vanished from city streets—especially when you needed one.

After hunting for about ten minutes, he finally found one in a convenience store that had signs in the window advertising Coca-Cola in Chinese and green tea in English. He swiped his credit card and dialed Allie's cell phone. She didn't pick up. He tried again—still nothing.

He hung up and tried Julian's cell phone.

"Hello?"

"Julian, it's Connor. Have you heard from Allie?"

"No, but I haven't been in the office since about 4:00, and she doesn't have this number. What's going on?"

"I'm not sure. She texted me and said she was trapped at Deep Seven's dock and needed help. She said they'd tried the police, but they just talked to the guards at the gate and left. She also, ah, said there were North Koreans with nukes there."

"Wow. That's . . . quite a story. Did she give you any details?"

"No. Just a couple quick texts. I tried calling her just now, but she didn't pick up."

"Sounds like something's going on. I'll drive down to the docks and check it out."

"Be careful."

"Always am. That tracker is staying on a shelf in the garage so they'll think I'm home the whole time. Should I call you back at this number?"

"No. I'm at a payphone right now. One of my partners—" No time for the whole story right now. "My cell phone fell in the water. I'm going to get a new one now, and I'll call you when I've got it."

Half an hour later, Connor walked out of the Verizon store on Pine Street, holding a new phone. He dialed Julian's number as he made for the parking garage.

"Hello?"

"It's me. You at the docks?"

"I'm watching through a telephoto lens from about half a mile away. That place is lit up like a Christmas tree. Lots of big guys with crew cuts and guns. Can't say whether they're North Korean, but most of them are Asian."

"What are they doing? Can you see Allie?"

"I haven't— Hold on a sec, they're doing something down there. Okay, now I see something. Six armed men are taking a woman and two guys from one building to another. Looks like Allie, but I can't be sure. Now they're inside again."

Connor's pace quickened and sweat began to bead on his forehead despite the cool evening sea breeze. "Was it her? Was she okay?"

"Couldn't say for sure. I didn't get a good look, and they were a long way off."

"Any ideas on what to do next? Try the cops maybe?"

"Didn't you say Allie already tried them? Besides, what would we say—that we saw a woman who might be Allie and some guys with guns? No violence, no force, no indication that she was bound. Just a woman and some armed men who could be her security guards for all the police know. Sorry, but that's not going to get them in there."

"Well, what would?"

"Good question. I think we're on our own tonight."

Connor reached his Bentley and got in. "Okay, so what are we going to do?"

Julian sighed. "Wish I knew, man. Even if the Port cops did want to get involved, I'm not sure they could get into that place. It's got a better fence around it than most prisons I've seen, and I'll bet they've got more firepower in there than just a bunch of M-16s. You'd need a company of Marines. With air support."

An idea sparked in Connor's mind. He ignored it. It burst into flame and he tried to stamp it out. It was crazy, risky, self-destructive—everything he wasn't. But it would probably work. And if Allie was telling the truth about the North Koreans with nukes—

"Connor? You there?"

He took a deep breath. "Yeah, I'm here. Can you stay where you are for a while?"

"Sure, as long as you want. Are you coming?"

"I think so." He leaned over to the passenger side of his car, found the tracking device under the seat, and tossed it out the window. "But I've got a couple things to do first, and a . . . a decision to make. Just keep your phone on and let me know if anything happens."

"Okay."

"And pray for me, would you?"

"Absolutely."

"Thanks. I'll call you from the road."

He put the car in gear and pulled out of the garage, driving as fast as the traffic would allow. He navigated the narrow, clogged streets of San Francisco, the perpetually backed up Bay Bridge, and then I-580 heading east. Finally, the open highway stretched before him and he zoomed along.

Connor still wasn't certain what he would do when he reached his destination. However, his uncertainty was melting away fast, much as he wished it wouldn't. He turned the idea over in his mind, looking for flaws or alternatives. He found neither. There were huge risks—especially for him—but no flaws. It would work, and he couldn't think of anything else that would.

Every muscle in his body tensed as the idea bore down on him, becoming relentlessly real in his mind. His knuckles whitened on the steering wheel. His stomach tied itself in knots. He sweated. He prayed—silently at first, then aloud. "I'll do it if you want me to, Lord. I will. It's just that . . . well, there's a good chance I'll be dead or in prison when this is over. It's not just me, either. What about my family? What will happen to them when this hits the papers tomorrow?"

He felt like a soldier with a desk job in headquarters who has just been sent to the front line and told to run across a minefield and take out a machine gun nest on the other side single-handed. It was impossible, unreasonable. "God, is this what you want me to do? Really? *Really?*"

Silence rang in his ears and in his heart.

He sighed and gave up. The night flowed over him and he felt the Bentley's understated power purring through the car. His body began to relax. The tension drained out of him and he became philosophical, almost detached.

For the hundredth time, he remembered his meeting with Allie in the Bahamas. He told her she always had choices, but maybe that wasn't quite true. Maybe by the time we reach a critical decision, we've already made it. Maybe all the little decisions in life are like bricks, and those bricks pile together into walls over time. And when some crisis comes, those walls force us along whatever path we've already chosen. Even if that path leads over a cliff.

That's how he felt now. He had no choices, just this thing that needed to be done and the knowledge that he needed to do it. The path before him was hard, narrow, and all too clear.

64

THE MEN SHOVED ALLIE INTO A METAL CHAIR that chilled her wet skin through her clothes. They tied her hands behind her. Then they bound her ankles to the legs of the chair. They worked silently and efficiently, as if they'd done this a dozen times before. Maybe they had.

She was in a machine shop—or at least she hoped that's what it was. Drills, saws, and other tools hung from the walls or sat on a well-used work table in front of her. Three assault rifles and a box of bullets stood in a corner by the door. Allie forced herself not to wonder why they were there. Naked fluorescent bulbs buzzed overhead, bathing the room in an unnatural white light. The floor was gray concrete, marred by dark splotches around the chair and table.

Ed and Mitch were there too. They sat against the wall with their hands and feet duct taped together. Guards stood on either side of them.

The men who had brought her in left and a muscular, heavily tattooed man wearing a ski mask stepped forward out of the shadows. He had plastic gloves on his hands and was playing with a pair of pliers. He grinned and his teeth glinted. "Good evening," he said in heavily accented English. "It has been long time since I had opportunity to entertain a lady."

He stroked her hair and slipped his hand down her neck to her shoulder. His hand was cold and strong. She shuddered and shrank away as far as she could.

He held up the pliers. "Maybe we do this easy way." His fingers traced her collarbone, then stopped. He held up the pliers and clicked them together. "Or maybe we do it hard way." He chuckled in her ear and she could feel his hot breath. "Or maybe we do both. What you think?"

She wished she could die right then and get it over with. But she couldn't. All she could do was take whatever this animal wanted to do to her until he killed her. Knowing that gave her a sudden reckless defiance.

She turned and spat, hitting him right in the left eye.

He jerked his head back and shouted in a foreign language. Then he backhanded her so hard that the chair fell over. Her skull crashed into the concrete floor and she saw black spots.

Her head rang like the inside of a bell and the room swam.

"Hey, don't you want to know what I think?" Ed's voice called out, cutting through the fog in her mind. "I think you'd scream like a little girl if I ever got hold of you."

The masked man roared with laughter. "Your turn comes, brave boy. Now you watch. Maybe you not so brave when you sit in chair."

He bent over Allie and grabbed her shirt.

A staccato male voice spoke from somewhere nearby, issuing what sounded like a command, though she didn't understand the language.

Her tormenter turned his head and answered over his shoulder.

Another peremptory statement from the unseen speaker.

The torturer grunted. Then he reluctantly released Allie's shirt and picked up the chair and her, setting them upright as easily as if the seat had been empty.

He walked over to the table and Allie got a look at the man whose voice she had heard. The second man was Asian, in his mid-thirties, and had sharp features made sharper by a look of disapproval.

The man in the ski mask returned carrying a syringe. He grabbed Allie's arm and jabbed the needle into a blood vessel inside her elbow. It hurt and a drop of blood ran down her arm after he pulled the needle out, but the pain was distant and somehow disconnected from her, as if she was remembering it.

Within seconds, she felt the drug. Her brain, already dulled by blows from the torturer's fist and the floor, lost focus. Her thoughts wandered away from each other and she could not gather them back. She wished Connor would rescue her, but he hated her. She wished her father were there, then remembered he was dead. She was so alone. Her chin dropped down to her chest and she nearly started crying.

"Allison Whitman, why did you come here?" asked an authoritative voice.

She felt an instant urge to answer, and the words spilled out of her before she knew it. "To see what was going on, what you were doing."

"What did you think was going on?"

"I didn't know. That's why I came."

"Who sent you?"

"No one."

"Did Devil to Pay, Inc. send you?"

Warning bells went off and she knew she needed to be careful, but she couldn't quite remember how or why. She looked down and said nothing.

She heard a sigh, followed by footsteps. A hand grabbed her chin and jerked her head up, making the room spin. The second man's face filled her vision. He stared down at her with hard black eyes. "Allison, we know about Connor Norman and Clayton Investigations. Did they send you?"

She clenched her jaws together and said nothing. She knew that answering his questions would mean betraying Connor, and she would not do that. Not again.

Without the slightest change in his expression, he slapped her across the mouth. "Did they send you?"

She tasted blood, but kept her mouth shut. Looking into his eyes, she knew all at once that he couldn't make her talk. Neither could his friend in the mask. They might be able to make her scream, but that was all. Something had clicked into place deep inside her, something strong.

She might die in that chair, but she would not break. She knew it. She smiled, and he knew it too.

He let go of her chin and walked away. He nodded toward the masked man as he went. The two men talked in a foreign language again. Then the second man walked out.

As soon as he was gone, the torturer looked at her with a gleam in his masked eyes and started walking toward her. He flexed his arms, making his tattoos come alive.

As he approached her, she heard a buzzing sound. It started faintly, like a fly trapped in her skull. But it grew louder fast, and in a few seconds it was an overwhelming roar. At first, she thought the noise was inside her head, but everyone in the room suddenly started shouting. The tattooed torturer seemed to forget about her. He grabbed a rifle and dashed outside.

The roar rose to teeth-rattling volume. Then a high jackhammer sound started. Something exploded outside, and the shock wave buckled in one of the walls and peeled the roof back like the lid of a can of sardines.

Allie looked up just as something flashed across the night sky. It looked like a winged shark made of polished steel.

Then the wall collapsed and the building came down on top of her.

65

THE DOCKS VANISHED BEHIND CONNOR, and he was flying over the black waters of the San Francisco Bay. He pulled back on the stick, climbing and banking to the right.

His mind hummed with adrenaline and his hand shook on the stick. Part of him could not comprehend that he was actually doing this. It looked and felt just like another movie shoot. But those were real bullets in his guns this time, not blanks. Those were real buildings and ships and men down there, and he had just fired hundreds of rounds at them.

He looked back over his right shoulder at the Deep Seven compound. A black and red mushroom cloud rose from the remains of a gas or propane tank. The building closest to it was a collapsed ruin, and another building appeared to have lost a wall and part of its roof. Tiny figures ran aimlessly or pointed after him. None of them appeared to be hurt or dead. Good.

He was trying to disrupt whatever was going on down there and bring in the Port police—or better yet, the military. Shooting people—even bad people—was something he really wanted to keep to a minimum.

Air traffic control had been jabbering on his radio for the past several minutes. Time to bring them into the loop. "Oakland Center, this is November-one-niner-six-six-November. I am observing violent activity on a dock in the Port of Oakland. I am attempting to disrupt it. Please contact Port police, Coast Guard, and all other appropriate authorities immediately."

"Six-Six-November, turn right toward San Francisco Bay, bearing due west and climb and maintain five thousand feet. You will be intercepted by an Air Force F-16. Acknowledge."

"Not until I see Port cops on the ground. I have a friend down there, and I'm not leaving her."

"Six-six-November, there are F-16s inbound. If you do not leave the area immediately, you risk being shot down."

"Get some cops on that dock and I'll leave. Six-six-November out."

Connor clicked off the radio and turned to his Bluetooth headset. "How's it looking? What's going on down there?"

"Tough to tell," Julian's voice said in his ear. The volume on the earpiece was up as high as it would go, but the cockpit noise still almost drowned him out. "There's a lot of smoke and one of those buildings just came down."

"Which one was Allie in?"

Pause. "I'm sure she's fine."

A sick feeling welled up in him. "No, you're not."

"Don't think about it. Look, the best thing you can do for her right now is to get the cops in there. Focus, buddy. You need to focus."

Was Allie okay? The question burned in his mind, but he knew Julian was right. Worrying couldn't save her, but it could kill him. He said a quick prayer and then did his best to push thoughts of her away.

He leveled out the *White Knight* and swallowed hard. "Okay, I'm going in for another pass. "What do I hit?"

"There's a lot of activity around a semi. See it?"

Connor looked down. He saw a large unmarked white semi parked in the shadows between the ship's gangway and a large warehouse. Men scurried around it even as it began to roll forward.

"I see it. Whatever's in there must be pretty

important for them to try moving it right now." He nosed the P-51 down into a power dive. The night air roared over the old fighter's wings and the ground rushed up at him.

Men raced for cover as the plane approached. When he was about three hundred yards out, he noticed strobe-like flashes from the corners of buildings. A chill went through him as he realized they were shooting at him. Bangs and pings rattled through the plane as some of the bullets found their mark. He was very glad that he had left most of the plane's original battle armor in place—particularly the steel plates and bullet-resistant canopy protecting the pilot.

Connor let loose a burst from the six .50-caliber machine guns in the wings. Dust and debris flew into the air as the massive bullets hit the ground, digging furrows in the asphalt and cement toward the semi's tractor. Men dove out of the truck, leaving it to roll forward on its own.

The stream of fire chewed into the cab. It didn't burst into a fireball the way vehicles did when Connor "shot" them on movie sets. Still, he was pretty sure he was hitting it.

Then he was past the truck. The dock flew by in a flash and he was over the water again. He pulled the plane up again, but it was sluggish and shook. He'd probably taken hits to his flight control surfaces. He looked to the right and left out of the Plexiglas bubble canopy, but he couldn't see his wings clearly in the dark. Hopefully the damage wasn't too bad.

He made a wide turn to the right, staying well out of range from the dock. "Did I get it?"

Julian whistled. "Oh, yeah. It's smoking, and it looks like Swiss cheese. They're not driving that thing anywhere."

"Any sign of cops yet?"

"Nope, but it's only been about five minutes."

"Really?" He let out a shaky laugh. "It feels like I've been up here for half an hour." He took a deep breath. "Okay, I'm going in for another pass. No target this time—I'll just buzz them."

He dove into the hornets' nest again, flying low and fast to make himself as hard to hit as possible. The ground fire started well before he was in range and there was more of it this time. The entire dock area sparkled with flashes like a stadium during the opening kickoff for a Super Bowl.

But the *White Knight* was going over 400 miles an hour—far too fast for an inexperienced marksman to hit from more than point-blank range. Bullets fired at the plane's nose would pass harmlessly behind its tail. To actually hit it, they would have to aim well in front of the aircraft—a skill few modern soldiers learned. He didn't hear any bullets hitting his plane.

After the pass, he climbed and banked again. A giddy euphoria swept over him. He grinned, then laughed. "Hey, Julian, I think I'm getting the hang of this!"

"Looking good! There's chatter up and down my scanner. Sounds like the police will be here in a couple of minutes. I also heard something about fighters from Fresno."

"Excellent! A couple more passes ought to do it, just to keep our friends on the dock off balance."

He made a wide turn and circled the dock for a few minutes, testing the ailerons, elevator, and rudder. The flight controls continued to be a problem, but nothing he couldn't handle. He swooped down again, firing a short burst into the water in front of the dock for effect. Men scattered for cover or fired up at him. But again Connor didn't notice any hits.

He had just started making yet another pass when his cockpit radio crackled. "November-one-niner-six-six-November, this is Falcoln 11 of the Air National Guard. Break off immediately or you will be shot down. Acknowledge."

"Acknowledged. I was wondering when you guys would show up."

"You will fly due west, climb to five thousand feet and circle over open water until we arrive. Then you will accompany us to Moffett Field. If you do not follow my instructions exactly, you will be shot down. Acknowledge."

"Acknowledged. You'll want to take a look at that dock before we leave."

He pulled up and turned west, waiting for his escort. There was a glint behind him and he saw two fighters streaking toward him. He was going 325 miles an hour, and the F-16s closed on him like he was standing still. One pulled alongside to his right, while the other stayed behind him.

Despite the repeated threats to shoot him down, Connor was deeply relieved to see the fighters. His part in this drama was ending. The military and police would take over now. He noticed that his hands shook on the plane's controls.

Just as the F-16 pulled up beside him, Julian's voice shouted in his ear. "There's something going on!"

"Yeah, I know." The F-16 to his right turned toward the Deep Seven dock and Connor paralleled his escort. Apparently the pilot was going to take Connor's advice about seeing for himself. "It's the military. They just ordered me to stop."

"No! Not in the air—on the dock!"

"What?" Connor pressed his head against the side of the cockpit, but the plane's nose blocked his view of the dock.

"Missile! Missile!" Julian shouted.

Connor caught a glimpse of something small flying up toward the two planes. He pushed the throttle all the way open and rolled to the right. The *White Knight* snapped over and out of the missile's path.

For a split-second, Connor thought he was safe. Then the lead F-16 exploded yards away. A wave of light, heat, and sound enveloped the P-51.

Connor dragged back on the stick, trying to keep the plane's nose up as it hurtled over the dock. The altimeter said he was at three hundred feet. He tried to turn left and away from the gunners below, but his rudder seemed to be gone.

Two hundred feet. Rattling, roaring, and garbled shouting filled his ears as he fought to keep the *White Knight* in the air. Bullets slammed into the canopy, making impact craters that looked like flattened snowballs.

One hundred feet. He was over the water again, so close that he could see small waves in the moonlight. No way he was going to be able to nurse the plane to an airport.

"Mayday! Mayday! Ditching at sea!" he shouted to whomever was listening.

Sixty feet. He slowed as much as he dared to lessen the impact, trying to keep the nose up the whole time.

Fifty feet. Forty. Thirty. He braced himself for the crash. "Dear God, please—"

The water came up and hit him like a wall.

66

Mitch's head hurt and his eyes stung, but he forced them open. He couldn't see the fire, but he could feel and hear it. The wall behind him was too hot to touch. The roar and crackle of hungry flames grew louder every second.

Dim red and yellow flickering lit the wreckage around him. The roof slanted down from one wall to the floor, like a giant lean-to. Wiring hung around them like jungle vines. Tools, bullets and debris carpeted the floor.

The woman—Allie—was still in the chair, but a beam lay across her and she wasn't moving. He tried to crawl over to her, but his hands and feet were still duct-taped together. Someone needed to help her—and him.

"Hey, Ed."

No response.

He looked around, but Ed was nowhere to be seen. He took a deep breath to call out, but smoke burned in his lungs and he choked. His head spun, but he tried again. "Ed!"

Even though his voice was little more than a loud croak, help came. A figure approached, but he couldn't make it out in the dim light and smoke. Strong hands grabbed his shoulders and dragged him backward along the wall.

They were outside and a cacophony of new

noises erupted. Sirens, shouting, gunshots, and explosions ripped through the air. Flashing red and blue lights competed with the bright white from the remaining lights on the security fence. Men ran all around him, shouting and carrying guns. Columns of smoke rose into the night sky. Floating fires and speedboat searchlights lit the water.

His rescuer pulled him out of the action and deposited him a few yards from the edge of the dock. "Thanks, Ed. I owe you, buddy. The girl is still in there."

He was alone. A chilly sea breeze blew over him. It made him shiver, but it was a welcome change from the smoke-filled heat in the building.

He heard a low moan beside him and turned his head. Ed lay beside him on the cold concrete. So who had rescued them? He looked around, but whoever it was had disappeared.

67

Allie FLOATED BETWEEN CONSCIOUSNESS AND unconsciousness, reality and unreality. Sometimes she was almost fully alert and knew that she was drugged and lying in a hospital room, hooked to an IV and a battery of monitors. But most of the time she was elsewhere.

The faces came and went. Sometimes they

crowded around her—Mom, Dad, Connor, Trudi, strangers with white coats and nameplates, the torturer in the ski mask. Other times they left her utterly alone and she felt she was the only one left in the world.

The pain, though, was always with her. Mostly it was a dull buzz in her head and left arm that troubled her sleep and never let her get quite comfortable. But if she moved too quickly or bumped her arm against something, it would come in great blinding jags that made her cry out.

Her dreams were vivid, and many of them involved interrogation. In one, she was back in the chair at Deep Seven and the two men—one with a mask and one without—were pounding her with questions in some foreign language, and then pounding her with their fists when she couldn't answer. Another time, she sat in a conference room at Doyle & Brown and Connor talked to her. She couldn't follow what he was saying, but she knew it must have something to do with her lies. His eyes were like golden-brown lasers that physically hurt her. She couldn't find a way to answer him, just apologize over and over as his eyes burned into her.

But the worst—and most vivid—dream involved Mom and Dad. They sat beside her bed, looking at her with loving, worried faces. Sometimes she saw Mom's face and sometimes she saw Dad's, but she always heard Mom's voice. Their questions weren't harsh or judgmental, just hurt and uncomprehending—and that made them worst of all. How had she gotten into trouble like this? Why hadn't she said something? How had all this happened?

Unlike in her other dreams, Allie answered them. The words poured out of her, gushing out through a broken dam in the depths of her soul. Old, stagnant words, kept bottled up too long. Sharp-edged questions of her own that had cut her like broken glass whenever she touched them over the years.

Why did Dad give her the awful secret of his death? Why did he make her lie? Those were his last words to her, to anyone. She was the one driving that night. Why couldn't she just say so and let the hurt out? Why? But no, Dad made her lock that secret away in a box. Was it any surprise that she learned to push other painful things into that same box? That was Dad's last lesson. Was it her fault that she learned it too well?

But then Connor was standing there looking at her like she was sewage and telling her it was her fault. That was so unfair. And it was even more unfair that he was right.

So she tried to fix things, but they kept getting more broken. And Jason Tompkins was still dead. And Dad was still dead. And . . . and . . .

She was crying then, babbling meaningless

sounds. Mom's voice was crying with her. Finally, she slipped into a deep and dreamless sleep.

Allie awoke—really awoke—for the first time early on a sunny morning. Fresh light slanted in through three windows and cast wide, bright rectangles across her bed, the sturdy guest furniture around it . . . and Mom. She lay in a recliner with a hospital blanket over her, snoring softly. Her faded blonde hair was pulled back into a ponytail and the top of a Cal Berkeley sweatshirt (a gift from Allie) was visible over the top of the blanket. She looked younger—sleep had smoothed away many of the care lines on her face.

Allie sat up—and instantly regretted it. Sharp pain knifed through her head and left arm. She gasped, which gave her a coughing fit. And that, of course, just made her head hurt more.

Mom opened her tired blue eyes. "It's okay, sweetheart. Just lie down. The nurse will be here in a minute. She pushed a button on a small box attached to a thick white cord. "I'm here. Mom's here. Everything is all right." She got up and walked over to the bed, hands held out.

Allie gingerly lay down again. "Hey, Mom. It's good to see you." Her mouth tasted like sour cotton. "Could I get some water? Maybe a cup of coffee too? Black."

The door opened and a thin Asian woman in a white uniform walked in carrying a clipboard. She looked at Allie and smiled. "Good morning." She glanced over at Mom. "Morning, Sandy."

The nurse looked back at Allie. "How do you feel?"

"Like I got hit by a truck. And I could really use a cup of coffee and some water."

The nurse laughed with grating perkiness. "Well, it sounds like you're back with us. Let me just ask you a few questions. What's your full name?"

"Allison Christine Whitman."

"Very good. Where are you?"

Allie looked around. "Beats me. Looks like a hospital room."

Nurse Perky gave Allie an approving smile. "That's right! Two for two. Now for the last one: who's that over there?" She pointed at Allie's mother.

"That's my mom. Her name is Sandra Whitman."

"Excellent! Doctor Andrews was hoping you'd start making more sense if we reduced your medication levels. He'll be in to talk to you on his morning rounds." Nurse Perky glanced at the monitors by Allie's bed and jotted something on the clipboard. She looked up and flashed another smile at Allie and her mom. "Bye."

"Can I get some coffee?"

But she was gone.

Mom folded her blanket and hung it over the back of her chair. "I'll get you a cup, honey."

"Thanks, Mom."

While she was gone, Allie collected her thoughts. She remembered going to Deep Seven, meeting Ed and Mitch, calling 911, and then getting caught. After that, things got patchy and jumbled. She recalled men questioning and hurting her. Then there had been an explosion and fire. That all made some sense, but she also remembered seeing Connor's plane, which made no sense at all. And her mind held dim images of him interrogating her too. Dad had been there too, and— An uneasy thought crept into her mind. What had Nurse Perky said about her making sense now? What exactly had she said while drugged?

Mom walked back in carrying two steaming paper cups. She handed one to Allie. "There you go, honey."

"Mom, I was wondering, um . . . Well, have you been here for a while?"

She nodded. "Mr. Clayton called me three days ago, and I got here as soon as I could. I've been in your room ever since."

"Did I—was I talking?"

She smiled. "Oh, yes. You had a lot to say, but most of it didn't make any sense. You also talked to people who weren't here. The doctor said the medication and your injuries made you confused. It was almost like you were half asleep, half awake."

Allie twisted her sheet in her right hand and looked down. "Did I talk about Dad?"

"You did."

Allie looked up at Mom's face. The care lines were back, deeper than ever. She looked exhausted. "What did I say?"

"You said a lot of things." She pressed her lips into a thin, pale line for a moment. "You said that he made you lie. You said you . . . you said something about his death."

"That it was my fault?" Her voice was barely a whisper.

"Yes."

Allie gulped her coffee, as if the hot liquid would make it easier to speak. It merely scalded her mouth and throat.

She coughed and took a deep breath. "It *was* my fault. I was driving."

There. It was out there. It was finally, finally out there. After all these years, the truth sat out in the open like a boulder that she had finally dropped from her shoulders. But would that boulder forever block the path that connected her and Mom?

Mom stared at Allie for several seconds, her mild eyes filled with pain. She pinched them shut. "Oh, Allie. You've carried that all these years."

Mom bowed her head, and Allie could see tears falling into her lap.

Allie felt her own eyes fill and her throat swell. "Dad made me promise not to tell you. He said you wouldn't understand. He wanted me to blame him, so I did and . . . and . . ." Her words dissolved into sobs.

"He was trying to protect you."

She nodded and buried her face in her sheets. Waves of agony swept over her. This was like having surgery done on her soul with no anesthetic.

"Allie, who is Jason Tompkins?"

She looked up and saw the reproach and fear in her mother's face. "I talked about him too?"

Mom nodded.

Allie took another sip of her coffee to calm herself. "Mom, there are some other things you should know. Actually, there are a lot of things."

For the next hour, Allie talked and her mother listened. Mom stopped crying but didn't otherwise react. She just sat there and absorbed what her daughter was saying with a blank look.

Allie filled in all the secret gaps in her life: Erik's meth use, Jason Tompkins's death, Blue Sea's blackmail, her fraud at Deep Seven, why she ran away, why she came back. Everything.

Then she reached the end and fell silent. It had been surprisingly easy. Once the first big confession was out, it was as if the cork was out of the bottle. She could pour it all out, and she had. Now she felt empty.

The two women sat quietly. The monitor beside the bed beeped softly and a bird sang outside the window.

Allie drained the cold dregs of her coffee. Awful stuff, even for a hospital. "I suppose you hate me now. It's okay—pretty much everyone I know hates me. I even hate me. I deserve it."

Mom reached over and took her hand where it lay on the damp sheet. "Oh, Allie. I don't hate you. I love you, sweetheart. I just . . . it's as if you've been a complete stranger and I just found out about it. I, I don't quite know what to think. But I don't hate you." She smiled and patted Allie's hand. "And I don't think that Mr. Norman hates you either. He's been in here every day for at least an hour."

"Really?"

"Oh, yes. We had some good conversations about you."

"What did—"

A sharp knock at the door interrupted her. Nurse Perky was back, and she had brought an equally chipper doctor with her. "Well, I understand you're feeling better, Allison."

She thought for a moment. "You know, I think I am."

68

KIM TAE-WOO, KNOWN TO MOST PEOPLE IN the west as Cho Dae-jung or David Cho, lay in his hospital bed, watching the ceiling. During the battle on the dock, he had suffered a superficial bullet wound, smoke inhalation, and some cuts and bruises. The smoke inhalation left him short of breath and prone to coughing fits, but he was getting better. He suspected that he could be released soon—if the Americans had any intention of releasing him.

He doubted they would. Two heavily armed guards stood inside the door, and whenever it opened he could see more men outside. As soon as he was well, he expected to be moved to a high-security prison somewhere. Perhaps Guantanamo or wherever the Americans kept terrorists these days.

That was all right. He had been prepared for much worse fates when he took this mission: torture, death, life in prisons much worse than Guantanamo. The Americans probably wouldn't even interrogate him much—he was already telling them everything they wanted to know. Well, almost everything.

There was a perfunctory knock at the door. Before Kim said anything, it opened and two men walked in. One was slender, white and wore a dark blue suit. The other was Asian, fat, and wore a rumpled gray suit.

"Good morning," the thin man said as he and his companion sat in guest chairs. The fat one put a tape recorder on the square bedside table, opened a small laptop computer, and nodded. "My name is Tim Jones," continued the thin man, "and this is Andy Ban. I'm with the CIA and Mr. Ban is with the South Korean National Intelligence Service. We're here to talk to you about the voyage of the *Grasp II* and related events."

"I already spoke to the government."

Jones nodded. "Yes, you talked to Homeland Security and the FBI. We're different agencies, Mr. Cho."

Ban leaned forward. "Which brings us to our first question. You're name isn't really David Cho, is it?"

"No."

"In fact, you are Lieutenant Young Moo-hyun of the South Korean Navy, correct?"

That was not correct, but Kim nodded.

"So, Lieutenant Young, why were you on board the *Grasp II* pretending to be North Korean?"

"Because Captain Ryu asked me to go on a secret mission."

"Who is Captain Ryu?"

"He was my commander during the mission. He called himself Mr. Lee on the ship."

"What did Captain Ryu tell you about the mission when he asked you to volunteer?"

"That we would strike a major blow against our enemy to the north."

"Anything else?"

"No."

Ban nodded and looked down. He typed energetically as Jones took over the questioning. "When did he first tell you that you would be impersonating North Korean military officers?"

"Two days before we came to America. He said we would have documents showing that we were—" he struggled for the right word "not military. Businessmen. We would also have secret papers saying we were North Korean soldiers."

"Did you find it strange?"

"I do not understand."

Jones leaned back and steepled his long white fingers. "Well, Lieutenant Young, weren't you curious why you would be going to America pretending to be North Korean soldiers pretending to be civilian businessmen?"

"I—" Kim coughed and then paused for several seconds to recover his breath and decide how to answer. "I trusted Captain Ryu."

"It did not occur to you that Captain Ryu might be planning to commit some outrageous act and make it look like North Korea was responsible?"

"He did not tell us the plan until we were on the ship. Then I knew."

"What did he say?"

"He said we would lift nuclear warheads from a sunken Soviet submarine. We would take them to America and explode them in San Francisco. He said we would do this on the same day America planned a test of the missile defense system in Hawaii. It would look like North Korea saying, 'Your missile defense cannot stop us.'"

"Did he really think that a warhead that had been underwater for twenty years would still work?"

"They were sealed in a missile, but he knew the bombs would need very big repairs. We had two engineers with us who worked to fix them. Even if they could not make the full chain reaction, they could explode much radioactive material over San Francisco."

Jones frowned. "But North Korea would deny any involvement."

"Yes, that is what Captain Ryu thought also. North Korea would deny that they had done this, but there would be American witnesses who would say they saw North Koreans do it. Captain Ryu told us to make 'mistakes' in front of the Americans—to leave North Korean documents where they could be found. Also, the captain said that when the money for the ship was investigated, it would look like it came from North Korea."

"I see. What did Captain Ryu think would happen next?"

"He said America would act the same way it acted after September 11. It would attack the terrorists' country and change its government."

Ban stopped typing and looked up. "He really wanted to start a war with North Korea?"

Kim nodded. "He said the South had lived in fear of the North for too long. He said our people should be reunited, like the Germans. Then—"

"But the cost of a war! The millions who would die!" Ban's face was pale and his mouth quivered slightly. "The North would destroy Seoul in an hour!"

"He thought the Americans would destroy the North in half an hour. America would think the North had attacked with nuclear weapons, so America would attack back with nuclear weapons. Some people in the South might die, but mostly the North's army. It would be destroyed before it could fight."

Silence filled the room for half a minute, punctuated by an oath from Jones.

Finally, Jones cleared his throat. That seemed to break the spell for Ban, who started typing again. "Do you know whether Captain Ryu was acting on orders from anyone?"

Kim didn't know, but it couldn't hurt to push the blame as far up the ladder as possible. The more trouble he could make for the South Korean militarists, the better. "Chain of command is very important to Captain Ryu. He would not do a thing like this without orders."

"Do you know who gave those orders?"

"For something this important, I am thinking the Blue House."

Ban stared at him. "The Blue House? You believe this plan was approved by the President of South Korea himself? Why? What evidence do you have?"

"Starting a war is a very big decision. A soldier, even a general or admiral, could not make it by himself."

Ban and Jones exchanged a look. "Thank you for your opinion, Lieutenant Young," said Ban. "We will look into this further." He nodded to the CIA agent.

"How much do you know about the company that owned the ship and dock facilities?" Jones asked.

"Very little. Captain Ryu worked with them."

"Do you know whether the company was aware of Captain Ryu's plans?"

"I don't. The men on the ship did not know, but I think some guessed."

Jones crossed his legs. "And the executives?"

"I don't know. If the bombs went off in San Francisco, many of them would die, so I don't think they knew."

"Yes, that makes sense."

"Captain Ryu once said he liked the company

because they did not ask questions and knew what to do to people who did."

Jones's eyebrows went up. "I see."

Ban leaned forward. "Let's go back to your story. What did you do when you learned Captain Ryu's plans?"

"While we were at sea, I could do little. I tried to help two crewmen send a message to the American navy, but they were caught."

"Granger and Daniels?"

"Yes. They thought we were North Koreans, so Captain Ryu said they must be locked in a hold until we are in America. Then we would let them escape after we exploded a bomb in San Francisco."

A look of sudden understanding came over Ban's face. "But you helped them escape early."

"Yes."

"And you gave them something?"

"Yes, a USB drive with files showing Captain Ryu's plans and that the North was not attacking." Another coughing fit interrupted him. "I am sorry. I must keep my speaking shorter."

"I understand. We'll let you rest soon. If Captain Ryu or the others discovered what you were doing, how would they respond?"

"To kill me."

Ban nodded. "You risked much, Lieutenant Young."

"I am a patriot, sir."

"You are indeed."

Jones stood up. "Well, we promised the doctor that we wouldn't keep you for too long. We may come back."

Ban put away his computer and stood. "Thank you, Lieutenant Young." He bowed and Kim nodded in response.

Jones and Ban left and Kim lay back on his bed. He looked out the window at the blue sky outside. Perhaps he would not go to Guantanamo after all.

69

IN SOME WAYS, CONNOR'S LIFE HAD GONE back to normal in the weeks since a nurse wheeled him out of the hospital. Reporters no longer called every hour. The CIA and FBI had questioned him to their hearts' content. He was back at work, and he even had a new false claims case that Max liked.

But there were big differences too. The biggest was that he now worked for the Law Offices of Connor Norman. After a wave of positive press coverage turned him back into an asset, Doyle & Brown's ExComm had dispatched Tom Concannon to try to lure Connor back to the firm. Did he want a corner office? An increased share of firm profits? How about a written guarantee that he would never be asked to take a case that made him uncomfortable?

Connor had turned Tom down as diplomatically

as possible. He had no desire to burn a bridge with a powerful firm like D&B but also no desire to walk back over it. A few months ago, he couldn't have imagined leaving the firm. Now he couldn't imagine going back, no matter what they offered him. The easy alliance between profit and principle that had characterized his career at the firm could never be rebuilt—at least not at Doyle & Brown. As he told Bill Fisher and Tom at Slanted Door, he had made a choice. And he did not regret it.

Not all the changes were positive. Connor's left leg was still in a walking cast that wouldn't come off for weeks. Worse, the *White Knight* was still on the bottom of the San Francisco Bay and would cost hundreds of thousands of dollars to repair once it was raised. But those were both temporary problems, and he couldn't let them distract him from the task at hand.

He focused himself on the meeting that had just started. He sat in his usual chair in conference room 11436 at DOJ, his foot resting on an empty chair. Max Volusca sat beside him with a tall stack of documents, questioning a hapless executive.

Today's lucky CEO was Sanford "Sandy" Allen of Blue Sea Technology. At Connor's suggestion, Allen had received a letter—not a subpoena— from Max inviting him to meet with DOJ about "irregularities in the bidding for the Golden Gate turbine project." Blue Sea's general counsel had written back that "Mr. Allen would be happy to discuss what he knows about Deep Seven Maritime Engineering."

The general counsel was a former tugboat captain named Alex McDonnell who picked up a law degree in night school. Connor suspected he knew more about practical admiralty law than he did about responding to government investigations, but he had been perceptive enough to look uncomfortable when he discovered Connor, a court reporter, and a videographer waiting in the conference room. And he had looked downright disturbed when Max put Allen under oath. Allen, however, seemed not to notice that anything was amiss.

The DAG wasted no time. "Thanks for coming in today, Mr. Allen. I'll get right to the point. As you know, we're investigating allegations of fraud in the Golden Gate turbine project."

"Good, good. I'm glad to hear it." Allen shook his snowy head with concern. "It's terrible what happened."

"What exactly happened, to your knowledge?"

Allen cocked his head to the side, as if he didn't quite understand the question. "Why, it was all over the news. It came out that Deep Seven was killing people and working with terrorists."

Max frowned. "Let me try again. What *exactly* happened, to your knowledge? How did the investigation of Deep Seven start? Did you or your company play a role in that?"

Allen smiled like a modest grandfather whose grandchild has just been praised. "We may have played some small role. I've heard that one of our former temporary employees helped uncover Deep Seven's crimes. As for me personally, I encouraged her to look around if she ever took a job at Deep Seven."

Max leaned back and folded his tree-trunk arms atop his massive stomach. "Did you give that advice to all your temps?"

Allen's smile faltered. "Ah, no."

"So why did you say that to this temp?"

"I . . . I'm not sure exactly why. She seemed curious."

"She wasn't the only one, was she?"

"Excuse me?"

"You were curious about her, weren't you?"

"I don't know what you mean."

Max snorted. "Yes, you do!"

Blue Sea's general counsel gave Max a stern look. "Counsel, please don't badger the witness."

Max ignored him. "Is it Blue Sea's practice to have a private investigator do a report on every temp they hire?"

Allen sat frozen. "A report?"

Max plucked a document out of the pile in front of him and slid it across the table. "A report like this one. Is that standard practice at Blue Sea?"

He handed a copy to the court reporter. "Exhibit one."

Allen went pale. "Where did you get this?"

Max's face darkened. "Answer my question!"

Allen looked to his lawyer. "I thought we were here to talk about Deep Seven."

McDonnell nodded. "That's right. We're here voluntarily. You don't have to answer any questions you don't want to." He looked at Max and thrust out his chin. He was a big man. Not as big as Max, but he looked like he'd been in more bar fights.

Connor turned to Max, waiting for the inevitable explosion—but Max didn't explode. Instead he lifted another document off his stack of paper and flipped it across the table into Allen's lap. "All right, you've just been served with a subpoena. Answer my question or go to jail."

Max was taking a calculated risk. In reality, refusing to answer his questions—even if asked pursuant to a subpoena—wouldn't result in jail time unless Max got a court order enforcing the subpoena, Allen ignored the court order, and the court held Allen in contempt. But there was a good chance that McDonnell didn't know how the process worked.

McDonnell took the subpoena from his client and looked at it for a moment. Then he glared at Max. "This is dirty pool."

Now Max exploded. "You want to know what's

really dirty pool?" he boomed. "Blackmailing temps to plant false evidence at a competing bidder to get their bid disqualified!"

Allen and McDonnell both jumped to their feet. "That's a lie!" shouted Allen. "We never did anything like that!"

Max stood and shoved a finger in Allen's face. "Be careful, buddy!" he bellowed in a voice that made Connor's teeth rattle. "Perjury is a felony, and you're under oath!" He dialed it back a few decibels. "But I'm a nice guy, so I'll give you another chance: did you or anyone else at Blue Sea blackmail Allison Whitman in order to get her to plant evidence at Deep Seven so that their bid would be disqualified?"

Allen looked at the stack of paper in front of the DAG, as if wondering what else might be in there. "Don't I have the right to remain silent?"

Max sat down and leaned back, making his chair groan. "Only if your answer might implicate you in a crime."

Allen's eyes stayed on the pile of documents. "I think I'll remain silent."

Connor wanted to let out a whoop of triumph. Exercising the right to remain silent couldn't be used against Allen in a *criminal* case, but in a *civil* case (such as a false claims case) it was fair game. Allen had just done the next best thing to admitting guilt. All that was left to talk about was money.

Max flipped through his notes. "All right. Well, if you're going to invoke the Fifth Amendment rights, I guess we're done for today."

Allen and McDonnell walked out as the court reporter and videographer began to pack up. They left a few minutes later.

Once they were alone, Connor stuck out his hand. "Nicely played, Max. They're dead men walking after Allen's performance today."

Max shook the proffered hand. "Thanks. Looks like Allie brought us another winner." He paused and looked Connor in the eye. "Might be the last one for a while, huh?"

Connor let out a sigh. "Yeah. The DA in Kansas is taking a really hard line. He wants her to testify against her ex-boyfriend next week *and* do at least a year in prison."

Max shoved his stack of paper—most of which was blank sheets intended to make the pile look bigger—into a box. "Can't say I'm surprised. DAs get elected for being tough on crime, especially crimes that get kids killed."

"I know. I thought they might be more reasonable because she came forward voluntarily and she's a hero for what she did out here."

Max scratched his jowls. "That earned her a get-out-of-jail-free card with our office, but we were only looking at stuff like perjury and obstruction of justice charges. Not murder or manslaughter."

Connor nodded. "Yeah, I see the difference. So does she. But a felony guilty plea, a year in jail, and a lifetime as an ex-con? There's got to be another way." He clicked his tongue and shook his head. "A year is a long time though."

70

"BEST BURGERS IN THE US OF A," ED declared as he put his tray down next to Mitch's.

Cho gave the bacon-guacamole Ed had recommended a doubtful look. "I have eaten McDonald's before. Is Carl's Jr. so much better?"

"Take a bite and find out."

When Cho continued to hesitate, Mitch chimed in. "You can trust Ed on two things: burgers and coffee. Not much else—and never let him set you up on a blind date."

Ed chuffed. "That was five years ago!"

"I still have nightmares. Anyway, he knows his burgers."

With that reassurance, Cho took a bite. A dollop of green goop came out of the other side of the bun, landing on his tray with a plop. His eyes lit up and he nodded. "Mmmm."

"Told you!" Ed crowed.

Cho swallowed and wiped his mouth with a paper napkin. "This is very good. Thank you."

Ed inclined his head. "Don't mention it. You

saved our lives. The least we can do is buy you dinner."

"I am sad I am eating here for first time at the end of my trip. There is no Carl's Jr. in South Korea." He took another bite.

"Or in North Korea, I'll bet."

Cho shook his head. "I think not," he said around a mouthful of burger.

Ed grinned and winked. "Oh, I'm guessing that you *know* not."

Cho stopped chewing and stared at him.

Ed turned and picked up a shopping bag. "That reminds me." He put the bag on the table. "Here's a little gift from Mitch and me."

Cho looked in the bag and lifted out a used video game console and a package of old games. He looked at them quizzically. "Thank you."

"Our pleasure," said Ed. "We thought you might want to practice your Nintendo skills. See, I was on a lot of jobs in South Korea in the eighties and nineties, when you were growing up. All the kids had Nintendos back then. You'd see 'em playing Gameboys on the bus, and when I went over to a coworker's house, you'd always—and I mean *always*—see a console by the TV if they had kids."

Cho nodded. "I remember."

Ed's eyebrows went up. "Really? You didn't act like it on the ship. Remember when we were playing Super Mario Bros. together? You acted like you'd never played a Nintendo before."

"I was acting North Korean."

"It was a good act. Really good. So good that people might think you really were North Korean. 'Cause, you know, that would explain a lot."

"I am happy my acting convinced you."

Ed nodded at the console. "My apartment is just a block away. What do you say we plug that thing in and you can show me how good you really are? I'll play Luigi, and you can have Mario."

Cho looked down at the console. "I must prepare for the flight to Korea. I have much to do. I am sorry."

Ed reached across the table and clapped him on the shoulder. "Don't be, comrade. Your secret is safe with us. You stopped a nuclear war and saved our lives. What do we care if you infiltrated the South Korean Navy while you were doing that? You think we'd turn you in?"

Cho stared at him for a second, then tossed back his head and laughed. "You are a funny man, Ed Granger!"

Kim Tae-woo sat in his hotel room near the Oakland Airport, staring at the Nintendo console Granger and Daniels had given him. What if one of the South Koreans had been paying attention when Granger had been teaching him to play

Super Mario Bros.? What if Granger and Daniels had talked to the CIA rather than him?

He shook his head. Future agents would need to be better trained. In the meantime, he needed to fill this hole in his knowledge.

He plugged the console into the hotel room TV set, inserted the Super Mario Bros. cartridge, and set out to rescue Princess Peach.

71

ALLIE AND CONNOR DANCED THROUGH A sparkling sea of black and white. They whirled, dipped, and swayed in perfect rhythm with each other and the music played by the excellent salsa band a few yards away. Connor expertly navigated them in and out among the couples on the crowded outdoor dance floor and kept Allie's feet safe from the governor, who was stomping away nearby.

She had never been to San Francisco's Black and White Ball, which took place in the Civic Center plaza every May. She hadn't planned to go this year either, but Connor surprised her with a ticket after a particularly rough negotiating session with the Salina, Kansas, DA's office.

Everyone at the ball wore black and white, so she had needed to do some shopping. She fell in love with a slinky white Vera Wang dress perfect for both dancing and sitting down afterward for dinner with members of Northern California's aristocracy. The dress was really too expensive, even for a night like this. Fortunately, Sandy Allen and Blue Sea paid for it with the first installment of the settlement Connor and Max beat out of them. The second installment might cover the diamond and sapphire earrings and necklace she wore.

Connor wore a tuxedo, of course. In a nod to the slightly eccentric spirit of the ball, he had picked one with a vintage Jazz Age cut. He looked like he had stepped straight out of an F. Scott Fitzgerald novel, except that he was a lot more sober and less depressed than any Fitzgerald hero she remembered.

The music slowed. Connor took her left hand with his right and slid his left around to her back. Her dress had no back, and his hand was warm against her skin in the cool of the night.

Allie looked up into his brown eyes. "I'm having a wonderful time. Thanks for inviting me."

He gave a sparkling, effervescent smile. "Thanks for saying yes. If you hadn't I'd have had to come here alone and spend the night dancing with my mom's friends."

"Liar."

"It's pronounced 'lawyer.' So, what happened to Trudi? Weren't she and her husband supposed to meet us here?"

"Their kids are sick, and she didn't want to leave them with a sitter."

He clicked his tongue. "Too bad. She's referred us half a dozen good cases, and I'd like to meet her in person."

After Allie's exploits splashed all over the news, she had told Trudi about Devil to Pay and her secret life as a whistleblower. She'd never be an invisible accounting temp again, so her *qui tam* career was effectively over anyway. Trudi had been hurt for about five minutes. After that, she spent two solid hours telling Allie about all the stories her other temps had told her about fraud they had seen at government contractors. A lot of those had been exaggerations or misunderstandings, but not all. Connor had more false claims cases going now than he ever had when she was his only source. And he insisted that all of them be brought through Devil to Pay so that Allie would get a percentage of the proceeds.

"She's a lot of fun. You'll love her, and Dave is great too." She paused. "Thanks for keeping me out of jail."

He shrugged modestly. "That was easy enough once I finally realized that Kansas has a brand new False Claims Act and an Attorney General's office with zero experience in false claims law. It wasn't too hard to persuade the AG's office that they'd rather have some free expert consulting than another inmate at the women's prison. Once the AG explained that to the local DA, the negotiations weren't too tough. I'm just sorry that you're going to have to spend the summer auditing contracts in a hot, sticky little cow town. I'm sure you'd much rather be on the beach at Tahoe."

"You know, I'm looking forward to it. I really am. Not the hot and sticky part, but going in there and helping these people. If I can find a couple of good cases for them and shake loose enough money to build a new school or something, it'll be a good summer." She thought about the prospects for a moment. "You'll probably laugh at me for this, but I'd actually choose this over Tahoe."

His smile returned, quieter and warmer. "My grandfather had a saying, 'You are what you are when the Devil whistles.' You show your true colors then, when you're under pressure and temptation. And ever since the Bahamas, you've shown pure gold, Allie."

A warm glow filled her from head to toe and she could feel the tears in her eyes. "I'd do it all again ten times over just to hear you say that. Thank God you were there for me, even when I screwed up." She let go of his hand and hugged him tight.

His arms came up and he held her gently. "He was there for you too, you know."

She didn't know how to respond, so she put her head on his shoulder and they swayed to the music. She closed her eyes and lost herself in the moment, wishing the band would play this song all night long.

But they didn't. The song ended and they stopped dancing, but Connor didn't release her. He continued to hold her close and she looked up into those warm, intelligent brown eyes that had caught her attention when they first met. There was something there she hadn't seen before— something that made her heart race. "Allie, I think this is the end of a beautiful friendship."

He kissed her. Somewhere, the music started again, but neither of them noticed.

Discussion Questions

1. A central theme in the book is how the characters react when they face hard choices. How did Allie respond? How did Connor?

2. Have you ever been in a situation where you were tempted to say that you didn't have a choice when the truth was that you didn't want to pay the price for making the right choice?

3. Late in the book, Connor reflects that "by the time we reach a critical decision, we've already made it. Maybe all the little decisions in life are like bricks, and those bricks pile together into walls over time. And when some crisis comes, those walls force us along whatever path we've already chosen." Do you agree or disagree? If you agree, will that affect how you make "little" choices in the future?

4. How does Allie change over the course of the book? What changes her?

5. How does Connor change? What changes him?

6. Was Allie's father right to tell her to blame the crash on him? If you think he was wrong, do you blame him for doing it?

7. As described in the following Author's Notes, the federal and state False Claims Acts allow whistleblowers to sue on behalf of the government and keep part of anything the government recovers. Had you heard of these laws before? If not, did their existence surprise you?

8. Advocates say that the False Claims Acts are important tools for fighting fraud. Opponents say they encourage frivolous lawsuits by disgruntled former employees. Who do you think is right?

9. Did you think Max Volusca was a good public servant? Why or why not?

10. Did Cho's true allegiance surprise you? Before reading the Author's Notes, were you aware of how much spying goes on between North and South Korea?

11. Early in the book, Connor says, "If you commit a crime, you should pay the price. Every. Single. Time. No excuses, no compromises." Do you agree with that statement? Is it fair? Is it merciful?

12. Does Connor's Christian faith affect his actions? Are there places where it should have affected them more?

13. Connor, like a lot of Northern California Christians, drinks alcohol. Did that bother you? Why or why not?

Author's Notes

I try to put as little fiction as possible into my novels. That's partly because I owe it to readers like you to get my facts right. But it's also because one of the things I enjoy most about being an author is talking to fighter pilots and scientists, poking around ROVs, visiting museums and labs, researching Russian submarines, and so on. I can't put all the fascinating things I find into my books, of course, but I do post a lot of them on my website: www.rickacker.com. I also have sample chapters from my other books, interviews, and other good stuff there, so be sure to stop by. You can also find me on Facebook and Twitter.

Here's the truth behind some of the key story elements in this book:

Allie's whistleblower lawsuits: Real false claims lawsuits usually involve less international intrigue than Allie's cases, but there's nothing fictional about the law involved or how lucrative these cases can be. Every year, *qui tam* whistleblowers like Allie uncover billions of dollars of fraud—and receive anywhere from 15 percent to 50 percent of the recovered money.

Whistleblower awards are generally in the millions of dollars, and I've been involved in cases where the whistleblower received over $100 million. You can learn more about false claims litigation by visiting the website of Taxpayers Against Fraud (www.taf.org) or the U.S. Department of Justice (http://www.justice.gov/usao/pae/Documents/fca process2.pdf).

The sunken Soviet submarine: The wreck of the Typhoon-class submarine is based on two real naval disasters. The first was the loss of the Russian submarine *Kursk* on August 12, 2000, which killed all 118 sailors on board. While the cause of the *Kursk* disaster has never been definitively proven, the most likely culprit was a chain reaction explosion caused by unstable VA-111 Shkvall torpedoes on the doomed sub. The same type of torpedo is used on Typhoon submarines. The second incident occurred on January 8, 2005, when the USS *San Francisco* smashed into an undersea mountain, killing one man and badly damaging the submarine. The accident was caused by a combination of bad charts, crew mistakes, and the fact that the submarine was not using its sonar, which is typical when a naval submarine is traveling submerged and does not want to be detected. The fictional Typhoon in this book sank when, like the *San Francisco*, it hit a seamount. The impact caused its VA-111 torpedoes to explode, ripping the sub's bow open like the *Kursk*'s.

Cho's spying: Despite the fact that the Korean War ended nearly sixty years ago, relations between North and South Korea remain extremely tense, and both countries routinely spy on each other. North Korea's Reconnaissance Bureau is particularly active and has sent numerous agents into South Korea with missions ranging from assassination to sabotage to infiltrating the South Korean military and government. The Reconnaissance Bureau's actions reportedly reach the level of outright terrorism, including an attack on a South Korean diplomatic delegation to Burma in 1983, the bombing of Korean Air Lines flight 858 in 1987, and the sinking of the South Korean ship *Cheonan* in 2010.

Wente, Slanted Door, and Gary Danko: These are all real Bay Area restaurants, and all are excellent. However, if you go to Gary Danko, don't expect the view Allie described to Connor. She got that detail wrong because, of course, she wasn't actually there.

Interview with Rick Acker

Please tell us a bit about yourself.

I write legal thrillers on the train to and from my job as a deputy attorney general in the California Department of Justice, where I prosecute corporate fraud cases like the ones described in *When the Devil Whistles.* I'm the father of four great kids and the husband of a loving and tolerant woman who puts up with being a single mother when deadlines loom or Notre Dame is playing. I'm also a decent breakfast cook, particularly if you're not picky about calories and fat.

What is your favorite Bible verse and why?

"I know how to be abased, and I know how to abound. Everywhere and in all things I have learned both to be full and to be hungry, both to abound and to suffer need. I can do all things through Christ who strengthens me" (Philippians 4:12–13 NKJV). Paul understood that no matter what circumstances he faced—freedom, prison, wealth, poverty, abundance, hunger—all that mattered was that he had the strength of Christ. He knew how to take both the good and the bad that the world threw at him because he had built his foundation on the Rock and couldn't be shaken.

What inspired the concept for writing When the Devil Whistles?

The cases I deal with every day. They're fascinating studies in corporate fraud, pride, and conspiracy. And the whistleblowers who bring them are no less interesting. I meet idealistic crusaders, amoral opportunists, angry layoff victims, and crazy conspiracy theorists. Sometimes they're right and sometimes they're wrong, but they're never, ever dull.

How did you choose the setting for your story?

Setting it in and around San Francisco was natural. We've got one of the most active (and interesting) corporate fraud practices in the country. The Bay Area also makes an excellent palette for adding color to a legal thriller: elite law firms making a living off expensive secrets, do-gooder aristocrats, quirky artists and musicians, risk-taking corporate executives with more money than ethics, and, of course, the spectacular scenery. Besides, I couldn't pass up a chance to show off my adopted home.

Is any part of When the Devil Whistles *factual?*

I put as little fiction as possible into my books. I tried to make everything in *When the Devil Whistles* factually accurate, from the corporate espionage tricks used by whistleblowers to the name of the receptionist at the Department of Justice's San Francisco office (thanks for doing a cameo, Ruby).

How long did When the Devil Whistles *take you to complete?*

About ten months from the first word until I sent in the manuscript, which is pretty typical for me.

Do you have a favorite character in When the Devil Whistles? *Why?*

That's a tough one. I like all the main characters for different reasons: Allie's sharp wit and deep conflicts, Connor's sense of honor, Ed's street (or sea) smarts and way with words.

How much research did When the Devil Whistles *take?*

The law-related parts took virtually no research, but other scenes were harder. I've never driven a robot submarine or flown a P-51, for example. I've also never handled a national security emergency. Fortunately, I was able to find people who have. They were generous with their time and helped me get my facts straight.

What was the most interesting fact that you learned while writing When the Devil Whistles?

I'm continually amazed at how few people know about the false claims laws described in *When the Devil Whistles*. Whistleblowers can receive bounties worth tens of millions of dollars for uncovering fraud on the government, but the fraud usually goes undiscovered and the bounties unclaimed because there's so little public awareness of these laws. Sigh.

What are some of the challenges you face as an author?

The biggest is trying to find time for everything. I'm a full-time lawyer and a father of four. Squeezing in time to write (let alone do research, marketing, blogging, etc.) is a continual struggle. If I didn't have a long commute, I probably wouldn't be a published author.

What aspects of being a writer do you enjoy the most?

All of it. I love writing a good scene, talking with fans, brainstorming with other authors, and digging into research. I even like doing edits. I'd do this job for free (hope my publisher isn't reading this).

What writing clubs or organizations do you belong to?

More than I really have time for: American Christian Fiction Writers, ChiLibris, Christian Authors Network, San Jose Christian Writers Group, and Logos Writers.

What were your favorite books as a child?

The Chronicles of Narnia, The Lord of the Rings, and anything by Ray Bradbury.

What is your writing style? (Do you outline? Write "by the seat of your pants"? Or somewhere in between?)

Um, yes. I outline, write SOTP, and often wind up somewhere in between. I start out with an outline that lays everything out neatly from the opening bombshell to the last twist. Then I get into the middle of the story and things happen. Characters wander in uninvited. Someone gets killed when I only intended a flesh wound. People fall in love when they were supposed to be just friends. So I take a deep breath, brew a pot of strong coffee, and do a new outline that will take the story home.

Do your characters begin to take on a life of their own as you write?

Oh, yes. Some of them also take on deaths of their own. That's always a hazard in one of my books.

What other new projects do you have on the horizon?

Here's a sneak peek at my current project: Lawyer Marie Derouen is trying to rebuild her life and career after her ex-husband was indicted for embezzlement and falsely implicated her in his crimes. She is assigned to defend a wealthy Miami importer who is accused of "disappearing" a teenaged girl years ago when he was a military officer in Guatemala City. He is handsome, charming, and seems honorable. And of course he denies killing the girl. Marie begins to fall in love with her client, but she senses that he is keeping secrets from her. Is she too suspicious because her ex betrayed her, or is her intuition about him right?

Who was the person who influenced you the most with your writing?

My high school English teacher, Mrs. York. She was the first person who didn't see my short stories and bad poetry as just a waste of time.

What message would you like your readers to take from When the Devil Whistles?

We can't hide from hard choices. How we face them defines us. As one of the characters comments, "You are what you are when the Devil whistles." Do you come running to him? Do you hide and hope he won't notice you? Or do you stand firm in the power of God?

What is your greatest achievement?

Raising four wonderful kids.

What is your goal or mission as a writer?

I try to write stories that readers can't put down and can't forget. I love it when a reader says something like, "I stayed up all night reading your latest, and it really got me thinking." In my view, good fiction should both entertain and challenge readers. I do my best to keep them on the edges of their seats until the last page and leave them with an insight about themselves, their Lord, or the world that will stick with them long after they put the book down.

What do you do to get away from it all?

I read, of course!

Center Point Publishing
600 Brooks Road • PO Box 1
Thorndike ME 04986-0001 USA

(207) 568-3717

US & Canada:
1 800 929-9108
www.centerpointlargeprint.com